Involved in the Moroccan caper are:

PENELOPE QUATTLEBAUM: a lusciously stacked career diplomat whose code number is 38-24-36.

BORIS ALEXANDROVICH KORSKY-RIMSAKOV: the world's greatest opera singer, an angel-voiced lecher and lush.

DON RHOTTEN (pronounced Row-ten): America's favorite TV newscaster, who's in constant terror of cracking the caps on his teeth or losing the rug that serves as his hair.

SHEIKH ABDULLAH BEN ABZUG: his religion forbids him to touch the fermented juice of the grape, a prohibition that, he discovers, does not apply to vodka.

MASH GOES TO MOROCCO
is an original POCKET BOOK edition.

Published by POCKET BOOKS

★M★A★S★H★
Goes to Morocco

Richard Hooker
and
William E. Butterworth

PUBLISHED BY POCKET BOOKS NEW YORK

A 701378

MASH GOES TO MOROCCO

POCKET BOOK edition published January, 1976

L

This original POCKET BOOK edition is printed from brand-new plates made from newly set, clear, easy-to-read type. POCKET BOOK editions are published by POCKET BOOKS, a division of Simon & Schuster, Inc., 630 Fifth Avenue, New York, N.Y. 10020. Trademarks registered in the United States and other countries.

*M*A*S*H*
Goes to Morocco

Chapter One

"And now," the master of ceremonies announced with great, if somewhat unconvincing, enthusiasm, "it's door-prize time."

The master of ceremonies was a pediatrician, or baby doctor, from down around Bangor, Maine, and that combination of sad affairs, in the opinion of Hawkeye Pierce, also known as Benjamin Franklin Pierce, M.D., F.A.C.S., was enough to drive any man to the bottle, as the evidence clearly suggested it had in this case.

Not that Hawkeye Pierce had anything against the bottle. It had its place, such as now. Dr. Pierce's hand held a plastic cup emblazoned with the name and logotype of Burble-Up, a citrus-oil-flavored soft drink which the bottler was touting as just the thing to foist on hospital patients in no position to complain and which he was passing out, free-of-charge, to all attendees at the State Medical Convention.

Dr. Pierce's cup, however, runneth over with a mixture of Burble-Up and a specially prepared gastric elixir, in the ratio of 50-50. The taste left a good deal to be desired, and Dr. Pierce would have much preferred to be sipping one of his famous 10-1 martinis; but that, under the circumstances, was unfortunately impossible. Dr. Pierce was in the company of his bride of many years, and the bride had issued a non-negotiable proclamation: "You will go forth to the General Meeting and drink nothing but Burble-Up."

The best he could do was what he was doing, drinking Burble-Up mixed in equal proportions with a gastric elixir prepared with great care in the pharmacy of the Spruce Harbor, Maine, Medical Center, for which Dr. Pierce served as chief of surgery. A half-gallon of 100-proof vodka had, under Dr. Pierce's stern professional eye, been decanted into stainless-steel laboratory bowls, which had then been placed into the freezing compartment of the pharmacy's refrigerator. When the temperature of the vodka had been lowered below 32 degrees Fahrenheit (zero degrees centigrade), it had been removed from the freezer. Small chips of ice were then dropped into the chilled mixture. Following the laws of physics, the ice chips had attracted the aqueous content of the vodka*, forming larger pieces of ice, which were then carefully extracted from the stainless-steel bowls and discarded.

The remaining liquid had then been carefully poured into standard eight-ounce prescription bottles. A few drops of food coloring were added to each bottle of what was now just about pure grain neutral spirits, giving some a foul-looking purplish color, and the others a revolting off-lavender tinge. The bottles were then sealed, and a standard label applied. The foul-looking purple bottles indicated that they had been prescribed for B.F. Pierce by John F.X. McIntyre, M.D., "for use as needed for gastric distress." The off-lavender bottles indicated they had been prescribed for J.F.X. McIntyre by B.F. Pierce, M.D., for the suppression of acne. (Mrs. McIntyre had not been a medical bride, so to speak, quite long enough to wonder why her husband was worried about acne.)

Dr. Pierce's "gastric distress"—the manifestations of which were chandelier-rattling belches—was, like the technique of refining vodka, something he had brought to the medical profession from his undergraduate days at Androscoggin College. He had paid a classmate five dollars for instruction in the fine art of belching on de-

---

*For the uninitiated, 100-proof vodka is a 50-50 mixture of grain neutral spirits, the distilling industry's little euphemism for pure alcohol and water.

mand. It had been five dollars well spent. Only moments before the Bangor baby doctor had announced that it was door-prize time, Mary Pierce had, following a relatively mild symptom of gastric distress (a number three-level burp, on a scale of one to ten), fiercely hissed at him to "take his damned medicine."

The four, Drs. Pierce and McIntyre, and their brides, were seated in the next to the last row of the convention auditorium, a wife at each end to insure that neither husband could suddenly discover pressing business which required his presence elsewhere during this, the most exciting facet of the convention.

"The first door prize," the baby doctor m.c. announced, "presented by Godchaux-Dewey Pharmaceutical Laboratories, is a complete set of matched luggage, in genuine, leather-grained vinyl. It is to be awarded to the oldest physician among us."

"My pimples are bothering me," John Francis Xavier McIntyre, M.D., F.A.C.S., à la "Trapper John," announced suddenly.

"Physician, heal thyself!" Hawkeye commanded.

"Don't mind if I do," Trapper John (who had been so-called after a conductor on the Boston & Maine Railroad had found him, in his college days, with a coed, who loudly proclaimed she had been trapped in the gentlemen's facility aboard a Boston-bound train) said. He added another ounce of lavender liquid to his Burble-Up.

"How is that supposed to help?" his bride, by name Lucinda, asked. "Why don't you rub it on your face?"

"Ssshh!" Trapper John said, putting his finger to his lips.

A tiny, fragile-appearing old gentleman came quickly, if somewhat unsteadily, down the aisle of the convention room.

"How old is he, anyway?" Hawkeye asked.

"All I know is that he won the oldest-doctor luggage when I came to my first convention as an intern," Trapper John said.

"He must have a houseful of luggage," Hawkeye said.

"Ssshh!" Mary Pierce said.

"No, he doesn't," Trapper John said. "He sells it back to the suitcase store. He wins the same set over and over, year after year."

Then they both got to their feet, clapping loudly and whistling between their teeth as the aged physician mounted the stairs to the stage. He turned and bowed to acknowledge the applause.

"You should be ashamed of yourself!" Mary Pierce hissed.

Hawkeye let her have a number-six burp.

"And will you take your medicine?" she hissed, furiously.

"Anything you say, my dear," Hawkeye replied, in his best Clark Gable diction. He took a deep swallow from his Burble-Up cup and then refilled it from his medicine bottle.

The prize-awarding went on and on. It was a sad manifestation of one of the greatest unrequited love stories of modern times, that of the ethical pharmaceutical manufacturers* for the medical profession.

It has, of course, nothing to do with the cold fact that unless the medical profession chooses to prescribe a certain drug, the manufacturer might as well not manufacture that particular drug. Ethical drug manufacturers cannot, in the manner of publishers and furniture manufacturers, conduct overstock or fire sales—or even going-out-of-business sales—making their wares available to the public at rock-bottom, even sacrificial, prices.

But to reiterate, it is not the crass commercial fact that unless the doctors prescribe their product, the manufacturers simply cannot sell it. It is rather a simple case of unabashed admiration for those who have taken the oath of Hippocrates, for their skill and knowledge, their

---

* Ethical pharmaceutical manufacturers are those who make drugs dispensed by prescription only. Manufacturers of non-prescription drugs and nostrums, such as aspirin and hemorrhoid suppositories, however, are not necessarily unethical.

charm, their good looks, their genius, their love of their fellowman and their all-around godlike qualities that causes the Ethical Drug Manufacturers to dispatch platoons of high-paid, well-educated, chosen-for-their-charm representatives (known as "detail men") to pay homage and court to anyone legally licensed to append M.D. to his name.

These surrogate lovers carry enormous, suitcaselike briefcases (quite similar to those used by airline captains to carry all their bureaucratic flight paraphernalia), loaded down with small tokens of admiration and love. There are pen-and-pencil sets, calendars, thermometers, framed homilies to hang on waiting-room walls for the edification of the patient and even such things as cocktail shakers and umbrellas. (There is also, of course, an absolutely free supply of sample medicines, together with a paean of praise to their efficacy written by a brother M.D. in the employ of the manufacturer.)

This pagan ritual reaches an apogee whenever two or three practitioners of the healing arts are gathered together in the name of medicine. When this occurs, all the stops on the organ are pulled out. A conventioneering doctor putting his hand out to see if it's raining will have three martinis and a Rum Collins in his palm before the first raindrop can strike. If a doctor is seen casually glancing at the entertainment advertisements in the hotel lobby, he can expect to find two tickets—for fourth- or fifth-row aisle seats—in his mailbox ("courtesy of Grogarty-Lipshultz Ethical Pharmaceuticals, manufacturers of Ipso-dipsomaniasis, the highly acclaimed specific for Black Plague") when he asks for his room key.

The door-prize awardings, a standard ritual at medical conventions, provide a splendid opportunity for these people to make sure that no one is left out; that every surgeon, as well as every orthopedist, every pathologist as well as every otolaryngological surgeon, every general practitioner as well as every neurosurgeon receives some token of the deep and abiding affection of the ethical drug manufacturer.

Door prizes are awarded every possible category. There is a prize for the oldest surgeon, another for the youngest and one for the physician closest to the average. There is a prize for the physician with the most hair, and the least hair; the largest mustache and the smallest; the one who has sired the most children; the one married the longest and the one most recently married. There is a prize for the surgeon with the shortest fingers, and the one with the longest. There are even prizes for the doctors who have won the most prizes and, just to nail it down neatly, a special prize for that physician who has managed to evade being awarded anything at all.

Drs. Pierce and McIntyre had spent long hours at the convention doing some serious plotting, based on careful and extensive research, with the idea in mind of receiving no prize at all. This, they realized, would really make them stand out among their fellows.

Their first step had been to register at the convention under fictitious names. With a perfectly straight face, Dr. Benjamin Franklin Pierce had told the joyously smiling blonde resting her ample development on the registration table that he was Dr. Louis Pasteur, and then introduced his close associate, Aloysius J. Roentgen, M.D., the well-known radiologist.

As the convention progressed, they had carefully avoided writing their names down anywhere, including on bar and restaurant tabs. On those few occasions when they had been trapped in a corner by detail men with pens extended, they had signed either the names of Drs. Pasteur and Roentgen or the names of rival detail men, taken from the lapel-identification badges ("Hello, Doctor! I'm Jerry G. Goodsport of your Friendly Mammoth International Drug Manufacturers' Monopoly) those luminaries were considerate enough to wear.

All is not peaches and cream for the detail men. Rather quickly, they had run out of things to give away. They strive, of course, for individuality, as well as something that will make the recipient remember (at least vaguely) the name of his benefactor after the convention is over.

The ordinary things (sets of luggage, stereos, golf clubs) given away at conventions can be given away only once. It would hardly do for a doctor to compare his Magna-Woofer Quadraphonic Hi-Fi with the Zoomerino Quadraphonic Home Entertainment Center given his competitor in the G. & O. game and find it wanting.

The unwritten rule among the competing detail men was that they should never knowingly offer as a token of their admiration for the medical profession a door prize similar to that being offered as a love-gift to physicians by the competition.

It was for this reason that Mr. Alphonse T. Hammerschmidt, proprietor of the Girdle the Globe Travel Service, Ltd., was able to solve a little problem that had been gnawing at him for more than a year.

Mr. Hammerschmidt had a year before put together a nice little profitable tour group, which took 88 members of the Greater Maine Retail Butchers & Sausage Stuffers Association through fifteen glorious never-to-be-forgotten days in North Africa. By paying in advance for the tour, which departed from Boston, Massachusetts, on board Air Mali's luxurious (and only) DC-6 for the Canary Islands, thence to Casablanca, and finally to Fez, Morocco, he had been able to get a good price for the group from *Bienvenu à Merry Morocco* Tourist Agency, which handled all in-Morocco details.

There had been a last-minute catastrophe, however. Max Detweiler, proprietor of Max's Maximum Meats, Inc. (a well-known butcher shop in Waterville, Maine), had once too often been told by a customer that the price of meat was outrageous. He had thrown a frozen leg of New Zealand lamb at Mr. C. Alton Whaley, a previously mild-mannered English teacher at Waterville High. Mr. Whaley had thrown the leg of lamb back at Mr. Detweiler, striking and breaking his right, or slicing, hand, and then had proceeded to the police station where he charged Mr. Detweiler with assault with a deadly weapon. The charge, of course, was ridiculous, and was later changed to "assault with intent to do bodily harm"; but Mr. Detweiler thought that his best interests would be served by cancelling his and his wife's fifteen-glorious-never-to-be-forgotten-days-in-North-Africa tour. Pending trial, he was forbidden to leave Waterville's city limits.

Mr. Hammerschmidt had naturally cheerfully refunded his money, and then applied for a refund from Air Mali and the *Bienvenu à Merry Morocco* Tourist Agency. Ten days later, he was informed that while a cash refund would not be forthcoming, he had a credit on their books for two passages—Boston to Fez and return, and fifteen days of accommodations in various hotels within Morocco.

He had written angry letters, threatening never to give Bienvenu a dime's worth of future business unless he got a refund, but Bienvenu had stood firm. Hammerschmidt had tried, even valiantly, to sell the accommodations. There seemed to be very little interest by anyone in Waterville in going to Merry Morocco; and Hammerschmidt, while not entirely abandoning hope, was getting quite close to it.

And then the Gods had smiled on him again. A detail man stopped by his place of business. Not only did he purchase first-class accommodations to American Samoa, where the American College of Tonsil, Adenoid and Vas Deferens Surgeons were holding a convention, but he took the fifteen-glorious-never-to-be-forgotten-days-in-North-Africa package off Hammerschmidt's hands.

It would, he said, make a splendid door prize for his company to give some deserving, chosen-by-random healer at the State Medical Convention. With a little politicking, he even managed to arrange with the committee for the package tour to be awarded last. This was something of a prize position—to be last. It was awarded to a doctor selected from among those doctors who had been at last year's convention, but whom the press of his duty to his fellowman had kept from attending this year's convention.

"God," Trapper John said, taking some more acne medicine, "we forgot all about that!"

"Keep your fingers crossed," Hawkeye replied. He hiccuped.

"I told you to take your medicine," Mary Pierce whispered fiercely.

"That was a hiccup," Dr. McIntyre said, "not a burp—a regrettable side effect of this otherwise marvelous medication."

"May I have the envelope, please?" the baby doctor from Bangor said. A representative of House, Water and Grumbacher, Certified Public Accountants, hired to remove any suggestion at all of hanky-panky in prize-awarding, came from the wings, wearing a top hat, white tie, tails and high, black mesh stockings. (It was, of course, a female representative of House, Water and Grumbacher.)

The baby doctor from Bangor tore open the envelope.

"Oh, this is wonderful," he said, coyly. "I can think of no one who would more enjoy fifteen glorious never-to-be-forgotten days in Merry Morocco with his wife than the winner!"

"He's talking about you, Trapper," Hawkeye said. "You're always complaining out loud about being as thirsty as a camel."

"The winner," the baby doctor said, "is that distinguished surgeon, the co-proprietor of the Finest Kind Fish Market and Medical Clinic . . . whose card says he was unable to be with us because he mistakenly sutured his fingers together . . . Dr. Benjamin Franklin Pierce."

A loud groan came from deep within Dr. Pierce's chest.

"Is there anyone here who would be willing to claim Dr. Pierce's prize for him?" the baby doctor asked, waving the airplane tickets over his head.

Mary Pierce rushed down the aisle, pausing only long enough to inform the Oldest Physician Present that she would be willing to take his luggage off his hands, and up onto the stage.

Dr. John Francis Xavier McIntyre rose to his feet and began to sing "The Sheikh of Araby." Dr. Pierce snatched what looked like a six-ounce medicine bottle from Dr. McIntyre's hand, tilted it to his mouth and drained it.

Mary Pierce, now on the stage, grabbed the microphone from the baby doctor from Bangor: "I would like to thank all those who made this possible," she began.

Drs. McIntyre and Pierce collapsed in their seats, one apparently suddenly struck hysterical, and the other apparently in agony.

Chapter Two

When His Royal Highness Prince Hassan ad Kayam, heir-apparent to the Sheikhdom of Hussid and chairman of the Council of Ministers of Petroleum of the Pan-Arabic Oil Consortium, saw the internationally famous opera singer, Maestro Boris Alexandrovich Korsky-Rimsakov, across the polished marble floor of Paris's Hotel George V, his heart fell and his gastric juices started to boil. He reached inside his gold embroidered robes for his roll of Tums for the Tummy.

It wasn't that His Royal Highness didn't like the singer. Quite the contrary. Hassan and Boris were the best of friends, and had shared many jolly escapades together. These usually involved long-legged, well-bosomed blonde females, in which His Highness had long had an interest, but with whom, pre-Boris, he had had little success, despite an income estimated by *Fortune* Magazine at $30,000 (pre-devaluation) weekly.

Long-legged, well-bosomed blonde females (as well

as short-legged, flat-bosomed brunettes; amply bosomed, short-legged, red-haired females; et cetera, et cetera) gathered around Boris Alexandrovich Korsky-Rimsakov like moths around a candle flame. Boris's rejects provided his pal with more feminine companionship than, pre-Boris, he would have dreamed possible, and he had had a rather active imagination.

Normally, His Royal Highness would have been delighted at the sight of his friend whom, until this moment, he had believed to be in New York City singing the title role in *Otello* at the Metropolitan Opera. Especially since Boris was in the company of two blondes, a redhead and a brunette.

But these were not ordinary circumstances. His Royal Highness was in the company of Sheikh Abdullah ben Abzug, absolute ruler of the Abzug tribe and the 15,000 square miles of granite mountains, desert and subterranean oil deposits of the Abzugian Sheikhdom.

Sheikh Abdullah ben Abzug was a sheikh of the old school. When he had boarded His Royal Highness's helicopter for the flight to Marrakech where His Royal Highness's Douglas 707 was waiting to fly them to Paris, it had been not only Sheikh Abzug's first helicopter flight as well as his first airplane flight, but the first time in his sixty-eight years (or sixty-nine, there being no accurate registry of births—or for that matter of anything else—in the Sheikhdom) that he had stepped foot on anything—land, carpet, Rolls-Royce, whatever —that he did not own.

Originally a nomadic tribe, the Abzugians had moved across the great desert after the Great War of 1802 to their present homeland. You will recall that Sheikh Mohammed the Merciful (1770–1806) had methodically slaughtered all adult males (fourteen and older) of those tribes which had surrendered to him after the Battle of Ungawallah, on June 11, 1802, and then had marched after the fleeing Abzugians with the same purpose in mind.

By the time the Camel Corps of Mohammed the Merciful caught up with the Abzugians in December of that year, they had reached the ridge of mountains separating the Sahara Desert from what is now Morocco and had established what proved to be impenetrable defenses. The Siege of the Mountains (1802–1806), which terminated only upon the death of Mohammed the Merciful, is the longest sustained military operation in Arabian military history, although not, of course, the only spectacularly unsuccessful one.

During the Siege of the Mountains, Sheikh Ahmed the Wise (sometimes known as Ahmed the Suspicious), who had not been willing to surrender to Mohammed the Merciful and who had led the trek across the desert to the mountains, died and was succeeded by his son, Abdu ben Ahmed, who was later to be known as Ahmed the Shepherd. The appellation had a double meaning. It made reference to both his devoted sheepherding of the Abzugians and to the means by which he established the Abzugian economic base. Recognizing that sheep and goats were essential to the survival of his people and that he had none to speak of, Ahmed the Shepherd, even before the death of his father, proceeded to rectify the situation.

In a series of daring raids, the Abzugian Camel Corps swept out of the mountains into what is now Morocco and returned with large flocks of sheep and goats taken at sword point from the Moroccan tribes. In obedience to the exhortation in the Koran to "go forth and multiply," they also brought back with them whatever women they happened to encounter. Each male Abzugian was allotted three females.

This naturally angered the tribes in Morocco, and a series of attacks was launched against the mountain redoubt; but these (which lasted until about 1840) met with no more success than had the attacks on Mohammed the Merciful.

Gradually, a détente with their Moroccan neighbors evolved, much of it based on the role of the female vis-à-vis the Moroccan and Abzugian cultures. The Abzugians, whose 3-to-1 ratio had produced a viable socioeconomic life-style, were perfectly willing to take excess females from the Moroccans, whose 1-on-1 ratio (monogamy) had produced a far less efficient (and apparently less satisfying) social structure. The Abzugians sometimes went so far as to take excess Moroccan females in lieu of sheep or goats but, normally, the Abzugians demanded at least 50 percent of their annual tribute in livestock.

During the French Occupation of Morocco, the détente between the Moroccans and the Abzugians was greatly strengthened. Sheikh Beni ben Mohammed (grandfather of the present Sheikh) permitted Moroccans fleeing before the French Foreign Legion to find refuge in his mountain redoubt. After several valiant, but quite futile, attempts to crush the Abzugian Redoubt by the French Foreign Legion (the last on May 19, 1909), it was decided to pacify the Abzugians only after the rest of Morocco had finally been brought peacefully and for all time under the French Tricolor. They were classified a "backward tribe" by the French and, for this reason, the precise boundaries of the Sheikhdom have never appeared on maps.

(François-Marie Alexander Hautetblance, when a distinguished French lieutenant general, told the story of his own service as a young officer in the region. He asked his captain where he could expect to find the Sheikhdom of Abzug. "Ride out toward the mountains," his superior told him. "When one of those barbarians shoots you between the eyes with one of our rifles, you know you're at the border.")

One of those to whom the Sheikh of Abzug gave refuge was His Royal Highness Ali ben Hassan of Hussid who, while serving as an officer in the British Army, was being pursued by the Turks during World War I.

As soon as he was able to return to his own side, he sent to the Sheikh a solid-gold wristwatch, self-winding, from Switzerland. The Sheikh had seen watches before, of course, interesting little devices that went tick-tock, tick-tock, which he had taken from the French, but never before had he seen one that would continue to do this day after day, week after week. All the others had stopped going tick-tock, tick-tock after the sun had come up twice.

As a token of his appreciation for the tick-tock, the Sheikh sent His Royal Highness some things he considered of value: two camels, four goats, one well-breasted Berber guaranteed to be a virgin, plus a hand-woven prayer rug.

Thus began the relationship between the Sheikhdom of Hussid and the Sheikhdom of Abzug. Aside from friendship, however, it had been a sort of economic one-way street. The Hussid Sheikhdom had sent teachers and doctors to Abzug, and the Abzugians had sent the Hussids more sheep, goats and prayer rugs, the word having passed as tactfully as possible that there was already a surfeit of virgins in Hussid. And then, after oil had been discovered under Hussid's shifting sands, just before World War II, the word was passed that there was a sufficiency of goats and sheep, too.

The time had now come, as the Sheikh of Hussid rather bluntly told his son and heir, His Royal Highness Prince Hassan ad Kayam, to drag the Abzugians into the twentieth century. The Wise Men had spoken, the Sheikh said. All seismological data gathered to date had been run through the computer and there seemed to be little question that a hundred feet or so below Abzug's soil were large pools of oil and large deposits of natural gas.

It wasn't that His Hussidic Majesty objected to paying for the entire national Abzugian budget (Rolls-Royces and all, it was in the Hussidic budget under "petty cash"), but rather an honest belief on his part that the Abzugians would be much better off if they were paying their own way.

He instructed his son to first get Sheikh Abdullah ben Abzug's permission to drill for oil; then to arrange for the drilling, supervising it himself; then to arrange for the sale of the oil; and then for the other necessities, pipelines, refineries, and so on.

When His Royal Highness Prince Hassan ad Kayam spotted Maestro Boris Alexandrovich Korsky-Rimsakov across the polished marble floor of the George V, His Highness was on Step One of the plan to bring the Sheikhdom of Abzug into the Twentieth Century, and he wasn't doing very well.

The Sheikh had passed the helicopter flight from his capital to Marrakech in prayer. With his head bent to the prayer rug, he had not, of course, been able to see out of the helicopter. He had spent the first thirty minutes of the Marrakech-Paris flight in prayer, until he developed a crick in the neck and got to his feet. The Sheikh had, at first, been fascinated with his new surroundings, although he had some difficulty in understanding why it was absolutely impossible for him to ride the rest of the way walking on the wing.

But then he happened to glance downward from 30,-000 feet and seen the cloud cover, like so much cotton batting, between him and the earth. He had said nothing at the time, but had obviously been lost in his own thoughts for the rest of the flight.

In Prince Hassan's Cadillac limousine, en route from Orly Field to the George V Hotel, he finally spoke, to announce that, having considered all things, when the time came for him to leave this place, he would do so on ground transportation. If Allah had intended man to fly like the birds, he would obviously have given him wings. He, Sheikh Abdullah ben Abzug, would return to his Sheikhdom as God intended; that is, by Rolls-Royce.

Neither, he announced, after being shown the fifth-floor Royal Suite of the George V, did he think that such surroundings would do. He was reluctant to give his reasons at first, saying that he would, for the time being, be perfectly content to sit here in the lobby of the hotel watching all the strange people. Finally, however, just before Hassan spotted Boris and Boris spotted Hassan, he gave his reasons.

For all of his life, but especially in the last twenty years, he had had the habit of rising in the middle of the night to void his bladder. A man doing that in the middle of the night, five floors up, was running a risk a wise man would not take.

The Sheikh was sure that his friend Prince Hassan would be able to make other arrangements for him.

The Sheikh had brought with him, as in the Arab custom, his personal bodyguard. As the Sheikh had sipped his tea and confessed his concern about his nocturnal necessities, the bodyguard, a 250-pound, six-foot-two-inch Son of the Desert had suspiciously eyed the patrons in the hotel lobby with a frown of disapproval that would have done credit to the U.S. Secret Service. When he saw Boris Alexandrovich Korsky-Rimsakov, he had a triple reaction. The first was the admiration of one large man for another. Boris was three inches taller and forty pounds heavier than the bodyguard. Furthermore, he had a magnificent beard: black, thick, curly, shining, the sort of beard every Arab wishes he could have. The first two reactions, therefore, were pleasurable. The third was quite the reverse. This huge man was approaching Sheikh Abdullah ben Abzug and Prince Hassan with a broad smile on his face. Protocol required that Sheikh Abdullah be approached, especially by infidels, by crawling on the stomach.

The bodyguard pulled his knife from his waistband.

"Hassan, you old camel thief," Boris Alexandrovich Korsky-Rimsakov cried loudly, "am I glad to see you!"

"Excellency," Prince Hassan said quickly, in Arabic, "the man who approaches us means no harm. He is well-known to me."

"Infidel, isn't he?" the Sheikh said. "But look at the *size* of him! There's Arab blood in him for sure."

"Hello, Maestro," Prince Hassan said.

"Put the knife away," Sheikh Abdullah ben Abzug said. "This infidel bastard is a friend of Prince Hassan's."

"Now see here, hooknose," Boris Alexandrovich Korsky-Rimsakov said, in fluent Arabic, "any pal of my pal Hassan is a friend of mine, but knock off that infidel-bastard business, O.K.?"

"You are an Arab," Sheikh Abdullah said. "You speak Arabic. You must be an Arab."

"What I am," Boris said in Arabic, "is a genius—musically and intellectually. I speak . . . let's see . . . eleven languages." He sat down in one of the armchairs. It creaked ominously under the load. He snapped his fingers to attract the attention of the waiter. The sound rang like a rifle shot in the large room, causing a waiter bearing a silver tea service on a tray to stiffen and jerk, spilling the whole thing on the floor.

"I admire your women," Sheikh Abdullah ben Abzug said to Boris, nodding his head toward the Baroness d'Iberville and Esmerelda Hoffenburg, the ballerina, who were smiling in his direction, waiting where Boris had left them near the reception desk. "Are they for sale?"

"I think you could probably work something out with the Baroness," Boris said, "but Esmerelda has a boyfriend just as rich as Hassan."

"Your Excellency," Hassan said, "among the other strange customs of the infidels is a prohibition against selling females."

"How strange," Sheikh Abdullah said.

"Some of them," Boris said, "actually believe in equality of the sexes."

"Astonishing!" Sheikh Abdullah said. "And how do you cope with this?"

"I just laugh at them," Boris said.

The waiter appeared.

"I thought you were home with your father," Boris said to Hassan.

"And I thought you were in New York singing *Otello*."

"You speak of the opera by Giuseppe Verdi?" Sheikh Abdullah asked.

Hassan looked at him in surprise, even shock. The last thing he expected Sheikh Abdullah to be familiar with was Italian opera.

"Why, yes, Your Excellency," he said, "we do. Are you familiar with *Otello?*"

"My grandson," the Sheikh said, and his eyes lit at the very thought of the boy. "Omar ben Ahmed, has developed a taste for Western music. Most of it, of course, pains the ears. But he has a phonograph recording of that opera which I have come to admire. There is one singer, a man whose very voice tells you that hundreds of healthy children have sprung from his loins, whose Allah-given tones make up for all the female caterwauling one must also hear."

"I see," Hassan said.

"You say you sing in this opera," the Sheikh said to Boris. "Has it been your very good fortune to have heard the golden-toned lion of which I speak, a man by the name of Korsky-Rimsakov, sing?"

Boris Alexandrovich Korsky-Rimsakov got to his feet. The bodyguard, mistaking his intention, unsheathed his knife again. Boris put his right hand on his chest, inhaled and opened his mouth. The final lines from scene 4, act 4, *"Cold now, yea, even as cold as thy chastity, most fit for heaven. Desdemona! Desdemona! Ah, Dead! Dead! Dead!"* came out of his throat.

The chandelier over the main staircase trembled. The plate-glass mirror behind the assistant manager's counter cracked and then crashed in a thousand shards to the marble floor. The Baroness d'Iberville slumped to the ground in a swoon.

"Boris Alexandrovich Korsky-Rimsakov at your service," he said. He bowed slightly from the waist toward Sheikh Abdullah and then sat down.

The Sheikh stared at him in disbelief for a moment, tears running down his cheeks. Then he slipped a nineteen-carat cut emerald, mounted in platinum and surrounded with a dozen small (nothing larger than a half-carat) diamonds, from his index finger and gently pressed it into Boris's hand.

"I don't want your ring," Boris, startled, said, in English. "It'd make me look like a fairy film producer."

"Take it," Hassan hissed, in English. "Say thank you and take it. I'll explain later."

"The ring does not please you, oh golden-voiced one?"

Sheikh Abdullah asked, a look of concern (and perhaps of about-to-be-injured pride) on his face.

"Oh, sure, Sheikh," Boris said, slipping back into Arabic. "Thanks a lot. Just what I've always wanted."

"You must come with me to my home," the Sheikh said, "and sing for my grandson."

"Well, I'll see how the schedule looks, Sheikh," Boris said.

"Boris, here they come," Hassan said in alarm. He gestured toward the lobby door, opening onto Avenue George V. A thin line of hotel employees and gendarmes was about to fall beneath a crowd of about two hundred middle-aged, amply built Parisian women who had needed only the ninety seconds of Verdi that Boris had sung to know that he was somewhere in the neighborhood; to find where; to throw modesty, decorum and everything else aside to satisfy their deep hunger to see him; and, if the Gods were smiling on them, perhaps even to touch him.

A look of genuine concern crossed Boris's face.

"What did you let me sing for?" he demanded angrily. "You know what always happens! The last time this happened, by the time I got away I was wearing nothing but one garter and a jockstrap."

He took off at a dead run for the rear of the hotel.

"You go with him, Your Excellency," Hassan said, suddenly making up his mind. "I'll stay here and fight a rear-guard action."

"Ahmed will stay with you," the Sheikh said. "Sell your life dearly," he ordered. Allah will reward you for it in heaven!" He drew his own dagger and, with surprising agility for a man of sixty-eight (or sixty-nine), ran after Boris, vowing in his mind that before the Infidel Women got the Golden-Voiced One, they would know they had been in a fight with a man.

It was not the first time that his fans had pursued Boris Alexandrovich Korsky-Rimsakov into the George V, so the hotel management was prepared for this invasion, even though it was unexpected.

Boris boarded an elevator, holding the door open
with his hand long enough for Sheikh Abdullah ben
Abzug to get in with him, and then rode the elevator
down to the subbasement. Tucking the Sheikh's arm
into his, he made his way through a maze of steampipes,
water drains and the like, around the electrical generating
system to a heavy, bolted steel door. A hotel employee
unlocked it, and Boris and Sheikh Abdullah went through
it. A panel truck, lettered HOTEL GEORGE V GARBAGE
DESPOSEMENT, sat there, engine running. Boris and
Abdullah got into the back, which had been outfitted
with two armchairs and a bottle of Dom Perignon '54
in a silver cooler. The door closed.

The truck drove up the ramp and onto Avenue George
V, tooting its horn and making its way slowly but surely
through the frantic mass of women and the gendarmerie
attempting to bring them under control. The panel truck
drove up Avenue George V to the Place de General
Charles de Gaulle (formerly Place de l'Étoile), circled
the Arc de Triomphe, then drove the quarter of a mile
down Rue de la Grande Armée, where it turned off
and finally drove into the courtyard of one of the elegant
apartment houses that line both sides of the street.

It stopped. The driver jumped from behind the wheel,
ran to the rear of the truck and opened the door.

"All is well, Maestro," he said, bowing as he opened
the door.

"It went very smoothly this time," Boris Alexandrovich said. "My compliments to the management."

"Our pleasure, Maestro," the driver said.

"Where are we?"

"We're at my pad," Boris said. "Come on in. Hassan
will be along in a little while. You and me'll have a
little belt until he shows up."

"A little belt?" Sheikh Abdullah asked, somewhat
confused.

"Something to keep the pipes greased," Boris said.
He tossed the now-drained bottle of Dom Perignon '54
into a garbage can. "You never can fly on one wing,
as I always say."

Sheikh Abdullah was disturbed to the point that he didn't notice that the elevator which they now boarded took them to the top floor of the building. He allowed himself to be shown to a large, tastefully furnished living room and installed on a couch.

"What's your pleasure, Sheikh?" Boris asked. "Some more of the bubbly?"

"My friend," the Sheikh said, "I do not wish to insult your magnificent hospitality, but I follow the teachings of the Prophet. . . . "

"Which prophet is that?" Boris asked, politely.

"Mohammed," the Sheikh explained. "And the Prophet teaches that his followers should not partake of the fermented grape."

"He certainly has a point," Boris said. "Not to worry, Sheikh." Boris turned to a large bar, poured three ounces of a clear liquid into a glass and handed it to the Sheikh.

"And what is this?"

"It's a health drink I have sent from Yugoslavia," Boris said. "It's sort of plum juice. They call it slivovitz."

The Sheikh took a healthy swallow and winced, his eyes closing, as the slivovitz hit tongue, mouth and throat accustomed to nothing stronger than orange juice and tea.

"It has a strange flavor," he said, looking with something close to envy at Boris Alexandrovich, who tossed his glass down neat, gave off with a pleasureful belch and patted his stomach in appreciation. He then poured another glassful.

"It grows on you," Boris said. "It does wonders for the appetite and settling the stomach."

The Sheikh was fully aware that medicines and tonics often had an unpleasant taste. Possibly this foul-tasting, burning liquid was the elixir which gave this angel-voiced lion of a man his strength. And not only the strength to sing, the Sheikh realized, after a moment, but to have all those females clamoring for his services. If that was the case, certainly a moment's unpleasant taste and a burning sensation was a cheap enough price to pay.

Sheikh Abdullah raised the glass of slivovitz to his

lips and, in the manner of a man taking medicine, downed it with a grimace and squinting eyes. Oddly enough, it didn't taste as bad or burn as painfully now as it had with the first swallow. And its medicinal, tonic qualities were now quite evident: a warm, entirely pleasant glow began to spread from Sheikh Abdullah's throat and stomach all over his body.

"Forgive my bad manners," Sheikh Abdullah said, "but could you possibly find it in your heart to spare an old man another draught of your marvelous elixir?"

"My pleasure, Sheikh," Boris said, refilling both their glasses. He raised his glass to his lips and, in his own tongue, offered the dedicatory incantation of his infidel faith. The least that good manners dictated that he do, Sheikh Abdullah realized, would be to offer the dedicatory incantation himself. It was the first English phrase that had ever passed his lips: "Mud in your eye," he repeated, solemnly.

"You're all right, Sheikh," Boris said to him in Arabic, patting him warmly on the back. "What was it you said brought you to Paris?"

"It was an invitation I could not refuse," Sheikh Abdullah said, "from the son of an old friend. He wishes me to go into the oil business." He took another swallow of the slivovitz. The elixir now seemed to have an entirely new, wholly pleasant taste.

"Well, you'd better watch out," Boris said. "Unless you know what you're doing, you can lose your shirt in the oil business."

"You are not suggesting that Hassan ad Kayam is less than honest?"

"Hassan is as honest as the day is long," Boris said.

"I am pleased to hear you say that," the Sheikh said.

"Not too bright, but honest," Boris said.

"I had the same feeling myself," the Sheikh said. "You know others in the oil business?"

"As a matter of fact," Boris said, pausing to freshen the Sheikh's glass, "one of my dearest friends happens to be in the oil business: Horsey de la Chevaux."

"That sounds French," the Sheikh said, deeply suspicious.

"No," Boris said, "he's an American—like me."

"You are an *American?* From your name, my friend, I thought perhaps you were Russian."

"Way back, I suppose," Boris said, "on my father's side. But I am an American."

"Mud in your eye," the Sheikh said solemnly, hoping he had the pronunciation correct. He tossed down the slivovitz.

"Mud in *your* eye," Boris replied, smiling and tossing down his slivovitz.

The Sheikh was pleased. This giant of a man liked him. The elixir made him feel twenty, even thirty, years younger. There seemed to be only one problem.

"My dear friend," the Sheikh said, "I grovel at your feet in my shame."

"What seems to be the problem?" Boris asked.

"We have drunk all of the elixir," the Sheikh said, nodding at the empty bottle. "Now you have none for yourself!"

"There's plenty more where that came from," Boris said, grandly. "But what do you say we get out of here and find some action?"

"Action?" the Sheikh said. "I regret I do not understand."

"I, too, have a prophet," Boris said, getting somewhat unsteadily to his feet. "Dr. T. Yancey Mullins, of Manhattan, Kansas."

"Allah has many names and many faces," the Sheikh intoned. "Mud in your eye."

"Precisely," Boris said. "Dr. T. Yancey Mullins teaches that man must exercise regularly, even religiously."

"Forgive me, my friend," the Sheikh said, as they staggered toward the door, "but is that such an original idea?"

"There is exercise, and then there is exercise," Boris said, as they entered the elevator. "In what will certainly rank with the discovery of penicillin and the X-ray as major breakthroughs in medical science, the Sage of Manhattan, Kansas, has discovered the best and most beneficial exercise of all."

"And what might that be?" the Sheikh asked, as they emerged in the lobby of the apartment house, lurched through it and out onto the Rue de la Grande Armée, where they entered a taxicab.

As they rode up the hill to the Arc de Triomphe, and down the hill to la rue de Pierre Charron, Boris told him of Dr. T. Yancey Mullins's theories.* Sheikh Abdullah ben Abzug could not have been more delighted.

"And we are going to exercise here?" he asked. "What is this place?"

"This is the Crazy Horse Saloon," Boris explained, as he led him across the sidewalk. "I always like to start out here, and then see what happens."

"I am completely in your hands, my friend," the Sheikh said.

Chapter Three

Within two hours of the disappearance from his Rue de la Grande Armée apartment of Boris Alexandrovich Korsky-Rimsakov, who was last seen in the company of His Highness, Sheikh Abdullah ben Abzug, the matter

---

* For further reading, see: *Sexual Intercourse: Man's Most Beneficial Exercise* (499 pp., New York, 1974; $9.95) and *Strength and Health Through Constant Coitus* (405 pp., illus., New York, 1975; $10.95); both by Theosophilis Yancey Mullins, M.D., Ph.D., D.V.M., D.D.

came to the official attention of the Deuxième Bureau of the French Government.

The Deuxième Bureau is for the French what the F.B.I., the C.I.A., the D.A.R. and the Ralph Nader Organization, all rolled together, are for the Americans. Whenever the peace, security, national prestige or financial stability of the French Republic is in any manner affected, the Deuxième Bureau is ordered into action.

The disappearance of two foreigners would have been enough in itself to trigger Deuxième Bureau action, but the case at hand went much further than that. These were not two ordinary, run-of-the-mill foreigners. Sheikh Abdullah ben Abzug was traveling, as a sovereign head of state, on a special diplomatic passport. More important, he had been in the company of His Royal Highness, Prince Hassan ad Kayam, heir-apparent to the Throne of Hussid, from which Sheikhdom the French Republic obtained thirty-eight percent of its petroleum needs.

The pressure from the French Foreign Ministry and the French Ministry of Petroleum Procurement upon the Deuxième Bureau was, understandably, enormous. However, it was nothing like the pressure brought to bear by L'Académie française and the French National Opera Association in terms of intensity or completely unveiled threats. Boris Alexandrovich Korsky-Rimsakov who, for two years, had been classified as an Official National Artistic Treasure of France, was scheduled to sing the title role in Jacques Offenbach's opera, *The Tales of Hoffmann,* at Paris's French National Opera House in two days.

It was to be a gala, charity performance, for the benefit of St. Imogene's School for Girls. St. Imogene's, a small school in the Maritime Province, had enjoyed 260 years of peaceful obscurity until just recently, when Mademoiselle Bernadette St. Croix, a recent graduate who had found postgraduation employment as a chambermaid at Le Grand Hotel St. Bernard, had caught the eye of a visiting politician and shortly thereafter had become Madame le President of the Fourth Republic.

The word had come down from the Elysée Palace

that if Madame le President wanted to stage a benefit opera for the benefit of her old school, Monsieur le President felt that nothing should be allowed to stand in her way. Any government servant who felt otherwise would probably be happier serving his country in the Senegalese desert.

The major problem in staging the performance had been Boris Alexandrovich Korsky-Rimsakov, star of the Paris Opera and Official National Artistic Treasure of *La Belle France.* It was generally agreed that unless *Cher* Boris Alexandrovich, as he was fondly known, was on stage to sing the role of Hoffmann, ticket sales would not be as satisfactory as they could be. *Cher* Boris Alexandrovich's appeal to French womanhood was well-known. When he sang a role in which he could bare his chest, it was possible to add a fifty percent surtax. The surtax was allegedly to pay for the erection of the Korsky-Rimsakov protective curtain, a heavy wire mesh arrangement needed to protect the singer and the rest of the cast from the shower of hotel-room keys and other items which sailed stageward from the audience in tribute to both his manhood and art during the performance.

Actually, almost all of the surtax could be applied to profits. Furthermore, when *Cher* Boris Alexandrovich was to sing with his chest in sight, it was possible to charge *performance spectaculaire* prices for tickets (twice the normal price) without a murmur of disapproval from his fans.

The effect of all this was that, presuming Korsky-Rimsakov sang *Hoffmann,* St. Imogene's School would receive as their share as much money as if the opera had simply been turned over to them, and the opera (because of the twice-the-normal-price tickets) would have a full house at standard rates. Everybody would be happy, especially Madame et Monsieur who occupied the Elysée Palace.

The problem was that Maestro Korsky-Rimsakov was in New York City. The Metropolitan Opera's most generous offer to him to sing *Otello* had coincided with a deep yearning on the part of the singer to return to the land of his birth, whose uniform he had worn in Korea, at least long enough to partake of a native delicacy of his youth—bagels and lox, which was not available in Paris at the level of gustatory excellence common along New York's Third Avenue.

And so he had agreed to sing, one performance only, at Lincoln Center, presuming the Metropolitan was willing to meet his simple needs during his stay. A floor in the Waldorf Towers was set aside for his use; round-the-clock Carey limousine service was arranged for; the Tactical Riot Squad of the New York Police Department was assigned to protect him from his fans; and the color-television sets in both the limousines and the hotel suite were specially rigged so that he would not, even while changing channels, ever be forced to look at Walter Cronkite.

(All of this was in addition, of course, to the standard contractual provisions for a Boris Alexandrovich Korsky-Rimsakov peformance, which included his choice of orchestra conductor, stage designer, chorus manager, fellow performers, and the right of approval of the guest list for the Spontaneous Appreciation Party which followed the performance.)

It was recognized by the Paris Opera that their problem of getting him back from New York to sing *Hoffmann* was far greater than it would have been if it had simply been a matter of keeping him in Paris. Keeping him in Paris required only that the director of the Opera have a little man-to-man chat with him, to impress on him his obligation to his art, the necessity of exercise to maintain his art and then to provide him with suitable exercise companions.

Extraordinary, even desperate, measures were going to be necessary to get him back from New York. Under the circumstances (Hell hath no fury like that of a sixty-two-year-old French husband of a twenty-year-old bride scorned), they were quickly provided. Air France made available a Concorde supersonic jet. It was outfitted with the little things *Cher* Boris Alexandrovich was

known to like: Iranian caviar, Dom Perignon '54,
Camembert cheese, a tape player, a supply of his own re-
cordings and, of course, the Baroness d'Iberville and
Esmerelda Hoffenburg, the ballerina.

Esmerelda Hoffenburg distracted the Tactical Riot
Squad guarding *Cher* Boris Alexandrovich by perform-
ing *Salome's* "Dance of the Seven Veils" on the steps
of St. Bartholomew's Church, which is across the street
from the Waldorf Towers. (Their distraction was complete. Esmerelda's choice of *Salome* was spur-of-the-
moment; and she was nearly through before she realized that she had been wearing but three layers of clothing, rather than the requisite eight, when she began.)

With the eyes of New York's Finest locked in rapt
fascination on Esmerelda, as she, in the cant of the
trade, "winged" removing the last four (now wholly
imaginary) veils, it was a simple matter for the Baroness
to entice *Cher* Boris Alexandrovich into the limousine
of the French Ambassador to the United Nations. She
knew from long experience that it would be best to attract
Cher Boris's attention by holding a bottle of Dom
Perignon '54 in one hand and a caviar cracker in the
other. There were far more women in his life who attempted to gain his affection by stripping off their
clothes than there were women who offered caviar.

Once *Cher* Boris Alexandrovich was inside the limousine, Esmerelda quickly scooped up her garments
(except her underpants, which unfortunately had
become snagged on the church bulletin board), trotted
gaily across the street and got into the limousine. They
were far up Park Avenue before the Police Riot Squad
closed their mouths.

The Baroness and Esmerelda were not surprised
when *Cher* Boris Alexandrovich readily agreed to go
for a little ride with them in what they described as
"their plane." He was, he told them, with typical Korsky-
Rimsakovian modesty, one of the charter members of
the Mile-High Club and, now that he'd had a little caviar
and champagne, would be delighted to personally sign

their qualification cards for forwarding to club headquarters.

He was, however, slightly annoyed when the plane
landed several hours later and he looked out the window
to see ORLY rather than JOHN F. KENNEDY.

"What the hell is this?" he demanded. "Have I been
zooming around the clouds with another drunken Frog
at the controls?"

"Boris, darling," the Baroness said, "forgive our little
trick. We need you."

"Need me?" he replied, tartly. "You've just had me.
Twice. Each. There is such a thing as too much exercise,
you know, even for someone in my superb all-around
physical condition. I suppose all the caviar is gone,
too?"

There was only a half-pound of caviar and one
jeroboam of Dom Perignon '54 left, barely enough to
stave off starvation and dehydration as they rode into
Paris in the Baroness's Daimler.

On the way, Boris agreed to sing *Hoffmann,* provided
he had their solemn, unqualified assurance that singing
was all that he had to do. "I will," he said, "have to
go directly from the stage to the airport if I am to be
on time to sing *Otello* in New York. I will have no
time to squander on the President's mistress."

"They are now married, *Cher* Boris Alexandrovich,"
Esmerelda corrected him.

"I knew that man wasn't to be trusted," Boris said.
"He has beady eyes and wears a rug. It doesn't surprise
me at all that he's gotten married." He looked out the
window and saw where on the Champs-Élysées they
were. "Turn left on Rue Pierre Charron," he said to
the driver. "Take me to the George V."

"I had hoped, *Cher* Boris Alexandrovich," Esmerelda said, "that we could go to my apartment." After
being jabbed painfully in the ribs by the Baroness, she
added, "All of us, of course."

"I know what you hoped, my dears," Boris said, "but
you have had all the exercise I can spare. I now re-

quire sustenance—a small steak and perhaps three or
four dozen oysters."

As a matter of fact, Boris was tempted to accept
Esmerelda's invitation. He felt the need for a little more
exercise. He had already planned to write Dr. T. Yancey Mullins personally to inquire whether the good
doctor's research into high-altitude exercise paralleled
his own. It probably had something to do with partial
weightlessness, or perhaps the high oxygen content of
the artificial pressurization; but his own experiences
(which he would publish pseudonymously in *The Journal of the Mile-High Club*) suggested that high-altitude
exercise was not as debilitating as exercise at sea level.

He knew, however, that any further exercise at this
time with the Baroness and Esmerelda would tend to
give them the impression that their services were somehow
special. They had, he reminded himself, already received
twice as much exercise as he normally permitted. If he
gave them any more, they would become insufferably
smug and arrogant. It had happened to him many times
before. Once he had had to hide out for three weeks
in a Trappist monastery.

They did not, as he hoped they would, remain in
the Daimler when he walked into the George V, but
trailed after him, already presuming that they had special
privileges. He was delighted when he saw Hassan and
some other A-rab in the lobby. Hassan was always so
grateful for his discards.

The pressure on the Deuxième Bureau to locate Boris
Alexandrovich Korsky-Rimsakov and Sheikh Abdullah
ben Abzug, therefore, had come from what are known
as "the highest quarters." Leaves were canceled. Two
companies of the Gendarmerie Nationale were placed
at the disposal of the officer-in-charge, and the Police
Commissioner for the city of Paris was personally ordered
by the President of the Republic himself to place his
entire force at the orders of the Deuxième Bureau.

It was all to no avail. Checkpoints at rail and air
terminals, and along all roads leading out of the city

turned up nothing. The vice squad, considerably embarrassed, reported that they had checked every hotel register in the city and come up with nothing. The Gendarmerie Nationale, armed with photographs of the singer and a police-artist's sketch of Sheikh Abdullah ben Abzug, checked every saloon, bar, bistro and Wimpy Burger stand in Greater Paris, and got nowhere. Boris and the Sheikh had apparently vanished from the face of the earth.

On the afternoon of the second day, however, there was a development at once encouraging and baffling. The assistant manager of the Paris Opera received a telephone call from a person alleging to be the missing singer. His telephone, of course, was connected to a tape recorder, a standard procedure when the very real possibility of kidnapping had to be considered.

The message ("This is Boris Alexandrovich Korsky-Rimsakov speaking. I will require a box for this evening's performance. The President's box will do.") was brief, the words appeared slightly slurred and, at first, it was believed that it was simply a hoax. But when the tape was replayed in the laboratory of the Deuxième Bureau and run through the audiospectographic computer (where it was compared with the singer's voice patterns taken from phonograph records), all doubt was removed. It was Korsky-Rimsakov's voice. He, at least, was alive. They could only hope against hope regarding Sheikh Abdullah ben Abzug.

At seven forty-five that evening, three gendarmes on duty in front of the Opera jumped in front of a battered Volkswagen bus which came onto the Place de l'Opéra, and by its flashing turn signals, indicated its outrageous intention to join the line of glistening Rolls-Royce, Citröen, Mercedes-Benz and Daimler limousines discharging their formally dressed passengers at the main entrance of the Opera.

The gendarmes, blowing their whistles furiously, managed to stop the Volkswagen bus, which, on closer examination, appeared to be not only driven by a United States Marine in full dress uniform, but jammed full of other ornately uniformed Marines and their female companions, none of whom could be called ladies unless of-the-evening was appended to the appellation.

At this point, the canvas sunroof of the Volkswagen bus slid back, and Boris Alexandrovich Korsky-Rimsakov's massive head and shoulders appeared.

"Get out of the way, you chinless idiot!" he screamed at the gendarme sergeant. "Boris Alexandrovich Korsky-Rimsakov is here!"

The whistles stopped blowing. A hush fell on the area—even those Parisians whose enjoyment of opera comes from standing outside the police barriers and offering pungent observations about those who actually enter the building.

Boris put his fingers into his mouth and whistled, attracting the attention of the chauffeurs of the two limousines—a Citröen and a Cadillac—nearest the official discharge point. "All right, Alphonse," he bellowed to the driver of the Citröen, "move it out of there." He pointed a finger at the second chauffeur. "And, you, Gaston, hold it right there!" A place was thus created at the official discharge point into which, following instructions from the vehicle commander, the Volkswagen bus quickly moved.

Boris had, of course, been recognized. The general manager and two of his assistants, on hand to greet the Very Important People, came to the curb itself as the Volkswagen's side door slid open.

Two Marines and their female companions emerged, and then *Cher* Boris Alexandrovich himself. He graciously acknowledged the applause of the crowd, raising his hands over his head in the manner of politicians accepting the nomination of their party for high political office. Then he turned back to the Volkswagen bus.

"O.K., Abdullah," he said, "there'll be time for more of that later. Out you go!"

His Royal Highness Abdullah ben Abzug, supported on one side by still another U.S. Marine and on the other side by a rather plump mademoiselle with frizzy red hair, stepped onto the sidewalk.

"We are honored," the general manager of the Opera said, somewhat in shock, "to have you with us this evening, Your Highness."

"Up yours," Sheikh Abdullah said grandly. "Mud in your eye." He had learned much English in the last two days, which he had spent in an apartment on the Rue Monsieur. It had been rented cooperatively by eight members of the United States Marine Guard Detachment of the American Embassy. He and his friend Boris had met these splendid young men at the Crazy Horse Saloon, and one thing had followed another (mostly elixir drinking and exercise).

"I called before to arrange for a box," Boris said to the general manager. "I presume it's ready for my guests?"

"Yes, of course, Maestro," the general manager said.

"Then what are we standing around on the sidewalk for?" Boris demanded. He linked arms with Sheikh Abdullah and, trailed by the ladies His Highness now thought of as "The Broads" and the detachment of Marines, they marched up the grand staircase of the Opera, between the lines of the Garde Nationale whose dress uniforms were almost, but not quite, as splendiferous as those provided the U.S. Marines.

The box set aside, as a precautionary measure, for *Cher* Boris Alexandrovich was not, of course, the Presidential (formerly Imperial) box. The President himself and Madame President were occupying that one. Sheikh Abdullah ben Abzug was led to the box immediately adjacent. He set his bottle of slivovitz carefully on the box's railing and sat down somewhat heavily.

"I gotta go change, Abdullah," Boris said. "I'll see you afterward."

"Mud in your eye," Sheikh Abdullah said, gesturing regally with his hand for one of "The Broads" to come kneel on the floor beside his chair.

By now, he had been spotted by the President himself, who exhaled in deep relief that His Highness was safe.

Then he stood up and leaned across the opening between the boxes.

"May I say how delighted I am to see Your Highness safe and sound," he said.

Sheikh Abdullah smiled and raised a friendly hand of greeting. "Your mother wears army shoes," he said. "Mud in your eye."

There was a flurry of excitement as someone was passed through the thick lines of security men (once they had him safe and sound, no chances were being taken) and given access to the box.

His Royal Highness Hassan ad Kayam entered the box.

"Oh, there you are, Hassan," Sheikh Abdullah said, in Arabic. "Where have you been all this time?"

"I trust you are well, my friend?" Hassan said.

"I am well," Sheikh Abdullah said. "Mud in your eye. And I have made a decision."

"What decision is that?"

"I have decided to permit oil exploration and exploitation," the Sheikh said.

"I'm delighted to hear that," Hassan said.

"Would you like one of these?" Sheikh Abdullah asked, gesturing at the redhead behind him and the blonde kneeling beside his chair. "My friends and I have more than enough to go around."

"Not just now," Hassan said. "You say you are going to go ahead with the oil development?"

"Put it from your mind," the Sheikh said. "All problems are solved. I have personally spoken on the telephone with Mr. Horsey de la Chevaux, the good friend of my dear friend Boris Alexandrovich, and he is at this very moment flying in the first technicians from someplace called Louisiana."

"I am delighted to hear that, Your Highness," Prince Hassan said, without very much enthusiasm at all.

"Mud in your eye," the Sheikh intoned. He leaned forward to smile at the President of France. He caught the eye of the President's wife.

"Up yours," he said, in his warm, benevolent tone. "Your mother wears army shoes."

And then the house lights dimmed and the conductor raised his baton.

Chapter Four

The Annual Report to Stockholders of Chevaux Petroleum International (64 four-color pages, 8 by 10 inches, circ., 34,560) has on its first inside page the following statement: "Founded in 1954 by Mr. Jean-Pierre de la Chevaux in Louisiana, Chevaux Petroleum International and its subsidiaries now operates in 119 countries around the world and, under Mr. de la Chevaux's enviable leadership, has increased its volume of business and profit figures each year since its founding."

That's the truth, but not, as the lawyers say, the whole truth and nothing but the truth.

Neither is the caption under the Bradford Bachrach photograph of Mr. de la Chevaux which fills page three of *The Annual Report to Stockholders:*

Col. Jean-Pierre de la Chevaux, founder, chairman of the board and chief executive officer of Chevaux Petroleum International, is descended from the very earliest Louisiana settlers. He founded the corporation shortly after returning from military service in Korea, during which he was decorated with the Distinguished Service Cross, the Silver Star and the Expert Combat In-

fantry's Badge, not to mention three Purple
Hearts for wounds received in action. In addition
to his business activities, he is a well-known leader
in charitable and fraternal affairs (especially the
Knights of Columbus, in which organization he
has long held high office) and yet finds time for
the fine arts. Among his many friends in the arts is
Mr. Boris Alexandrovich Korsky-Rimsakov, the
opera singer, whose annual appearance in New
Orleans to open the season at the Daisy-Mae de la
Chevaux Memorial Opera House is the major fea-
ture of the New Orleans social-cultural season.

The truth again, but nothing like the whole and unvarnished truth.

Horsey de la Chevaux did indeed earn the D.S.C.
and the other medals in Korea, but not as a colonel.
He was at the time a sergeant of the 223rd Infantry
Regiment, and was seriously wounded while leading his
platoon up Heartbreak Ridge. He was carried off the
ridge by Pfc. Bob Alexander, the nom de guerre of
Mr. Korsky-Rimsakov, who was then serving as his
Browning automatic rifleman.

Although the nature of his wounds was such that
loss of his right leg seemed inevitable, military surgeons
at the 4077th Mobile Army Surgical Hospital (MASH)
managed to save the limb. After a lengthy hospitalization,
Sgt. de la Chevaux was medically retired from the Army
with a thirty percent pension, and returned by Greyhound
bus to his ancestral lands in the Mississippi Delta, an
area known locally as Bayou Perdu.

The land, indeed, had been in the De la Chevaux
family for generations. The title to the land had come
to a long-forgotten ancestor from His Most Catholic
Majesty, Louis XIV, of France. It had remained in the
family, largely because the 16,000-acre tract was mostly
underwater much of the time, and officially described
in later years by the U.S. Coast and Geodetic Survey
as "marsh and swamp, unfit for agriculture or human
habitation."

The De la Chevaux family manse was a clapboard shack precariously perched on pilings over the swamp. Transportation between the nearest road (three miles distant) and the community of Bayou Perdu itself, a half-mile away, was by water—specifically, by hollowed-out cypress log, known as a "pirogue." The community of Bayou Perdu consisted of: six houses, identical in all respects to the De la Chevaux home; St. Antoine's Roman Catholic Church, a clapboard shack above which had been raised a Cross to mark its religious function; Pepe La Roche's General Store & Muskrat Skin Buyer; and the largest building in town—two clapboard shacks joined by a ramp—housing the Bayou Perdu Council, Knights of Columbus which, since the population was entirely Roman Catholic and the male population, without exception, members of the K. of C., filled the function of social center.

Mr. de la Chevaux, then known to his friends as "Horsey," had barely reaccustomed himself to being home—to spending his days poaching for deer and tending his still and his nights in the warm companionship of his fellow Knights of Columbus (of which he was Knight Commander of the Golden Fleece)—when the first surveyors appeared.

Actually, the surveyors who appeared, in National Guard amphibious tanks, were the second set of surveyors dispatched to the area by the State Highway Department. The first set of surveyors, who had arrived in swamp-flies (small, flat-bottomed vessels, powered by aircraft engines mounted aft), had been driven off with rifle fire by the inhabitants of Bayou Perdu in the mistaken belief they were agents of the Alcohol Revenue Department.

When the amphibious tanks appeared, Horsey de la Chevaux, who had been, after all, "a non-commissioned officer of the very highest ability and valor" (so said his D.S.C. citation), knew that this particular battle had been lost before it got started. Not even the heavy .50-caliber machine guns he had thoughtfully shipped home in pieces from Korea for use against *Les Revenues* would be of any good against tanks.

Flying a white T-shirt atop a cypress pole, Horsey, whose leg was still a little stiff, had poled out in his pirogue to meet the Revenuer tanks. Intelligence had been faulty. The occupants of the tanks were not after the stills at all (as a matter of fact, before they left, they had purchased twenty-one gallons of the local brew), but simply surveying the land. There was money from Washington, with which the state of Louisiana planned to construct a four-lane super-speed highway between Texas on one side and Mississippi on the other. The route of the projected road ran right through the De la Chevaux land holdings.

Horsey de la Chevaux was not at all interested in selling any of his land, even for such a practical purpose as a highway; but there didn't seem to be anything at all that he could do about it. When he consulted Father François LeGrand, pastor of St. Antoine's, Father François explained the legal principle of eminent domain to him. The state had the right, the good Father said, to take his land from him, paying fair market price, whether or not he wanted to sell it, if they could go to court and demonstrate that the public need would thus be better served.

"Take the land, O.K.," Horsey had replied, fingering the Garand M-1C sniper's rifle he had also sent home from Korea as a souvenir. "But dem bastards still be building dere highway when Sweet Jesus make duh Second Coming."

Father François was a persuasive man, and Horsey was dissuaded from engaging in guerrilla warfare against the duly constituted Highway Construction Authority of the state of Louisiana. The condemnation proceedings proceeded according to bureaucratic custom. For a 100-yard-wide swath through his land, Jean-Pierre de la Chevaux would receive $60,000.

(This figure was described by State Senator Elmer J. Morfutt, New Orleans Democrat, as "an unconscionable rape of the treasury," but the money was paid nevertheless, an appeal by the state to the United States Court of Appeals for the Fifth Circuit having been denied.)

Horsey de la Chevaux got back on the Greyhound bus and rode into New Orleans for his check to make those purchases his newfound wealth would permit. He even made television, in that minute-long "Today's Chuckle in the News" spot. Holding onto the microphone stand with one hand and clutching a quart bottle of Old White Stagg Blended Kentucky Sour Mash Bourbon in the other, Horsey had stared somewhat fish-eyed at the television lens while the newscaster explained Mr. de la Chevaux's recent good fortune.

"And how," the newscaster asked, laying his hand in a gesture of friendship on Horsey's shoulder, "do you intend to spend your money, Mr. de la Chevaux?"

"Getcherpawsoffme," Horsey replied somewhat thickly.

"I beg your pardon?" the newscaster said, pulling Horsey a little closer, so as to make a better television image.

Horsey, shaking himself loose from the newscaster, now said, each syllable perfectly clear, "Keep your paws off Horsey de la Chevaux, you lousy fairy."

Somewhat stunned, the newscaster fumbled for a moment and then finally blurted, "How do you plan to spend your money?"

"Oh, dat," Horsey said, and paused thoughtfully. "Three tings," he said. "I go by duh Sears, Roebuck. I get an outboard motor for the duh pirogue," he said, and searched his memory before continuing. "An' I get a new saw," he said. And then for the benefit of those who might not understand what kind of a saw he was talking about, he mimicked the noise by putting his tongue between his lips and blowing. It was a credible duplication of the sound, even if it did give the newscaster something of an unexpected alcohol bath. "And . . . oh, yeah," Horsey concluded, "Sears, Roebuck gonna come and drill me a new water well."

It was, everyone agreed, a pleasant little laugh, exquisite counterpoint to the grim and ominous news of the day.

Three weeks later, Horsey de la Chevaux was back on television, again clutching a bottle of Old White Stagg (this time a half-gallon) in one hand and hanging on to the microphone with the other. But this time he wasn't the last-minute laugh—he was the top of the news. Sears, Roebuck's water-well-drilling crew had been a failure, water-wise. What their simple little drilling rig had tapped was what the *Oil & Gas Journal* described as "the largest find of natural gas in the history of the industry."

It was, of course, generally presumed that the phrase "a fool and his money are soon parted" had been coined with Horsey de la Chevaux in mind. He would soon be sweet-talked out of his oil and gas and be back poaching deer and making moonshine.

This did not happen. In the words of Boris Alexandrovich Korsky-Rimsakov, in an interview in *Fortune* some years later, "Just because he looks and sounds like that doesn't mean he *is* a moron. Horsey is one of the sharpest men I've ever known. Otherwise, he would have been carrying that damned Browning automatic rifle and I would have been the sergeant in Korea. Ergo sum, in other words."

The statement came after the fact. By the time Mr. Korsky-Rimsakov was interviewed, Horsey had parlayed his initial $1,500,000 royalty advance into an enormous fortune, the exact extent of which no one knew. His method of successful oil exploration, allegedly the most closely guarded secret in the oil industry, was actually simplicity itself. Horsey de la Chevaux had simply roamed the world's swamps, from Venezuela to Borneo. Using a tin can nailed to a stick, he would obtain a sample of the muck on the swamp floor and then sniff the muck. If the smell was similar to that of the muck from the bottoms of the swamps in the Bayou Perdu area, he would nod, and a well would be put down. His wildcat well success rate was 62.8 percent, five times the industry average.

Horsey's experience with payday millionaires in the

Army, furthermore, had made him aware of the pitfalls
of sudden wealth. While he did, of course, share his
good fortune with his fellow Knights of Columbus, he
did so with forethought and care. He instituted an on-the-
job training program for his friends and neighbors. To
a man, they took to oil-well drilling as if they had
been born for it, as indeed, the job titles seemed to suggest. (Oil-well workers are known as roughnecks.) Within
ten years of the founding of Chevaux Petroleum, all
rig bosses, tour bosses and mud men employed by the
firm were members of the Bayou Perdu Council, K. of C.

A fleet of Chevaux jet aircraft, operating out of the
newly built Bayou Perdu International Airport, carried
them and their families to Chevaux operating locations
around the world.

. Mr. de la Chevaux, who had accepted a colonelcy
on the staff of the Governor of Louisiana mainly because
it carried with it the prerequisites of adorning his auto-
mobiles with flashing lights and sirens, was careful not
to disturb the generations-old work traditions of his
neighbors. Phrased simply, this was the custom of working no longer than was necessary to acquire sufficient
money to pay the next month's booze and food bills.
The work schedule that evolved was one month on and
two months off, a system which also served to provide
enough employment for all those in Bayou Perdu who
chose to seek work.

There were, of course, major social changes in Bayou
Perdu, most notably the Archbishop Mulcahy Memorial
School, a first-grade-through-high-school educational
facility, named for the distinguished clergyman (then
an Army chaplain) who had comforted Horsey while
he was hospitalized in Korea. Staffed with the finest
teachers money could import from France (English
was regarded as an unimportant second language in
Bayou Perdu) and instantly certified by Horsey's friend
the Governor, the Archbishop Mulcahy Memorial
School began to raise the educational level of the community rather spectacularly.

The clapboard, connected shacks which had housed

the Bayou Perdu Council, K. of C., were replaced with a 1.85-million-dollar Council Building, complete with bowling alleys, kitchen facilities and the longest bar east of the Mississippi, "a Victorian treasure" according to National Heritage, which had bitterly protested its removal from a hotel being torn down in San Francisco, California, and shipped by air to Bayou Perdu.

Horsey de la Chevaux recognized the importance of the Bayou Perdu Council, Knights of Columbus, in maintaining Bayou Perdu community spirit. He saw to it that the uniforms of the group (which had been acquired fifth-hand from a movie-theater chain, and which had first seen light at the 1939 New York World's Fair) were replaced by the most splendiferous uniforms available from Brooks Brothers of New York.

After several unfortunate crashes between the Cadillacs, Lincolns and Chrysler Imperials, with which the Bayou Perdu Council Knights had recently equipped themselves, and Louisiana State Highway Patrol cars, Horsey saw to it that the official dictum was issued by the Grand Council of Knights Superior & Extraordinary of the Council. It required all Knights to travel to and from K. of C. functions in official K. of C. transportation.

Horsey then got in touch with the people who make Greyhound buses and arranged for the production of four special buses. Outside (except for their flaming-yellow color scheme), they were identical to deluxe Greyhound buses. Inside, however, there were differences. The seats had been obtained from the firm which had equipped Presidential jet aircraft; there were sanitary facilities; bars; and a projector and screen for movies en route. When the driver touched the horn button, six large chrome-plated trumpet horns on the roof played "Onward, Christian Soldiers."

There were, however, some problems. As a wise man once said, "It is possible to take the Cajun out of the swamp, but getting the Cajun out of the Cajun is a horse of another color."

The Bayou Perdu Council, K. of C., was something of a thorn in the side of the other Councils of the Knights of Columbus. The generosity of the Bayou Perdu Council could not be faulted. They had a "Matching-Dollar Charitable Program," which saw a dollar contributed to K. of C. charities for every dollar that passed across the Victorian Treasure Bar, for every dollar spent on an outing (the Bayou Perdu Council were ardent supporters of what they called the New Orleans Saints Footsball team) and for every dollar spent on uniforms.

Neither could fault be found with their religious devotion. The Bayou Perdu Council participated in more religious ceremonies and festivals than any other Council in Louisiana or Mississippi. And as the Archbishop himself pointed out, it didn't really matter that the eagerness to participate was based largely on their desire to show off their uniforms and to participate in the post-festival drinking. The point was that they were there.

What bothered the other Councils of the K. of C. was a certain lack of dignity and a certain informality on the part of the Bayou Perdu Council, K. of C. Many felt that the image of the entire organization was seriously damaged, for example, by the participation of the Bayou Perdu Council in K. of C. parades. Council after Council would march down the street, preceded by drum majors, drum majorettes, baton twirlers and fine marching bands playing "The Stars and Stripes Forever," the "Washington Post March" and other such rousing pieces, all of it combining to paint a splendid portrait of the patriotism and discipline of the K. of C.

And then the Bayou Perdu Council would appear (often to wild shouts of appreciation from spectators) with their band. The band consisted of three bass drums, two tubas, a xylophone, four Jew's harps, a steam calliope and a sousaphone. There were but two numbers in the band's repertoire: "There'll Be a Hot Time in the Old Town Tonight" and "When the Saints Come Marching In," which were rendered with great, if somewhat unskilled, enthusiasm.

The Archbishop had readily admitted, when meeting with delegates from outraged Councils, that he too suspected that the Bayou Perdu bandsmen had fortified themselves with intoxicants for the rigors of the march; and that the spectacle of the Bayou Perdu drum major leaving his post to force his unwanted amorous attention upon Miss Estelle Grogarty, head baton twirler of the St. Paul's Council Marching Band, was indeed conduct unbecoming a Knight of Columbus.

He had, the Archbishop said, already had a stern little chat with both Knight Commander of the Golden Fleece de la Chevaux and with Father François LeGrand, the Bayou Perdu Council's spiritual adviser, and he would speak with them again.

Privately, the Archbishop had little hope that he would be able to do any good. After the unfortunate incident during which the Bayou Perdu Council, in full uniform, had stormed onto the football field in Dallas, Texas, with the announced intention of hanging to the goalpost a referee who had ruled for the Cowboys and against the Saints, he had staged a full-scale inquisition into Bayou Perdu Council behavior and discipline.

Knight Commander of the Golden Fleece de la Chevaux was the picture of an admitted sinner and penitent. He announced that he deeply regretted any embarrassment the Bayou Perdu Council had caused the rest of the Knights of Columbus, and instantly offered the resignations of all concerned from the organization.

That was not the response the Archbishop had expected.

"I hardly think it's necessary to go quite that far, Horsey," he said.

"It's all right, Archbishop," Horsey said. "We been talking about starting our own Knights anyway."

"I beg your pardon?"

"Duh ting is, Archbishop," Horsey had explained, "we're French, comprenez? Columbus was an Eye-talyan."

"But Columbus discovered America," the Archbishop said.

"No, he didn't," Horsey said. "Columbus found some dumb little island and thought it was India. Louisiana was discovered by Bienville, and Bienville didn't think it was India. We're going to form the Knights of Bienville. We already been talking wit' duh guy from Brooks Brothers about uniforms."

With the profound wisdom and infinite tact for which the Archbishop is so well known, Horsey de la Chevaux was dissuaded from disassociating himself and the Bayou Perdu Council from the Grand Consistory of the Knights of Columbus to form the Knights of Bienville.

It was not, as some sorehead in the Consistory was heard to mumble, because of the financial contributions of Mr. De la Chevaux personally and the Bayou Perdu Council generally to the Archdiocese, although this may have had some effect.

It was, instead, because the Archbishop wished to retain some control over the Bayou Perdu community. Although the Archbishop was sure that it was pure coincidence and had nothing whatever to do with the discovery of the gas field, the Episcopals, Baptists, Seventh-day Adventists, Christian Scientists and the Ethical Cultural Society had all established missions in Bayou Perdu shortly after the first well came in. It was far better, in the Archbishop's judgment, to have the Bayou Perdu Council lurching down Canal Street, roaring drunk, playing "There'll Be a Hot Time in the Old Town Tonight" on the steam calliope under the moral restraint of the K. of C.—no matter how fragile that restraint might be—than to have them behaving like little angels under the moral guidance of somebody else.

Over the years, in fact, the Archbishop and Horsey de la Chevaux had become rather close personal friends. In some ways, they were very much alike, completely honest men wholly devoted to the welfare of their flocks. Through Horsey, the Archbishop had come to know Mr. Boris Alexandrovich Korsky-Rimsakov, whose fan he had long been. By reminding himself that the creative genius responsible for the Sistine Chapel and other works of piety in the Vatican had hardly been a candidate for Sainthood, His Eminence was able to overlook, if not quite forgive, the opera singer's rather unusual concept of sexual morality.

The regard between the two was mutual. When the opera singer opened the New Orleans opera season each year, it was his custom to warm up, so to speak, by dining at the chancellery with the Archbishop and to, as he put it, "sing for his supper" by offering post-dinner renditions of "When Irish Eyes Are Smiling," "The Rose of Tralee" and other such works dear to the Archbishop's ears before going to the opera house.

The Archbishop, therefore, was pleased but not surprised to receive a call from Mr. de la Chevaux on his private, unlisted line, announcing that he had just spoken to Boris Alexandrovich Korsky-Rimsakov in Paris, and that the opera singer had asked him to pass on his warmest regards to the cleric.

"That was very good of Mr. Korsky-Rimsakov," the Archbishop replied. "When you next see him, please extend my warmest regards."

"Next week, Your Eminence," Horsey replied.

"Oh, he's coming here? Or perhaps you're going to Paris?"

"As a matter of fact, we're both going to Morocco," Horsey said.

"How interesting," the Archbishop said. A sixth sense, developed after long years of dealing with his flock, told the Archbishop that there was more to the Morocco trip than Horsey and Boris standing around on the desert watching the camels. "May I ask why?"

"I'm going to sink a couple of wells for a friend of Boris's," Horsey said.

"Is that so?"

"Someplace called Abzug," Horsey explained. "Ever hear of it?"

"As a matter of fact, I have," the Archbishop said. He had only that day seen the report of the Vatican Council on Missions. After attempting to do so for 135 years, the Good Missionary Brothers had finally succeeded in getting Sheikh Abdullah ben Abzug to grant them permission to open a mission station. The mission station was to be limited to providing veterinary service to Abzugian camels, but it was a foot in the door; and the Archbishop did not have to use much imagination to envision how quickly and how firmly the door could be slammed shut again if the Abzugian national dignity should be offended—by, for example, playful off-duty employees of the Chevaux Petroleum Company chasing Abzugian virgins around the mountaintops.

"Horsey," the Archbishop said, thoughtfully, "would you be offended if I suggested that you take Father François along with you? I'm sure he would be as interested in seeing Morocco as I would, and he could, of course, provide a little spiritual guidance for the boys."

"Father François left about an hour ago for Borneo," Horsey said.

"I'm very sorry to hear that," the Archbishop said, meaning every word of it. "Perhaps I could find some other priest . . . "

"You mean for the spiritual guidance? Not to worry," Horsey said. "I just got off the phone from talking to the Reverend Mother Emeritus . . . you know, Hot Lips?"

"I have the pleasure of the lady's acquaintance," the Archbishop said.

"I was giving her Boris's regards, too," Horsey went on. "And when she heard that we was all going to be in Morocco together, she asked was there space for her on the plane. So I told her, sure . . . we're taking one of the 747's . . . and she's going."

"How nice," the Archbishop said. "Well, nice talking to you, Horsey."

"I'll send you a postcard," Horsey said. "Or maybe one of them houris the Arabs seem to like so much."

"Good-bye, Horsey," the Archbishop said. "Have a nice flight." He hung up his private, unlisted telephone and immediately picked up another instrument. His private secretary came on the line.

"Sister," the Archbishop said, "would you please get me the Secretary of State in Washington? This is, I am afraid, in the nature of an emergency."

Chapter Five

When the telephone call from the Archbishop of New Orleans came to the office of the Secretary of State, the Secretary was in conference with a distinguished solon, the Hon. Edwards L. "Smiling Jack" Jackson (Farmer—Free Silver, Arkansas).

The Secretary and Smiling Jack were neither friends nor professional associates, although the Congressman's press agent, whom the taxpayers paid $32,500 annually plus a long list of prerequisites, spent much time, effort and a good deal of the taxpayers' money trying to give that impression.

The cold truth of the matter was that the Congressman had something on the Secretary, specifically that the Secretary had been arrested in Spruce Harbor, Maine, at three o'clock in the morning, charged with "creating a public nuisance." The very charge was subject to many different interpretations, none of which were at all flattering to the man charged with executing the foreign policy of the United States.

"Creating a public nuisance" meant different things in different places. In Cambridge, Massachusetts, where the Secretary had been employed before entering public service, those charged with "creating a public nuisance" were those who had been unable to find a rest room at a time of urgent personal need and who had been apprehended, so to speak *flagrante delicto,* in close proximity to an alley wall. In other places, the charge implied littering, failure to curb one's dog, indecent exposure, public drunkenness or marching in a parade without having previously secured the necessary permit.

What the Secretary had been doing, fully clothed, all buttons buttoned, zippers zipped, dogless, standing in one spot, when he had been placed under arrest by Chief of Police Ernie Kelly personally was singing.

While the good burghers of Spruce Harbor, Maine, normally had nothing at all against singing (indeed, Spruce Harbor's Boob-a-Doob-a-Boo Barbershop Quartet had placed fifth in the state competition), they did not appreciate and would not tolerate, a cappella renditions of "Roll Me Over, Yankee Soldier" on the courthouse steps at three in the morning.

It had seemed at the time a splendid idea. The Secretary of State had been in Spruce Harbor on an international diplomatic mission* of the highest sensitivity and importance. Students of diplomacy, of course, are well aware that far more, diplomacy-wise, can be accomplished over a cheering cup than over a barren conference table.

The conferees had informally assembled at a well-known Spruce Harbor gourmet restaurant, the Bide-a-While Pool Hall/Ladies Served Fresh Lobster & Clams Daily Restaurant and Saloon, Inc., Stanley K. Warczinski, Sr., proprietor.

Innkeeper Warczinski, having been informed by Dr. Benjamin Franklin "Hawkeye" Pierce, one of the local healers, of his once-in-a-lifetime opportunity to dispel, once and for all, the popular notion that a Polish Banquet consisted of two Poles sharing a can of beer and a hot dog, had pulled out all stops, gustatorily speaking. The lobsters and the clams came in a steady stream from the Warczinski kitchen; and a wide variety of intoxicants, ranging from the local home brew through a half-gallon bottle of Grand Marnier to earthenware jeroboams of

---

* The details are available, for those with a professional interest in behind-the-scenes diplomacy, or simply for the insatiably curious, in *M*A*S*H Goes to London*, New York, 1975.

imported Polish vodka, came from the Warczinsky Cellars on the strong shoulders of Stanley Warczinsky, Jr., Director of Beverage Services. For the occasion, he had tied the key to his Kawasaki motorcycle on a bootlace and hung it around his neck in the classical manner of the sommelier, or wine steward.

When the meeting (to skip lightly over the somewhat boring details) had been satisfactorily concluded, it had, of course, been Toast Time, which period of compliment-passing cum tippling had lasted at least two hours. Following Toast Time, several participants in the conference, including the Secretary of State, had decided to raise the cultural level of Spruce Harbor by staging a small vocal recital on the steps of the County Courthouse.

Through the good offices of Dr. Pierce, the incident had been kept out of the newspapers and, through the influence of Mrs. Mary Pierce—who had once happened to run into Chief of Police Kelly and a young woman known as "Tootsie Baby" at a Fraternal Order of Police Convention to which Mrs. Kelly had been unable to come—the record of arrest had been expunged from official police records.

The expunging had been accomplished simply, by tearing out that page from the loose-leaf notebook which served as Spruce Harbor's Police Arrest Record, or "blotter."

L. Bryan Fowler, Congressman "Smiling Jack" Jackson's Administrative Assistant (which is what Congressmen call their press agents), had not participated in the a cappella recital. He had taken a little nap under the footsball machine before the others had been struck with the inspiration to sing, and had learned of the recital and arrest only after being awakened the next morning by Mrs. Warczinski, who had, as was her long-standing habit, begun the day by wetting down the floor of the establishment with a fire hose.

(Under the circumstances, Mr. Fowler was forced to accept Mrs. Warczinski's statement that she had no idea he was, in her words, "crapped out" under the footsball machine, and that there had been nothing personal in the hosing. He later applied for, and received, compensation for his ruined suit from the U.S. Treasury. It had, of course, been ruined in the execution of his official duties.)

Once awake, L. Byran Fowler immediately made inquiry as to the whereabouts of Congressman Jackson. At first disbelieving Mrs. Warczinski's assertation that the Congressman and "the little fat drunk with the funny accent" had been tossed into the local slammer, he soon came to believe that such a miscarriage of justice in these remote-from-Washington backwoods was indeed possible.

He went (after, first, of course, changing his suit) immediately to the police station. He witnessed Chief Kelly ostentatiously ripping the Arrest Record sheet in half for the edification of Mrs. Pierce and, immediately recognizing that the Arrest Record was an important historical document which otherwise would be irretrievably lost to the nation's scholars, managed to get it out of the wastebasket, and with a little Scotch tape, to reassemble it.

Since the Congressman was rather busy in England, it wasn't until they had been back in Our Nation's Capital for a week that Mr. Fowler showed Smiling Jack his historical discovery. As he suspected, the Congressman was profoundly grateful for Fowler's deep dedication to the preservation of historical artifacts. Immediately upon Fowler's turning over of the Arrest Record to him, Smiling Jack signed the necessary documents recommending that Mr. Fowler receive a Sustained Superior-Performance Award of $2,500 from the Civil Service Commission. The Congressman also arranged with the Speaker of the House for Mr. Fowler's job title to be changed from Administrative Assistant to Executive Administrative Assistant, which carried with it an additional honorarium of $5,500 per annum.

"If the people expect good government," as Smiling Jack so often said, "they have to expect to pay for it."

Smiling Jack then thoughtfully had the document

Xeroxed and sent a copy to the Secretary of State as a little souvenir of their labor together in solving the nation's diplomatic problems. Smiling Jack had only recently met the Secretary of State personally. He had been aboard an Air Force Sabreliner about to take off for England on Congressional business (the phrase is "junketing") when the plane had suddenly been commandeered for the use of the Secretary. Since there was room for them all, Smiling Jack had been permitted to go along.

From what he had seen of diplomacy in the week they had been together, it was a far more fascinating field of government than that (the Committee on Sewers, Subways and Sidewalks) in which he had spent his sixteen years in Congress.

When he approached the Speaker of the House, however, volunteering to give up his seniority (he was third in line to become Chairman of the Committee on Sewers, Subways and Sidewalks) in exchange for a transfer to the Foreign Relations Committee, he had run into something of a blank wall.

"I've had my eye on you for years, Charley," the Speaker had begun.

"That's Edwards, Mr. Speaker," Edwards L. Jackson corrected.

"Of course. I've had my eye on you for years, Congressman Edwards," the Speaker went on, "and you're doing a bang-up job in the Sewers."

"It's Congressman Jackson, Mr. Speaker," the solon had corrected him again. "And I would like to broaden myself."

"What better place to broaden yourself, my boy, than in Sewers, Subways and Sidewalks?" the Speaker had said, making his little joke. "The House needs someone of your expertise standing on the curb, so to speak, ready to jump in and assume command should, God forbid, your seniors in Sewers go down to defeat at the polls."

Smiling Jack had been around long enough to know that absolutely nothing he could say was about to change the Speaker's mind. But he was not discouraged. Had he not shared the rigors, and yes, the dangers, of actually serving abroad with the Secretary of State himself, in far-off London? A word from the Secretary to the Speaker would be of more value than anything he could think of, including the first thing he had thought of: getting down on his knees and begging.

He congratulated himself on his original assessment of the Secretary's over-all importance within the governmental infrastructure when three months passed before an audience could be fitted into the Secretary's busy schedule for him. But, finally, the big day came. He dressed himself with care, in what he thought was appropriate attire for someone who wished to serve his country in the diplomatic game. He put on his newly acquired wardrobe (homburg, a morning coat, striped pants, patent-leather shoes and spats), carefully brushed his silver locks into place and took a taxi to the State Department Building.

A Deputy Assistant Under Secretary of State for Protocol greeted him with the news that something unexpected had come up. The Ambassador from the People's Democratic Republic of Glomorra (a small island off the English coast which was recently granted independence from the Isle of Man and admitted to the United Nations only the day before) was in town to present his credentials to the Secretary of State and, regrettably, there was no room for the Congressman at the official luncheon. Would the Congressman prefer to try again another day?

The Congressman would not. Smiling Jack sat in one of the chrome-and-leather Barcelona chairs outside the Secretary's office, dusted off his homburg and his patent-leather shoes with his handkerchief and settled down to wait just as long as necessary for his audience with the Secretary.

Three-and-a-half hours later, after first expressing surprise that the Congressman was still "out here," the Secretary's secretary flung wide the door to the Secretary's office.

"The Honorable Jackson Edwards, Radical of California," the secretary formally intoned.

"That's the Honorable Edwards Jackson," the Congressman hissed, "Farmer—Free Silver, of Arkansas."

"Whatever," the Secretary's secretary said.

"Mr. Secretary," Smiling Jack said, flashing his famous smile, "how nice to see you again."

You godda weird sense humor," the Secretary replied. "You know dat?"

"I'm afraid I don't quite understand," Smiling Jack said.

"I got dat Xerox in the mail. You tink dat's funny?"

"I had hoped you would be amused," Smiling Jack said.

"So vat's on your mind?" the Secretary said.

"I have come to offer my services, Mr. Secretary," Smiling Jack said.

"I vas afraid it vas something like dat," the Secretary said. "You guys on the Hill are just gonna have to learn that there's not enough embassies around to pass one out to every Congressman vats gets vhipped in duh elections. Senators, ve can take care of, but there's just too many Congressmen."

"I have every confidence, Mr. Secretary, that I shall be returned to office at the polls," Smiling Jack said.

"Vhere did you say you vere from?"

"I have the honor to represent the fine people of Swampy Meadows, Arkansas," Smiling Jack said.

"They don't have newspapers and TV out there?"

"Mr. Secretary," Smiling Jack said, determined not to be sidetracked into a political discussion when he had the Fate of the Nation, diplomatically, in mind, "what I need is your recommendation."

"For vhat?"

"A word from you in the Speaker's ear would, I feel sure, be enough for him to arrange my transfer to the Foreign Relations Committee."

"You been at the sauce again?" the Secretary said. "You tink I don't have enough trouble vit dose nebbishes vithout you should be vith them?"

At that point, the telephone buzzed, and the Secretary picked it up.

"So?" he said.

"Mr. Secretary, the Archbishop of New Orleans is on line fourteen. He says it's an emergency."

"Vonderful!" the Secretary said. "Put him through." He turned to Smiling Jack. "You gotta excuse me," he said. "Trouble vith the Vatican."

"I'll wait, if you don't mind," Smiling Jack replied.

"It's a secret matter," the Secretary said. "You shouldn't lissen."

"Not to worry," Smiling Jack said. He put his index fingers in his ears and closed his eyes.

The Secretary shrugged one of his famous shrugs and picked up the telephone.

"So, Archbishop, how's by you?" he said.

"Mr. Secretary," the Archbishop said, "some rather distressing intelligence has recently come to me, which I felt it my duty to pass on to you."

The Secretary sat up erect in his chair. He had only the week before failed again in secret negotiations to place the Vatican Intelligence Service under contract to the C.I.A. He had high hopes that close association with the Vatican Intelligence Service would see some of their accuracy, speed and all-around professionalism rub off on the C.I.A. which, surely and demonstrably, needed it.

"So tell me," he said.

"Are you familiar with the Sheikhdom of Abzug?"

"So, who isn't?" the Secretary replied.

"I have just learned that Sheikh Abdullah ben Abzug has completed arrangements for oil exploitation of his country," the Archbishop said.

"Archbishop, this is straight? You trust your source?"

"Absolutely," the Archbishop said.

"Archbishop, I vouldn't vant this to go any further but, between you, me and duh Lyndon B. Johnson Memorial, I had a little talk with Sheikh Abdullah ben Abzug myself about Abzugian oil. He told me then that the next time a Yankee Imperialist Infidel Bastard brought the subject up, he vas going to turn his oil over to duh Russians. I thought he vas bluffing. I guess he vasn't."

"It's worse than the Russians, I'm afraid, Mr. Secretary."

"The Chinese? *Oy vay iz mir!*"

"Worse still, I'm afraid," the Archbishop said, trying to break the news as gently as possible. "Chevaux Petroleum!"

For a long moment, the Secretary said nothing. Then, as tears started to run down his cheeks, he shook his head to get control of himself and asked, desperately, "You're sure, Archbishop? No chance of a mistake?"

"I just spoke with Horsey myself," the Archbishop said.

"Oh, my God! Vhat could be vorse?"

"Chevaux is taking with them the Reverend Mother Emeritus of the God Is Love in All Forms Christian Church, Inc., as spiritual adviser."

"*Dat's* vorse," the Secretary admitted.

"Perhaps the Reverend Mother will be of some solace in case some of the men face Abzugian justice for insulting the throne," the Archbishop said. "Religious counsel sometimes helps those facing execution."

"I forgot about dat," the Secretary said, suddenly remembering the Abzugian Code of Conduct for Infidel Bastards Visiting Abzug. It was simplicity itself. One member of any group of people was placed in charge and named Sheikh pro tempore. He was responsible for seeing that none of his group violated any of the 1,004 Abzugian Criminal Canons, ranging from "adultery, commission of," to "xylophone, unauthorized playing of," the violation of which were punishable by death.

Should such a violation occur, in the interests of speedy justice, the Sheikh pro tempore was summarily executed. In former times this was accomplished by being tied to four horses spurred in different directions and, more recently, in the interests of a merciful death, by a specially designed guillotine which sliced lengthwise, rather than off the top.

The Secretary was aware that he had at the moment

no legal right to restrain Chevaux Petroleum Company from going to Abzug or, for that matter, anywhere else in the world they wanted to go. To bar Americans from travel to any specific location required Congressional action; and there had been no such action with regard to the Sheikhdom of Abzug for the very good reason that no Congressman had ever heard of it.

He had, on the other hand, standby authority to "temporarily" forbid Americans to travel anywhere where their lives would be in danger. The moment the eight-foot knife dropped on one of Horsey de la Chevaux's Cajuns he would have proof of the danger, and he could order the rest of them out instantly, using the Marine Corps, if necessary, to enforce his order.

Diplomacy was really a tough business, he thought. Here he was, cold-bloodedly looking forward to the death of some innocent Cajun, so that the lives of a hundred others could be saved.

And then his eye fell on Congressman Edwards L. "Smiling Jack" Jackson (Farmer–Free Silver, Arkansas).

"Congressman?" he said, now smiling his famous, warm smile. There was no response. Smiling Jack still had his eyes firmly pressed together and his index fingers in his ears. The Secretary threw a copy of *The Washington Post* at him, knocking one finger out of an ear. "Congressman!" he said, sternly.

"Yes, Mr. Secretary?"

"Did I understand you correctly, my dear Congressman, to say dat you would like to serve your country diplomatically?"

"Yes, sir, Mr. Secretary," Smiling Jack said, getting to his feet and coming to attention.

"How does Sheikh pro tempore sound to you?" the Secretary asked. Then, without waiting for the Congressman to form a reply (Congressmen always take forever to form replies, except when asked how they feel about Motherhood or the American Flag), he turned back to the telephone.

"Archbishop," he said, "I think maybe I'm on top

of this. I very much thank you for the tip, Archbishop, and I'll make it up to you somehow."

"I am happy to be of service, Mr. Secretary," the Archbishop said.

"And, if you see her before she goes, please give my best regards to Hot Lips," the Secretary said.

"You mean, the Reverend Mother Emeritus, of course," the Archbishop said. "Good-bye, Mr. Secretary." He broke the connection with his finger, flashed his secretary and, when she came on the line, he said, "Get me Hot Lips on the phone, will you, please, Sister?"

Chapter Six

The Secretary, despite what you might hear from certain soreheads who have wound up, so to speak, with the shorter stick following negotiations with him, is not really cold-blooded, steel-hearted, ruthless and unfeeling.

Within three days of his appointment of the Hon. Edwards L. "Smiling Jack" Jackson as official Sheikh pro tempore for all American nationals within the Sheikhdom of Abzug, the delighted, even joyous, smile on his face began to pale. On days four and five, there was a further deterioration of the smile and, by day six, his sleep troubled by rather detailed nightmares in which a terrified "Smiling Jack" Jackson was dragged, screaming and weeping, by hooded-and-robed Arabs to a giant guillotine, he was prepared to bite the bullet.

On the morning of day seven, as the first thing on his schedule, he ordered his secretary to place a person-to-person call to Dr. Benjamin Franklin Pierce, chief of surgery of the Spruce Harbor Medical Center in Maine.

The following dialogue transpired:

"Dr. Pierce."

"One moment, please," the Secretary's secretary ordered in the grandly imperious manner of a bureaucratic flunky employed by a high-ranking bureaucrat. "The Secretary of State is calling."

"He's not here."

"Who's not here?"

"Dr. Pierce. The last we heard, he was in the South Seas."

"I thought you said you were Dr. Pierce!"

"Why would I say something like that? I told you, Dr. Pierce is in the Antarctic."

"I thought you said the South Seas."

"The Antarctic is about as far south as you can get. Didn't you study geography in school? What kind of a bureaucrat are you, anyway?"

"Who are you?"

"Somebody who never heard of the Secretary of State."

At that point, the Secretary of State picked up his extension and, recognizing the voice, broke into the conversation. "So, Hawkeye, how's by you? Lots of nice rich patients, I hope?"

"Trapped!"

"Mr. Secretary, this . . . this *person* says that Dr. Pierce is in the South Seas, or Antarctica."

"What's on your mind, Tubby?" Hawkeye asked. "Ooops. That slipped out. I should have known better than to ask."

"I'm vell, thank you," the Secretary said. "Yourself?"

"Until the phone rang, I was feeling great," Hawkeye replied. "Whatever you want from me, Tubby, the answer is no."

"And how's Trapper John? And his charming wife?"

"On to you, Tubby," Hawkeye said. "On to you. We're not going anywhere. Lay that Middle-European charm on somebody else."

"A little medical advice," the Secretary said, entreatingly. "Is dat too much to ask, for old time's sake, from a dear friend?"

"Take two aspirin, go to bed and call somebody else in the morning," Dr. Pierce said. "How's that, dear old friend?"

"You been around, Hawkeye," the Secretary pressed on. "Tell me, vhat do you know about duh guillotine?"

"Contemplating ending it all, are you?" Dr. Pierce said. For the first time, there was an element of hope in his voice.

"Actually, I'm vorried about a friend," the Secretary said.

"Sure, you are," Dr. Pierce said. "What do you want to know about a guillotine?"

"If it cuts right down duh middle," the Secretary asked, "instead of across the neck, is it still a guillotine?"

"Interesting question," Hawkeye said. "Let me think on it, and I'll get back to you either this year or next."

"Hawkeye, please!" the Secretary said. He couldn't see him over the telephone, of course, but the tremolo in his voice was enough for Hawkeye to have a good, clear mental image of the Secretary's face.

Hawkeye, following in the path of the world's most coldhearted political leaders, gave in rather than have the memory of the Secretary's mournful eyes, pursed lips and quivering jowls on his conscience for the rest of his life. He told himself there was no shame because the face which had melted Golda Meir's heart was also melting his, even over the telephone.

"O.K., Tubby, what's this all about?" Hawkeye said. And the Secretary began to tell him. It was not a violation of the security of the United States, but rather an act, even a courageous act, taken by the Secretary of State

in the interests of the security of the United States, or
at least in the interests of keeping alive one of its Congressmen.

"I'm very much afraid that the Honorable Edwards
L. Jackson is in great danger of losing his life by the
guillotine," the Secretary said.

"Is that the distinguished Arkansasian solon with
the wavy silver locks who was with us in England?"
Hawkeye asked.

"Dat's duh vun," the Secretary said.

"The one who told the Queen that although some
of his dearest friends were English, he didn't think he'd
want his daughter to marry one?"

"Vun and duh same," the Secretary said.

"And he's going to be guillotined? In public?"

"It looks dat way," the Secretary replied.

"How many tickets can you get me, Tubby?" Hawkeye
asked. "And I'm sure Trapper John will want to be
there, too."

"Vat I'm trying to do is keep dat from happening,"
the Secretary said.

"There is no finer human quality than mercy," Hawkeye said piously and then added: "But there's a time
and a place for everything, as I always say."

"You gotta minute, Hawkeye? Let me tell you about
it?"

"You're not going to believe this, Tubby," Hawkeye
said, "but this very minute I was about to leave the
office on a very long trip."

"A trip? Vhere to?" the Secretary asked, suspicion
in every syllable.

"Would you believe Merry Morocco?" Hawkeye
asked, doubtfully.

"*Merry* Morocco?" the Secretary replied. "Dat's vhat
you said, *Merry* Morocco?"

"It's in Africa, someplace," Hawkeye said. "Mary
and I won a trip at the State Medical Convention. First
time in years that we'll have a chance to go away alone
somewhere together."

"Morocco?" the Secretary repeated. "I heard dat right, Morocco?"

"Merry Morocco is what it says on the tickets," Hawkeye said. "Maybe they changed the name."

"For a million dollars, I vouldn't think of interfering vith your trip," the Secretary said. "You should excuse the call at this important time. Travel in good health! Bon voyage! Mazel tov!"

"What are you up to, Tubby?" Hawkeye demanded, suspiciously.

"You suspect me, your Secretary of State, of being *up* to something? Shame on you!" the Secretary said. "Nice talking vith you, Doctor. Have a nice trip."

The connection went dead. Hawkeye hung the phone up and stared at it for a long moment, searching his mind (and his mind, frankly, was just about as devious and cynical and wildly imaginative as the Secretary's) for a logical reason for the Secretary's delight at the news he was en route to Merry Morocco, and for the Secretary having so suddenly shut off the conversation.

Then, shrugging his shoulders, he stood up and walked out of his office. He could think of nothing he had ever done and no one he had ever known that had any link at all, however remote, with Merry Morocco. The only thing he knew for sure about Merry Morocco was that it was far away. It was so far away, in fact, that the AAA-1 Handy-Dandy Telephone-Answering Service had told him, somewhat archly, that they hoped he understood he would be without their service as long as he was there.

That had been crushing news. For as long as he could remember, with the notable exception of Korea during the unpleasantness there, the AAA-1 Handy-Dandy Telephone-Answering Service had been part of his life. Over the years, they had acquired a fine skill in contacting him at all hours and in all places—just as he stepped under the shower, for example; or just as he swung the driver over his shoulder on the first tee; or as Stanley K. Warczinski set a pitcher of beer and two chicken lobsters in front of him.

This thought cheered him. If the AAA-1 Handy-
Dandy Telephone-Answering Service frankly confessed
they would be unable to reach him while he was in
Merry Morocco, it seemed logical to assume that neither
would the Secretary of State.

He underestimated the Secretary of State. No sooner
had the Secretary hung up on Hawkeye than he had
flashed his secretary again. "Come in wid your liddle
book," he said. "A message to Morocco, I got to send."

Hawkeye, knowing none of this, made his way down
the corridor of the Spruce Harbor Medical Center until
he came to the Doctor-Finding Board. This device, which
had a much longer, possibly more accurate nomenclature,
consisted of: a long list of the physicians catering to the
patients of the medical center; a long line of little, sliding
gadgets which slid to one side or the other exposing
the words "In" or "Out"; and a greenish blackboard
on which the doctors were supposed to write, presuming
they were going to be "Out," where, precisely, they were
going to be while "Out."

With great pleasure and a certain not unattractive
flourish, Hawkeye wrote "gone to Merry Morocco" on
the blackboard after his name. He didn't think anyone
would believe it, but he felt sure it would brighten otherwise dull conversations in the Physicians', Nurses' and
Medical Technicians' Coffee Shoppe.

Then he got into his car and drove home. It was
his intention to pick up his bride and their luggage,
and drive to the Spruce Harbor International Airport
where the proprietor, Wrong Way Napolitano, had arranged for their aerial passage between Spruce Harbor
and John F. Kennedy International Airport in New York
for the connecting flight via Air Mali to the Canary
Islands and Merry Morocco.

When he turned off the road into his driveway, his
path was blocked by a barrier consisting of John Francis
Xavier McIntyre, M.D., F.A.C.S., who was sitting atop
a pile of luggage. When he saw Hawkeye's car, he rose
to his feet and extended his right hand, palm outward,
in front of him in the manner of a traffic cop.

Hawkeye rolled down the window and stuck his head out.

"I'm very touched that you came to wish me bon voyage," he said, "but your duty under the Hippocratic oath clearly indicates you should be at the hospital working at your trade. I know that I'm irreplaceable, but you'll just have to do the best you can."

"Why, hello there, Dr. Benjamin Franklin Pierce, M.D., healer of the sick, world traveler, last of the big spenders and father of four kids with the measles," Dr. McIntyre replied.

"What's that supposed to mean?"

"You know," Trapper John replied, "little, red spots on the skin and a big QUARANTINE courtesy of the County Health Department on the door." He turned and pointed to the door on which, indeed, was an eight-by-ten sheet of cardboard with the legend QUARANTINE printed on it in big, red letters.

"If this is your idea of a joke, McIntyre," Hawkeye said, rather threateningly, "forget it. I'm going to Merry Morocco, period."

"Yes, you are," Trapper John said. "Do you think we're going to have a good time, sweetie?"

"What do you mean 'we'?"

"Guess whose kids have been playing with whose kids?" Trapper John replied. "The correct reply will get you two weeks with me."

"I spent sixteen months with you in Korea," Hawkeye replied. "That's enough for a lifetime."

"The question is not whether you're going to spend the next two weeks with me, but where," Trapper John said.

"If you think you're going to weasel out of two weeks' work simply because your nasty contagious offspring have infested my little angels, you've got another think coming."

"I'll lay it out for you, simply," Trapper John said, picking up the luggage and carrying it to the car. "Mary and Lucinda have decided to pool the kids, so to speak. My kids are there, too. They will do the Florence Nightingale bit on sort of a duty roster. The original idea was that you were going to move into my house."

"Whose stupid idea was that?"

"Your wife's, as I recall," Trapper John said.

"It does have some merit when you consider it carefully," Hawkeye said.

"But then my Lucinda suggested that since it was such a shame to waste the Merry Morocco tickets," Trapper John said, "and since the trip could not be rescheduled, maybe it would be a good idea if you and I went to Merry Morocco together."

"It was their idea?"

"I resisted the suggestion," Trapper John said, "that you and I would enjoy going off together alone, under the circumstances, far from our feverish, irritable, but not really too sick, offspring."

"And they swallowed it?"

"I was practically pushed out the door," Trapper John said.

"And we have two whole weeks?" Hawkeye asked.

"While you were dawdling at the hospital," Trapper John said, "I fixed everything. I had our golf clubs sent from the club to the airport. Not only do we have a cottage on the first green at Southern Pines, but Wrong Way knows an airline pilot who'll mail postcards from Morocco. I even went by the library and checked out some *National Geographic* magazines so we can report on what we saw."

"You're a genius!" Hawkeye said.

"Mary and the kids are in the window," Trapper John said. "Wipe that idiotic grin off your face and wave them a sad good-bye."

Five hours later, Eastern Air Lines deposited seventy-eight disgruntled travelers and two widely smiling physicians at John F. Kennedy International Airport. What was an hour-and-a-half's circling in the stack above the airport compared with the prospect of two uninterrupted weeks on the dark and immaculate greens of Southern Pines?

Whistling "Count Your Blessings" in duet, which

for some reason seemed to displease the other travelers,
Drs. Pierce and McIntyre skipped gaily down the un-
loading ramp, looking not unlike Judy Garland and
Bert Lahr heading up the Yellow-Brick Road in *The
Wizard of Oz.*

And then two sturdy gentlemen in business suits,
white shirts, ties and snap-brim hats stepped in front
of them, barring their way.

"Drs. Pierce and McIntyre, I presume?"

"My name is Camembert," Hawkeye said immediately,
"and this is Professor Roquefort." It was a technique
they had developed on a troopship when returning from
Korea. Since it had worked then, to keep them from
admitting to being doctors and thus passing the voyage
conducting the traditional military function known as
"Short Arm Inspection," Hawkeye had no reason to suspect it would not work now.

The two men, taken aback, stepped out of their way.
But one of them, suspicious by nature, suddenly reached
into his pocket and came out with two 5-by-7-inch,
black-and-white photographs.

"Ho, ho, ho," he said, bubbling over with all the
jolly goodwill that the Giant had demonstrated as he
watched Jack have at his beanstalk with his ax. "Having
your little joke, are you?"

Each of the sturdy gentlemen in the business suits
and snap-brimmed hats took a physician by the arm
and propelled him across the terminal with practiced
skill.

"Would it be all right if I asked where we were going?"
Trapper John inquired, politely.

"Aren't you supposed to take a little card from your
pocket and read us our rights?" Hawkeye asked.

"It's nothing like that, ho, ho, ho," the larger of the
sturdy gentlemen said. "What we are doing is expediting
your departure . . ."

"I think I smell a rat," Hawkeye said.

". . . at the special request of the Secretary of State
himself," the sturdy gentleman went on.

"One thing about you, Hawkeye," Trapper John said. "You got one hell of a smeller."

"There has been a slight change in our plans," Hawkeye said. "We're not going to Morocco, you see. We're going to Southern Pines."

"If the Secretary of State says we are to expedite your departure to Morocco," the sturdy gentleman said, "you ain't going to Southern Pines. You're going to Morocco."

"But we don't want to go to Morocco!" Hawkeye protested.

"Here we are," the sturdy gentleman said, leading them to a departure gate at which large, heavily armed border patrolmen stood in the places normally occupied by attractive women in airlines' uniforms.

"Two specials for departure," the sturdy gentleman announced.

"We've been expecting them," the border patrolman said. "Which are they? The jewel robbers or the white slavers? How come they ain't handcuffed? I wouldn't trust that long, skinny, ugly one as far as I could throw him."

"Nah," the sturdy gentleman said, "these are the two for the special flight to Morocco."

"Well, they look like white slavers to me," the border patrolman said.

"They're friends of the Secretary of the State," the sturdy gentleman said.

"That figures," the border patrolman said. "O.K., you two, follow me!"

"If it's all the same to you . . . " Hawkeye began.

"I said 'follow me,' " the border patrolman said.

Drs. Pierce and McIntyre raised their hands above their heads in the manner of prisoners and followed the border patrolman down a corridor, which turned into sort of a tunnel, and finally deposited them inside an airplane.

A 190-pound Air Force master sergeant, quite as large and nearly as ugly as the border patrolman, smiled at them. "I am Airwoman Betty-Lou Williams," she said. "Welcome aboard Air Force Three. We will depart

momentarily for Casablanca, and I am here to make
your trip as enjoyable as possible. Feel free to call upon
me for anything that will make this a pleasant flight
for you."

"Actually," Trapper John said, "we don't really want
to go to Morocco. Nothing personal, of course . . ."

"Go back into the V.I.P. cabin," she said, gesturing,
"and then sit down, shorty, and shut up. I don't want
no trouble outa you."

"Thank you kindly," Hawkeye said. "Yes, ma'am."

They made their way to the aft cabin, aware of the
sound and vibration of starting engines. As they sat
down and fastened their seat belts, the plane began to
move away from the terminal.

And then the door to the cabin opened again. Two
people stepped into the cabin. One was a small gentleman,
rising no more than five feet three from the floor. He
carried an enormous attaché case and peered at them
from behind large, black-rimmed glasses. The second
was M. Sgt. Betty-Lou Williams, who presented each
of them with a small, insulated container and a small,
waxed paper-wrapped parcel.

"Good evening, gentlemen," the little man in the large
glasses said. "I am Q. Elwood Potter, III. I am Deputy
Assistant Under Secretary of State for North African
Affairs. I am your official escort officer and, just as soon
as you have eaten your chicken soup and chopped-liver
sandwiches, prepared for you as a token of personal
friendship by the Secretary himself, I will begin the
briefing."

At that point, having broken ground, the pilot of
the airplane pulled back a little further on his stick,
and the nose of the aircraft rose sharply. This occurred
at the precise moment that Dr. Pierce, who was always
troubled with an extraordinary curiosity, opened the
insulated container.

Hot chicken soup (with lots of noodles and little
chunks of white meat) poured into his lap. He closed
the container, and then his eyes, and began to weep,
softly, but heartrendingly.

Chapter Seven

At this precise moment, all across the country, millions of eyes were focused on television sets. It was the Amalgamated Broadcasting System's "News Hour" and it was reaching its climactic moment. After fifty-five minutes of commercial messages, interrupted briefly and rarely by thirty-second segments of news, it was time for "The Rhotten Report." World-famous television journalist, Don Rhotten, was assigned precisely two minutes of time to explain to the viewers just what they had seen on the news portion of the program, and to explain what it meant.

"Punch in Rhotten," the director said, and the technicians did just that, electronically speaking. The monitors showed three different angles of Don Rhotten in what looked to the viewer like a newsroom with library. A battery of Teletype printers clacked audibly in the background, as yellow paper jerked out of them. Above the teleprinters was a wall of books. The books, actually, were fake, and leftovers from a popular dramatic series. Before that, they had served as a backdrop from touching scenes in which Fatherly Doctor Paul had counseled terminally ill patients about the joys of dying under his gentle care.

The teleprinters were hooked to nothing but the socket in the wall. They had been rigged so that when the RHOTTEN TWX switch was pushed, they typed line after line of X's, shifted lines, rang bells and generally gave the impression of legitimate functioning.

Don Rhotten himself sat at a desk, on which was a typewriter, a telephone, and what looked like a humidor for the tobacco for his ever-present pipe. What it was, actually, when viewed from Rhotten's position, was a prompting device. Rhotten did not give his nightly little lectures from memory, although it looked that way. What he did was read what had been written for him to say by a staff of writers, and which appeared on a small television screen hidden in the tobacco humidor.

"Take two," the director intoned; and that camera, Number Two, "went live." A little red bulb on the front of it lit up, telling Rhotten that that particular camera was "on the air" and transmitting his image all across the nation.

"Good evening," Rhotten said, taking his pipe from his mouth, and flashing his famous modest and unassuming grin at the camera. "I'm Don Rhotten, and this is 'The Rhotten Report.'"

(It should be noted parenthetically here that Mr. Rhotten is of Dutch ancestry, and that his name is pronounced Row-ten, rather than how it might at first glance, to the uninitiated, appear to sound.)

Rhotten, who, if nothing else, was an excellent "sight reader" (someone who can read, convincingly, out loud, material which he has never seen before), devoted 85 of the 120 seconds allotted to him to a rather skillful demolishment of the just-issued report of the Presidential Commission on the Problems of Aging, which had taken a bipartisan group of 130 scholars, economists, physicians and clergymen two years to write.

Rhotten (more precisely, the people who wrote his copy) disapproved. The scholars, economists, physicians and clergymen had wasted their time.

He took a puff on his pipe, a hooked calabash, to give the viewers five whole seconds to reflect on his profound observations, and then turned to glance at the prompter to read the final thirty seconds of opinions and news from the tobacco humidor.

"This reporter," he intoned solemnly, "has exclusively learned of secret United States support of the Sheikh of Abzug. At least one planeload of uniformed men left the United States today for the desert kingdom. The Pentagon flatly denies what my confidential, high-ranking sources saw with their own eyes, and the State Department actually refused to discuss this gravely serious matter with this reporter at all.

"But I'm not going to let the matter rest with a Pentagon and State Department denial. This reporter's bags are packed, and a station wagon is waiting at the studio door to rush me to the airport. Next stop, Abzug!"

His excitement was clearly visible to all his fans. In times of high excitement, his Adam's apple bobbed, and his voice took on husky timbre.

"Take three," the director said. The red light on Camera Two blinked out, and the light on Camera Three came on. Rhotten turned in his leather, upholstered chair to face it.

"This has been 'The Rhotten Report," he said. "Until we meet again, this is Don Rhotten."

"Roll the last film clip," the director said. Don Rhotten's image blinked off some 11,345,213 screens and was replaced by that of an even more impressive-looking male human being sitting in an even more impressive office.

"Good evening," he said. "I'd like to talk to you, confidentially, for the next few moments, about something of great importance that concerns all of us." He paused for dramatic effect, and then got to his feet. The camera zoomed in for a tight shot of his handsome, sincere-looking face.

"Hemorrhoids," he said, and held up the giant-family-economy-size box.

Don Rhotten saw nothing of this. The moment the red "on-the-air" light on Camera Three blinked off, he jumped up from behind his desk and angrily snatched the lavaliere microphone from around his neck.

"I want to see you!" he screamed at three men who had been standing by his set out of camera range. One

of them was so startled that he bumped into the flat
on which all the book spines had been so realistically
painted. It fell down, exposing the concrete-block walls
of the studio, a spaghetti maze of wires and cables, and
a startled little man in coveralls whose hot dog the falling
flat had missed by no more than two inches.

Rhotten surveyed the damage. He turned and faced
the trio again.

"I'm glad!" he screamed. "Do you hear me? I'm
glad!"

"Now, Don-Baby!"

"Don't you 'Now, Don-Baby' me, you four-eyed
creep!" Rhotten said. "I know when I've been sand-
bagged."

He stalked off the set to a door in the concrete-block
wall on which his name was painted under a silver,
five-pointed star. He stepped inside and slammed the
door.

The three men at whom he had screamed looked
at one another, shrugged and went to face the music.
Don Rhotten did not answer their knocks and, after
a moment, one of them timidly tried the door. It opened
a crack, and then the famous Rhotten voice was heard,
somewhat louder than usual: "How dare you disturb
me when I'm removing my contact lenses?"

The door was closed again quickly, and this time
the trio waited until it was opened from within. The
man who answered the door at first didn't look like
the man whose face had just, as he liked to phrase
it, "visited" 11,345,213 homes via the television tube.
He was wearing glasses, thick-lensed, thick-framed
glasses which magnified his eyes, giving him a guppylike
glower. The man on television had had a full head of
thick black curls. This man displayed a freckled, if
spotlessly clean, expanse of light-pink skin covering
a somewhat lumpy scalp. His only hair was a sort of
monk's ridge at the level of his ears.

It was only when he spoke that one could be sure
it really was indeed Don Rhotten.

"All right," he said, "get in here and figure out some

way we can explain why I'm still here instead of wherever the hell I said I was going."

"Let's talk about it, Don-Baby," the shorter, fatter member of the trio said.

"There's nothing to talk about," Rhotten said. "I ain't going, and that's it."

"Don-Baby," the taller, thinner member of the trio said, "think of the exposure!"

"That's precisely what I am thinking of. My exposure to a bunch of South Pacific savages who want me for their supper."

"Abzug's in Africa, sweetie," the third member of the trio said.

Mr. Rhotten did not immediately reply. He had, literally, his hand in his mouth. He emerged with what appeared to be a perfect, full set of shiny white teeth. It could have been a magician's illusion, for there was a full set of teeth (not, to be sure, as perfect or as shining white, but a full set) remaining in his mouth. It was not a magician's illusion. What Mr. Rhotten had removed from his mouth was a device known to the dental trade as "cosmetic prophylactics," and to their wearers as "caps." They are artificial teeth whose function is to hide their less attractive natural brothers over which they fit.

Mr. Rhotten dipped his caps into a glass of mild antiseptic (always kept in the same spot on the same table for this precise purpose) and then placed them carefully into a small leather-and-foam carrying case.

He ran his tongue over his real teeth for a moment, as if checking to see that they were all still there, and only then replied to the last explanation.

"That's even worse," he said. "I'm not going to Abzug."

"It's all laid on, Don-Baby."

"Unlay it off, then," Rhotten said. "I ain't going."

"You had a good time in Israel, Don," the second member of the trio said. "Don't you remember? Her name was Rebecca, or something like that."

"And what happened when she left? I had sand all

under my rug. Do you know what it's like to stand there in the hot sun with sand between your rug and your head?"

"We'll do all the shooting indoors, Don-Baby, I absolutely guarantee."

"I won't have to leave the hotel?" he asked, doubtfully.

"My word of honor," the man said. "Would I lie to you?"

"Come to think of it, yes," Don Rhotten said. "What's the name of the hotel?"

"The Abzug Hilton," the short, fat man said, too quickly.

"You know what my contract says, Seymour," Dan Rhotten said. "No Hiltons and no Howard Johnson Motels."

"Actually, it's not the Hilton," the tall one said. "Seymour was mistaken. We wouldn't violate the terms of your contract."

"I'm not a jerk, you know," Rhotten said. "I'm Don Rhotten. And Don Rhotten's contract calls for certain things in keeping with my stature and Neilsen rating."

"That's why we think you should go to Abzug, baby," the short one said. "The ratings."

"What do you mean, the ratings?"

"For the last two weeks, baby, you've been number four, after Smith, Rather and Cronkite."

"Smith's got an unfair advantage," Rhotten said, somewhat petulantly. "He can pronounce all those funny names. He's even been to most of them."

"Well, before he moved into the big time, he used to be a reporter," the short one said. "Real reporters have to go places all the time."

"There ought to be a law," Rhotten said. "No real reporters in front of the camera."

"Smith and Cronkite go way back, baby," the short one said. "You know that. It's sort of a grandfather clause. Once they're gone, that'll be the end of them. They're sort of like dinosaurs."

"Are Smith and Cronkite going to wherever the hell it is?"

"It'll be all yours, baby," the short one said, "an exclusive."

"If it's such a big story, how come they ain't going?"

"They don't have to go anywhere, Don. *They're* Number One and Number Two in the Neilsens."

"That's really disgusting, you know that?" Don Rhotten said. "You spend half your youth in speech and elocution classes, and then half your life getting made up, and what happens? Some lousy reporter beats you out in the ratings."

"Well, nobody's blaming you for that," the short one said. "We know you do your part, Don. Sincerity-wise, presentation-wise, you're number one. But you have to get out there where the news is breaking. What people want to see on the news is violence. And, no offense, what did you give them tonight? Old people. Who cares about old people?"

"That's not *my* fault," Rhotten protested. "*I* don't write 'The Rhotten Report.' "

"I know, I know," he said. "But the bottom line is the same. No violence, the ratings go splash."

"We got a new gimmick for you, Don," the short one said.

"What kind of a gimmick?"

"What you're going to report from Abzug is that you made a mistake."

"Don Rhotten made a mistake?" Rhotten said. "You're right. You are bananas."

"Think about it, baby," the short one said. "Be profound."

"Profound, shmofound, Don Rhotten doesn't make mistakes," Rhotten said.

"Hear me out," the short one said. "From what we hear, this Abzug is loaded with color."

"What kind of color?"

"Desert, mountains, camels, horses, guys in robes running around with rifles and swords . . . "

"That's all I need is some guy running around me

with a rifle. You know I'm afraid of guns," Rhotten said.

"You don't have to get near the guys with the guns. We'll put them on film and run them behind you on rear projection. Like I said, you won't have to get out of the hotel."

"I'm not saying I'm going, Seymour; but if I do, you better count on me holding you to that."

"I left out the best part," Seymour said. "You know how they handle their crime problem?"

"How would I know something like that?" Rhotten asked.

"The first time they catch somebody stealing, they cut off his left hand," Seymour said. "The second time they catch him, they cut off his right hand. And the third time, they cut off his head."

"You don't say?" Rhotten said. "Can you get that on film?"

"We had Kodak make us up some special film so the blood shows really red," Seymour said. "It'll make the competition's "Blood on the Highways" series look about as gory as an afternoon in kindergarten."

"Now you're cooking with gas, Seymour," Rhotten said, approvingly.

"I thought you'd like it," Seymour said, modestly.

"What did you mean about me making a mistake? What was that all about?"

"Well, do you remember what you said on the tube tonight?"

"You better fill me in, Seymour," Rhotten said. "I had other things on my mind."

"Well, it was sort of a teaser," Seymour said. "What you said was that your highly placed sources told you that a planeload of uniformed men took off for Abzug tonight. Remember?"

"Yeah, I think so," Rhotten said, searching his memory.

"And then you said that the State Department wouldn't talk to you . . . "

"I remember that," Rhotten said. "Wasn't that stretching credibility a little? I mean, I *am* Don Rhotten, and when I want to talk to somebody, I talk to somebody."

"That's the pitch," Seymour said. "People are going to be shocked that the State Department would have the chutzpah not to talk to Don Rhotten."

"You better believe it," Rhotten said.

"So people are already excited," Seymour went on. "So we go to Abzug. The departure business is all laid on. We got you a bush jacket and a hat with a wide brim from Austria . . . "

"That's *Australia,* Seymour," the thin one said. "*Austria* is Strauss and funny little hats; *Australia* is kangaroos and funny big hats."

"Right," Seymour said, although it was evident he was annoyed at the interruption. "Like I was saying, we got you this hat with the big brim and a bush jacket . . ."

"With a big brim, they won't be able to see my face," Rhotten protested.

"The cameraman will handle that with special lights," Seymour said. "Don't worry about it. So, like I was saying, we get fifteen, twenty seconds of you on film leaving the studio here. We got cops on motorcycles to escort the station wagon to the airport."

"Station wagon? Station wagon? Why can't I go to the airport in the Cadillac?"

"The *image,* sweetie. You're dashing off to the far corners of the world. You don't dash off to the far corners in a limousine."

"O.K.," Rhotten said. "But just to the airport. No station wagon when we get where we're going."

"Agreed. Anyway, we get fifteen, twenty seconds of you here, running out to the station wagon in your bush coat, with the hat, and then taking off for the airport behind the motorcycle cops."

"Maybe I could hold the hat in my hand," Rhotten said.

"Then you'd have to put the rug back on," Seymour protested. "I was just trying to think of you, sweetie."

"I'll put the rug back on," Rhotten said. "I'm prepared to make sacrifices for my career, too, you know."

"O.K. Then at the airport, we get another fifteen or twenty seconds of you arriving, behind the motorcycle cops, and rushing out to the airplane." He paused dramatically, and then went on: "We chartered Hefner's airplane, sweetie."

"No kidding? Broads and all?"

"Broads and all," Seymour said. "We can't keep it, though. It leaves the moment we get off. I did my best, but he rented it out to somebody else and I couldn't get him to break the deal."

"Then how the hell are we supposed to get back?"

"Trust me, baby. Would I leave you deserted somewhere in the middle of nowhere?"

"Go on, Seymour," Don Rhotten said.

"So you turn at the top of the stairs, take the pipe out of your mouth and wave good-bye to the people."

"That damn pipe again! That stupid thing hurts my mouth, and it's already cracked three sets of caps."

"But it fits, baby, you know that. The *image*. If *Cronkite* didn't have *his* pipe, he'd probably still be covering the stock market for some lousy wire service."

"O.K., so you got thirty, forty seconds of film of me. What do you do with it?"

"We run it tonight on the eleven o'clock 'News Roundup'; we run it on one of the late-hour talk shows; we run it again first thing in the morning on 'Top o' the Morning News'; and we run it again tomorrow night, on your regular spot."

"That's only 40 seconds out of 120," Rhotten said. "What about the rest?"

"We run that film clip of you getting that Honorary Doctor of Humanities degree from Harvard."

"Sounds all right," Rhotten said.

"And then," Seymour said, "a kicker like no other kicker in the history of television journalism!"

"What's that?"

"For two days, we keep building suspense. We got

the satellite for tomorrow. We show you getting off the airplane in Abzug, and into the Jeep . . ."

"What Jeep? You haven't forgotten, Seymour, what happened the last time you put me in a Jeep?"

"You got sick to your stomach," Seymour said.

"That, too," Rhotten said. "What I was talking about was cracking my caps. I forget where I was at the time."

"Israel, Don. The Jeep disaster was in Israel," the thin one said.

"Well, then, you remember how much trouble it was getting caps in Israel. What are we going to do in . . . where is it?"

"Abzug, Don," the thin one said.

"In Abzug, if I crack my caps?"

"We're carrying three extra sets of caps, sweetie," Seymour said. "And you only have to ride in the Jeep about fifty yards. All flat and level. No problem."

"So what's the kicker?"

"We fill the rest of the two minutes with color. Guys on camels, women in masks, that shtik. All you have to do is a voice-over. What we're establishing is that Don Rhotten is on the scene in this far-off place, getting to the bottom of the story the State Department and the Pentagon deny. Maybe, if we're lucky, they'll have some guy who just got caught stealing for the third time. That'll knock Smith out of the ratings!"

"But what's the kicker?"

"The third day, via satellite, Don Rhotten says that his personal reporting, on the scene, has convinced him that his highly placed sources misled him. The United States is not secretly aiding the Abzugians."

"Who were they supposed to be fighting, anyway?" Rhotten asked. "The Israelis or the Arabs?"

"Both," the thin one said. "They're at war with both sides."

"I'm supposed to say I was misled? How does that fit in with my image?"

"Honesty!" Seymour said. "You're an *honest* TV journalist, willing to publicly admit you made a mistake.

It'll be a first! It has never happened before. Durwood checked that out."

"And you absolutely guarantee that all I have to do is ride fifty yards in a Jeep, then in a limousine to the hotel, and don't have to leave the hotel?"

"You got my word of honor," Seymour said.

"To hell with your word of honor. I want it in writing," Don Rhotten said.

"You got it, baby," Saymour said. "Durwood, get Don his rug and the hat with the big brim!"

"Right, Chief," Durwood said.

"And then call downstairs and tell them to crank up the crowd of spontaneous fans. We'll be down just as soon as we get Don-Baby into his caps and rug!"

Don Rhotten was ready in just a few minutes. He rather liked his reflection in the mirror: the wide-brimmed hat, pinned up on one side, gave him a rather dashing appearance; the bush jacket added just the right flair.

Seymour handed him a metal box, which was about a foot long and eight inches square, with a strap and microphone dangling from it.

"What is this ugly *thing?*" Rhotten asked, examining it suspiciously.

"It's a tape recorder, Don-Baby. You push the button and talk into it. It records your voice."

"No fooling?"

"Yeah, the real reporters use them all the time," Durwood said. "They even work sometimes."

"I'll be damned," Rhotten said. "You don't even have to plug it in, huh? Where's the prompter? How am I going to know what to say?"

"Durwood'll hold up dummy boards, Don. No problem."

"I don't like this business of mingling with the fans," Don Rhotten said.

"It's only a couple of seconds, Don-Baby," Seymour said. "And then we're inside the station wagon and off to the broads on the plane." He paused. "One thing,

Don. You're supposed to hang that tape recorder from your shoulder, not carry it in both hands like that."

"Gotcha," Don Rhotten said, and flashed his famous smile. Then they all left the dressing room.

Chapter Eight

"Oh, God!" sang Boris Alexandrovich Korsky-Rimsakov, addressing not the Deity but the Muse. *"With what ecstasy you have set my soul afire!"*

He was answered with a chorus of feminine sighs, which Jacques Offenbach had not written into the opera.

"Like a divine concert, your voice has penetrated me!" Boris went on. Two large hotel keys came flying stageward through the air and a rather insubstantial pair of panties floated gently down from the balcony of the Paris Opera to have their brief moment of glory in the beam of the spotlight which followed the singer around the stage.

"With a gentle and burning fire my being is consumed!"

The lady beside Miss Penelope Quattlebaum gave a small moan, frothed slightly at the lips and slipped out of her seat as if it had been greased. Penelope Quattlebaum looked at her with mingled sympathy, horror and fascination as the lady's husband, giving every evidence that he was quite accustomed to his wife slipping into a coma in the Opera, hauled her back into the chair, held her in place with his arm and straightened, more or less, her hat on her head.

"Your glances into mine have poured their flame like radiant stars," the huge, bearded singer sang. He paused for breath, and was answered by another feminine chorus of sighs and terms of endearment.

"Disgusting, isn't it?" Miss Penelope Quattlebaum's escort, Mr. T. Dudley Dulaney, III whispered. Mr. Dulaney was, like Miss Penelope Quattlebaum, a member of the Foreign Service Corps of the United States of America. He was Deputy Fourth-Assistant Secretary of the U.S. Embassy, Paris, and among his manifold other duties was the custody of other junior Foreign Service Officers passing through Paris en route to or from other diplomatic posts.

Normally, what the others got was a check of their shot records, a hotel reservation and a copy of *Paris Tonight*! (published for free distribution by the Greater Paris Hôtelier & Innkeepers Association). T. Dudley had made an exception in Miss Penelope Quattlebaum's case. He had bought her lunch and dinner, and had high hopes of being able to buy her breakfast. The hotel room in which she was billeted was a three-room suite in the Crillon Hotel, next door to the Embassy. It was normally reserved for Foreign Service Officers in the grade of Minister and above,. junketing Congressmen and others high in the politico-bureaucratic hierarchy, for whom no expenditure of the taxpayers' money could be considered sufficient compensation for having to labor on alien shores.

As a Foreign Service Officer, Grade Seven, Penelope Quattlebaum was nominally entitled to somewhat less grandiose accommodations, such as "the businessman's special" at the Paris Hilton (a nine-by-twelve cubicle furnished with a single bed, a chair, a dresser and a three-foot-square shower). But Miss Quattlebaum was a rather unusual Foreign Service Officer. Not only was she a freshly commissioned member of the Corps, who needed a little sympathetic encouragement to get her over the shock of her first days outside the home country, but she was a *female* member of the Corps; and she was one, moreover, in the quaint patois of the Marine

Guard who had brought her to Mr. Dulaney's office, who was "stacked like a brick outhouse."

"Does this always happen?" Penelope whispered back as Boris Alexandrovich Korsky-Rimsakov drew breath into his lungs, which sent buttons popping off his costume.

"He seems to have a strange effect on French women," T. Dudley Dulaney whispered.

"Sssssssssssssh! You cultureless American barbarian!" the lady to Mr. Dulaney's right said, jabbing him painfully in the ribs with her umbrella. "The Maestro is singing! . . ."

"And oh, my be-lov-ed Muse," Boris sang, *"I feel the passing of your perfume-ed breath over my lips and over my eyes!"*

"I can't imagine why," Miss Penelope Quattlebaum whispered, spreading her perfumed breath over his ear. "I mean, what is he, besides three hundred pounds of perfectly proportioned male animal with teeth like pearls and the voice of a god?"

"Precisely," T. Dudley Dulaney agreed, and got himself stabbed with the umbrella tip again.

"Be-love-ed Muse," Boris sang, *"I am yours!"*

The response from the feminine portion of the audience was now mingled with ecstasy and sorrow. An animallike howl went up; there was another shower of hotel-room keys and intimate female apparel floating through the air, followed almost immediately by the sound of uncontrolled sobbing from those who, knowing the opera, were aware that Boris Alexandrovich Korsky-Rimsakov had just sung his last line.

There were a few more lines of the opera, but so far as the feminine fans were concerned, it was over. The applause began before Nicklausse could tell Stella that Hoffmann was dead drunk. The audience didn't want to hear that anyway.

Suddenly, one deep masculine voice, carrying over the wailing soprano, filled the house.

Penelope Quattlebaum was sure that her ears were playing a trick on her. She looked up behind her to the Diamond Circle and located the male who was shouting. He was in the box immediately beside the box of the President of the Republic, and he was an Arab in full robes. What he appeared to be shouting . . . but of course could not be shouting . . . was "Your mother wears army shoes!" over and over again.

The curtains closed, and then immediately opened again. Boris Alexandrovich Korsky-Rimsakov, who had sort of slumped into a chair after his last line, now rose and, with immense dignity, tinged with modesty, stepped to the footlights, smiled his dazzling smile, and bowed low. The applause and screaming rattled the chandeliers. He straightened. Something caught his eye. It was still another item of intimate feminine apparel, a pair of shocking-pink panties. He moved with an athlete's quick grace across the stage and snatched them from the air as they fell.

He held them in his right hand and bowed, and then rose and waved them again, over his head, as the audience went wild. This continued for a good thirty seconds; and then, with a gesture of graceful élan, he tossed the panties over his shoulder. He then raised both hands in front of him above his shoulder level and, smiling broadly, slowly lowered them. As the hands descended, so did the level of the roar of the crowd. By the time his hands reached the level of his waist, the only sound in the huge opera house was that of a man snoring somewhere in the fifth or sixth balcony. There was a sudden yelp of pain, and then all was silence.

"My children," Boris Alexandrovich Korsky-Rimsakov said, his voice filling the house, "for tonight only, I am afraid that I will not be able to stand here for the customary half-hour acceptance of your compliments."

There was a groaning roar of disappointment.

"I must take a plane to New York," he went on. This time the groan reached deafening proportions, and here and there were cries of *"À bas les Américains!"*

Boris raised his hands again and lowered them again, and again there was silence.

"I will, of course, return," he said. There was a roar of approval. He let it continue, even swell, and didn't raise his hands for silence even when a quintet of ladies in the first balcony began to sing "The Marseillaise." He watched with interest as a long line of page boys began to carry the traditional baskets of flowers on stage. He made a gesture with his hands, telling them to hurry up. The set was quickly filled with flowers, most of them long-stemmed roses. When the last basket had been deposited, he raised his hands for silence again.

"We are gathered here tonight not only to hear my magnificent, unequaled voice," he said modestly, "but also in the name of charity."

"*À bas la charité!*" a blue-haired lady on the distant side of fifty shouted suddenly from the Diamond Circle. "*Je vous aime!*" (A rough translation might be, "To heck with charity. I like you.")

Boris ignored the outburst. "The exact nature of the charity at the moment escapes me," he said.

The prompter hissed something from the prompter's stand. Boris didn't hear him precisely.

"I am informed it is St. Imogene's Home for Unwed Mothers," he said.

Madame le President, in the Presidential Box, stopped her husband in the very act of getting to his feet to correct and protest this defamation of his wife's alma mater, St. Imogene's School for Girls.

"We must allow genius," Madame le President said, "their little idiosyncrasies."

She told herself that this time there would be no ornately calligraphed expression of appreciation on stationery of the Elysée Palace. She would present her expressions of gratitude personally to the Maestro, just as soon as something called Monsieur le President away on the nation's business. She knew just what she would wear: the low-cut dress with the high hem, the one M. le President forbade her to wear because he said it made her look like a hooker.

"Which is," Boris went on, "a noble institution long

dear to my heart. With that in mind, my children, I am going to place these flowers on sale for ten francs a blossom, all proceeds to the fine unwed mothers at St. Imogene's. Bear in mind, my children, that I, Boris Alexandrovich Korsky-Rimsakov, have personally sniffed each flower."

He bowed again and, still bowing, stepped away from the footlights. The curtain came down suddenly, and the house lights went up.

"When are you going to Rome, darling?" Madame le President asked.

"I'd thought we would go next week," he said.

"I have a headache," Madame le President said. "You'll have to go alone."

As hordes of women rushed to the stage, pushing and jostling, each jeweled hand waving the currency of the country, Miss Penelope Quattlebaum and Mr. T. Dudley Dulaney made their way to a side exit catering to the upper classes and those authorized to affix a CORPS DIPLOMATIQUE plaque above their license plate.

It turned out to be another manifestation of Orwell's theory that some equal pigs are more equal than others. There were a hundred cars in the V.I.P. area, each with a C.D. sign on the bumper. But there was only one Cadillac limousine with a C.D. sign along with the flag of the Sheikhdom of Hussid flying from its glistening fender.

The Republic of France drew thirty-eight percent of its oil supplies from beneath the sands of the Hussid Desert. A dozen gendarmes, waving white batons and furiously blowing whistles, made sure that the Hussidic Cadillac was first at the exit.

Miss Penelope Quattlebaum watched with fascination as more gendarmes formed a line, linking arms, to make a path between the Opera House exit and the open door of the Cadillac. She was sure that she was about to see, up close, the President of the French Republic and his lady.

She saw, instead, Boris Alexandrovich Korsky-Rimsakov, still in costume, holding a jeroboam of Dom

Perignon '54 in his hand. He ran quickly to the limousine and got inside.

His voice, even more thrilling in close proximity, came from the car. Penelope Quattlebaum, a recent graduate of the State Department's Crash Course in Arabic for New Diplomats, was thrilled that she understood what he was saying: "For Christ's sake, Abdullah, get the damn lead out!"

All eyes moved to the door of the Opera. With great, even regal, dignity, raising first one hand and then the other to the crowd, His Royal Highness Sheikh Abdullah ben Abzug, followed by His Royal Highness Sheikh Hassan ad Kayam of Hussid, who held a bottle of slivovitz in each hand, emerged.

"Mud in your eye," Sheikh Abdullah solemnly intoned to those on the left, and then turned to those on the right. "Your mother wears army shoes," he said benevolently.

And then all three were in the back seat of the limousine. A siren howled; gendarmes furiously blew their whistles; the crowd parted. The limousine moved away from the Opera, past American Express, the Café de la Paix and, gathering speed, raced down Place de l'Opéra in the general direction of Orly Field.

Penelope Quattlebaum let out an audible sigh. This was what she dreamed a life as a diplomat in the service of her country would be. It was another world, from Emmaus, Pennsylvania, where she had spent the first seventeen years of her life, and from Slippery Rock, Pennsylvania, where she had been educated at the Slippery Rock State Teachers College.

It was a good omen. The first Arabs she had ever seen, except on television, were the nobility: men of education, culture and refinement who appreciated the opera. It was cruel and callous of her, she knew, but this was the life she wanted, not the life her parents wanted to give her. They meant well, of course; but the prospect of taking over the Quattlebaum Dairy Farm & Quarter Horse Ranch of Emmaus, Pennsylvania (she was the only Quattlebaum child) was stifling and unattractive to someone of her cultural and artistic hungers.

The gay, glamorous, rarified atmosphere of international diplomacy was, Penelope knew, what her soul had been crying for all these years, ever since she had seen Cary Grant focus his soulful eyes on a lady diplomat on "The Late, Late Show."

She had a long way to go, she realized. She had just been given a rude warning that the Crash Course in Arabic for New Diplomats had been woefully inadequate. Penelope had no idea what the Sheikh had been saying as he blessed the crowd. "Mudden yuri" and "yurmudder waresar mishus" had not been in either the "basic vocabulary" or in the "list of common phrases" at the language school.

She took her notebook from her purse and wrote the phrases down, so that she could, at the earliest possible moment, look them up in her English-Arabic dictionary.

"What are you doing, Miss Quattlebaum?" Mr. T. Dudley Dulaney asked.

"Writing down what the Sheikh said," she said.

"He said 'mud in your eye' and 'your mother wears army shoes,' " Dudley replied, somewhat taken aback.

"Yes, I know," she said impatiently. "All I'm trying to do, Mr. Dulaney, is increase my vocabulary."

"Certainly," Dulaney said. It was the first suspicion the Dulaney had had that the lady might be a little odd. He told himself that he should have suspected that she was a little odd. Who ever heard of a *gorgeous* lady diplomat?

His suspicion that she was strange was confirmed two hours later. He had passed the two hours plying her with brandy, which she said tasted just like "Papa's hard cider" and drank with great gusto. He was sure that he would be able to work his wicked way with her; but when he tried to put his arm around the back of the seat in his MG, she suddenly revealed a nasty, hitherto-hidden-from-sight character trait.

"You try that again, buster," she snarled, "and you'll be carrying your arm in a sling."

"I'm terribly sorry," T. Dudley Dulaney said. "I'm afraid you mistook my intentions."

"I didn't mistake your intentions," Penelope said. "I recognize a dirty, rotten, male-chauvinist, sexist, improper advance when I see one. There's a new breed of women afoot, Dudley, and you better not forget that we've come a long way!"

"I'm very sorry," T. Dudley Dulaney said, suddenly quite alarmed at what would happen should Foreign Service Officer Grade-Seven Penelope Quattlebaum report to someone that Foreign Service Officer Grade-Seven T. Dudley Dulaney had made improper advances toward her.

"Sorry's not good enough!" Penelope said. "Let me out of this car, you dirty, rotten, male-chauvinist, sexist pig!" They were stopped at the moment in traffic at the Rond Pont of the Champs-Elysées, which is about two blocks from the Crillon Hotel.

Penelope seized the opportunity to climb out of T. Dudley Dulaney's MG coupe. She stalked off in the direction of the Elysée Palace, the American Embassy and her suite in the Crillon Hotel.

That she headed in the proper direction was a fortuitous circumstance; for, the truth of the matter is that Foreign Service Officer Grade-Seven Penelope Quattlebaum was in her cups up to the tip of her pretty little nose. Although she manifested none of the ordinary symptoms of being smashed—slurred speech, staggering gait or hard-to-focus eyes and so on—she was actually far more in the arms of Bacchus than she had ever been in her life. T. Dudley Dulaney's campaign to get her loaded had succeeded, although Phase B of that plan was not to reach the fruition he had planned.

The curious effect that alcohol had upon her had surfaced only rarely before in her life, for the very good reason that Penelope Quattlebaum had partaken of the spirits only rarely.

On one previous occasion, when Penelope had been a freshman cheerleader at Slippery Rock, a young man with the same general purpose in mind as T. Dudley Dulaney had spiked her Seven-Up at the Down but Not Out Post-Game Get Together (Slippery Rock had gone down to defeat at the hands of Mauch Chunk 13-7) with gin.

Shortly after draining the third cup, Penelope Quattlebaum had assaulted the right guard of the Slippery Rock offensive eleven, one Victor C. Grumplebacher, by first kicking him in the shins, and then as he bent over to clutch the wounded member, by belting him in the eye with a small, bony fist.

At the time, her behavior was regarded as a manifestation of her disapproval of Mr. Grumplebacher's football prowess. He had tripped over his shoelace and fallen flat on his face six yards shy of the Mauch Chunk end zone, thereby losing the game. An excess of school spirit, in other words, rather than an excess of the fermented kind.

Two years later, far from the campus, at the wedding of her cousin Agnes Quattlebaum to H. Howard Albumblatt, D.V.M., Penelope had caused something of a stir. After spending some time by mistake at the "wet" punch bowl (there had been a "wet" punch bowl and a "dry" punch bowl in deference to the feelings of the Albumblatts, who had recently taken the Total Abstention Pledge), Penelope had first thrown a cup of punch at the Reverend Buckley Templeton Lewis, II, D.D., the handsome young cleric who had performed the nuptial ceremony, and then slapped his face.

The Rev. Mr. Lewis announced that he had no idea why he had been assaulted, but felt constrained to observe that when Godless people served the Devil's Brew at festive occasions, things like that were bound to happen. Penelope's father had taken the opposite tack. He rather loudly announced that not only was he highly suspicious of men who said they never took a drink, but also that he would feel no constraint whatever about taking a horsewhip to anyone who made an indecent advance to his little girl, Doctor of Divinity or not.

There had been other incidents involving Penelope, attractive young men and booze; but they had been so far separated by time and distance that no one, least of all Penelope, had thought about them in depth and reached the obvious conclusion.

In her cups, Penelope's quite natural interest in an attractive member of the opposite sex surfaced. The surfacing so shocked her (she was that rara avis, someone entitled, when the time came, to march with head high, and in virginal white, down the aisle) with its rather livid and detailed imagery, that she was suddenly filled with a blind rage directed toward the party responsible for the imagery.

Victor C. Grumplebacher, the Rev. Buckley Templeton Lewis, II, D.D., T. Dudley Dulaney and five or six others, in other words, had made a far more favorable impression upon Penelope than any of them, considering their encounters with her, would have been willing to believe.

Penelope made her way past the Elysée Palace, glowering furiously at the gendarmes on duty outside, and then came to the American Embassy. A Marine Guard was, as always, on duty outside.

"I am looking for the Crillon Hotel," she announced.

"If you can wait ten minutes, honey," the Marine Guard replied, "I would consider it an honor and a pleasure to escort you there personally."

He got a kick in the shin for his interest in tourist welfare; but since he was a Marine, he did not howl in pain, although tears ran down his rosy cheeks. Penelope went farther down the street and came to what appeared to be a hotel lobby. Her feet, encased for the past four hours in tight shoes, hurt. She decided that she would go into the hotel lobby, sit down for a moment and then resume her search for her hotel.

She made it to an armchair and slumped into it, not without attracting the attention of many people in the

lobby. It was not that she staggered or lurched. To
reiterate, as plastered as she was, she looked and behaved
as if she had never so much as sniffed a cork.

Once she had rested her feet, it seemed to her to
be a good idea to rest her eyes. She closed them.

A very tall, rather dark gentleman with a perfectly
cropped British-style, brush mustache, who had been
using one of the house phones and who had watched
with more than casual interest her appearance at the
hotel's door, was concerned.

He took the telephone from his ear and handed it
to another rather dark man, telling him, in French, "Stay
on here and see if you can stop the plane." Then he
walked to where Penelope dozed, snoring just a little,
in the armchair.

Up close, she looked even better than she had looked
when he had first seen her. As something of an expert
on European females, he quickly decided that she was
not French. (Her complexion was too perfect for that,
and she wore no powder or other facial make-up.)
German, possibly, but a bit too finely featured for that.
Scandinavian, probably. Even more probably, Swedish.
Unfortunately, the Swedish he knew was not suitable
for the first few words of what he hoped would be a
long conversation, a conversation leading to a long and
rewarding association. He did speak German.

"Excuse me, Fräulein," he said, in impeccable German, "may I be of some small assistance to you?"

Penelope stirred but did not awaken. Ever so gently,
the tall dark stranger touched her shoulder and pushed
her, ever so gently. When her eyes opened, he repeated
what he had said before.

Penelope Quattlebaum spoke, of course, since her
mother tongue, Pennsylvania Dutch, whose roots, as
linguists and philologists are well aware, lay with German, not with the language spoken in the Netherlands.

She understood what he was saying. She focused her
eyes on him. A wild, blind rage swept through her.

"Get away from me, you sex maniac," she said, in

Pennsylvania Dutch. "What kind of city is this, anyway, when a girl can't find her hotel without being accosted by every male-chauvinist, sexist pig on the streets?"

Pennsylvania Dutch, fortunately, does not readily translate in *Hochdeutsch,* or High German, which is the language the gentleman understood. All he really understood of the outburst was that she was looking for a hotel.

"If *das gnädige Fräulein* (roughly: "the charming miss") will give me the name of her hotel, I will be honored to send her there in my car," he said.

Penelope did not understand all of that, but enough to know that he had asked for the name of her hotel.

"The Crillon," she said. Certainly, there could be no harm in revealing that much.

"Aber, mein liebe gnädige Fräulein, das ist die Crillon," he said. (Roughly: "But, my dear, charming miss, this *is* the Crillon.")

Penelope got to her feet. A cloud of her perfume filled his nostrils.

"No thanks to you, you masher!" she said, this time in English. She looked at his face and into his deep, dark eyes. A dark-red mist of rage filled her very soul. Her right arm, the same one she had used to give Victor C. Grumplebacher the shiner that had become a permanent part of Slippery Rock football lore, swung in an arc toward his face. He reached out and stopped the swing with his hand by clutching her wrist. Unsuspecting, she was thrown off balance and fell into his arms.

They stood that way for a moment, immobile, and then Penelope finally remembered where she was, what she was doing and what, most importantly, she wished to remain. She suspended herself on one foot and sent the other sailing into the gentleman's shin.

With a howl of pain, he let her go.

"How dare you put your filthy, rotten, male-chauvinist, sexist-pig arms around me?" she said, and swung at him again, this time connecting, fortunately, with an open palm. The sound of the slap rang like a pistol shot through the corridor, and two assistant night managers came running, as did the man to whom the gentleman had earlier handed the telephone.

The mustachioed, tall, dark stranger raised his hand, and they all stopped in their tracks.

"This young lady," he said in French, "is a guest of this hotel. Please be good enough to see her to her room."

One of the assistant night managers was old enough to be her great-grandfather, and Penelope allowed herself to be led away as he very politely asked for her name.

The other night manager, very timidly, said, "Is there anything else I might do for you, Excellency?"

"Have a dozen long-stemmed roses delivered with her breakfast," he said. "No card."

"Certainly, Excellency," the assistant manager said.

The mustachioed gentleman turned to the man to whom he had given the telephone.

"What did you find out?" he asked.

"The French authorities have contacted the plane, Your Highness," the man said. "And there is word from your grandfather."

"Which is?"

"We are to return home immediately, Your Highness, so that we may meet your grandfather's guests and extend to them all hospitalities."

"Is that all?"

"There is something else, Your Highness. I have no idea what it means, but I am assured that it is part of the message."

"Well, what is it?"

"The last sentence of the message, Your Highness, is 'Mud in your eye.'"

The tall, dark man looked thoughtful for a moment and shrugged his shoulders. Then a look of genuine annoyance mingled with profound regret crossed his handsome features. He snapped his fingers to attract the attention of the assistant night manager who still hovered by.

"Make that two dozen long-stemmed roses," he said.

Then he turned on his heel and walked out the door. A Rolls-Royce was sitting at the curb. He got in, and the other man got in beside him. The chauffeur closed the door after them, and the car made an illegal U-turn and headed across the Place de la Concorde in the general direction of Orly Field.

Chapter Nine

As all this was going on, there was also extraordinary activity in the Elysée Palace. Monsieur le President had returned from the Opera in great high spirits. The sale of flowers, one at a time, from the fifty-one baskets of flowers delivered to, and personally sniffed by, Boris Alexandrovich Korsky-Rimsakov, had been a complete success. The coffers of St. Imogene's School, Madame le President's alma mater, were about to bulge.

And, although Madame le President had been naturally disappointed that *Cher* Boris Alexandrovich had not been at the post-performance reception, she had had a good time and had taken aboard several bottles of champagne.

Monsieur le President had high hopes of ending the evening in connubial bliss. As Madame le President (whom he referred to as "Mon Petit Chou-Chou," the loose translation of which is, unfortunately, "my little brussels sprouts," and does not quite reflect the tender affection implicit in the French version) prepared for bed, commenting again and again on the vocal artistry of the singer, Monsieur le President went into the Presidential bath, showered, liberally doused himself with eau de cologne and wrapped himself in a silk dressing gown.

No sooner had he entered the Presidential bedchamber, however, than the telephone rang. Not the white bedside telephone, which could be ignored or, under the circumstances, ripped from the wall and thrown out the window. What rang infuriatingly was the official, bright-red *téléphone pour les affaires d'état,* which was kept in a rather elegant piece of furniture used during *La Belle Epoque* to store a porcelain container for the personal use of Louis XIV.

"I suppose I must answer that," Monsieur le President said.

"Duty above all," Chou-Chou replied, understandingly.

He opened the cabinet and picked up the telephone.

"Yes, what is it?"

"M'sieu le President," his caller (whom he recognized to be the Deputy Chef de Cabinet of the Deuxième Bureau) said, "I hope I have not disturbed your sleep."

"Not at all," M'sieu le President said. "It was necessary for me to be awake to hear the telephone."

"M'sieu le President," the head of the Deuxième Bureau said, "one of the ushers attending Sheikh Abdullah ben Abzug at the Opera was not an usher."

"You call me in the middle of the night, disturb my sleep, to talk about an imposter usher? And who is Sheikh Abdullah ben Abzug? Was he that crazy Arab in the next box who insulted my wife?"

"The usher, M'sieu le President, who attended the Sheikh of Abzug was Col. René Françoise de la Montsacre—one of my men."

"Then why did not the good Colonel do something when that crazy Arab insulted my wife, the wife of your President, with the allegation that her mother wore army shoes?"

"Colonel Montsacre, M'sieu le President," the head of the Deuxième Bureau went on, "overheard the conversation between Sheikh Abdullah and Sheikh Hassan ad Kayam."

"That's the fat little one who kept leering at my wife?"

"Yes, sir."

"And what did those two Arab degenerates say about my Petit Chou-Chou?"

"May I remind M'sieu le President that France imports thirty-eight percent of its oil from the Sheikhdom of Hussid?"

"You think I don't know that?" M'sieu le President said. "Get to the point."

"Your Excellency will recall, I am sure, that the government, the Foreign Ministry, has been exerting great pressure upon the government of Morocco to insure that when the oil of Abzug is exploited it will be exploited for the benefit of France?"

"Yes, of course," the President said. "My dear Minister," the President said, "I am delighted that you bring me such good news, even at this ungodly hour. You have my thanks and my congratulations. And now, if there is nothing else . . . "

"Excellency, what Colonel Montsacre overheard was that the Sheikh of Abzug has decided to permit oil exploration by the Chevaux Petroleum Corporation."

"The details of the matter are none of my concern," the President said, "so long as it is a good French corporation, as Chevaux is . . . "

"M'sieu le President," the head of the Deuxième Bureau went on, "the head of the Chevaux Petroleum Corporation is Jean-Pierre de la Chevaux."

"And he wants a medal? O.K. Tell him he's as good as a *Chevalier de la Légion d'Honneur*. I'll even give it to him myself."

The head of the Deuxième Bureau bit the bullet: "Jean-Pierre de la Chevaux is an American!" he said. "You should excuse the expression!"

"Impossible!"

"He is an American," the head of the Deuxième Bureau repeated.

"How could you let this happen?" the President said. "What are we paying you for, anyway—to go around playing usher?"

"If Colonel Montsacre had not been . . . as you put it, Excellency . . . 'playing usher,' we would not know of this development. We would have been presented with a fait accompli."

"You mean, it's not finally settled?"

"It is not in writing, Excellency—not yet. But the Sheikh has given his word, and he has never gone back on it before."

"There is a first time for everything," the President said. "I presume, M'sieu le Minister, that you have a plan?"

"Yes, Excellency."

"Well, out with it. I'm a busy man and I need my sleep." He looked over his shoulder. Petit Chou-Chou, tiring of affairs of state, had slipped out of her peignoir and, wearing a rather transparent garment whose hem rose a foot above her knees, got into the bed.

"I don't quite know where to begin, M'sieu le President," the head of the Deuxième Bureau said.

"Start somewhere!" the President said sharply. "We're dealing with the future of France!"

"Well, from what we have been able to put together," he said, "the connection, the American Connection, so to speak, goes from Sheikh Abdullah to Sheikh Hassan to Boris Alexandrovich Korsky-Rimsakov . . . "

"The opera singer? *That* Boris Alexandrovich Korsky-Rimsakov? What's he got to do with it?"

"Papa," Petit Chou-Chou said, suddenly sitting up erect in bed, "is that *Cher* Boris Alexandrovich on the phone?"

"No, Mon Cher Petit Chou-Chou," the President said very gently, "we are just talking about him."

"Isn't that interesting?" she said. "What are you talking about?"

"As I was saying, Excellency, the connection runs from Sheikh Abdullah to Sheikh Hassan to the singer to Chevaux. The latter three are all friends."

"You're trying to tell me that opera singer outwitted the entire Foreign Ministry and is about to deliver the Abzugian oil fields to the Americans?"

"Yes, sir."

"Well, what do you plan to do about it?"

"The obvious thing, sir, would be destroy the bonds of friendship."

"Good thinking," the President said. "Have you a plan to do that?"

"The Arab culture places a good deal of emphasis on hospitality," the man from the Deuxième Bureau said.

"Get to the point," the President said.

"The Sheikh of Abzug, as a first step, has extended an invitation to both Chevaux, the man, and to the singer to visit him. His pride would be deeply injured if they didn't show up."

"That's a good idea," the President said. "The last I heard, nobody was quite sure where Abzug was, anyway."

"The Sheikh customarily entertains guests at the Mamoumian Hotel in Marrakech," the man from the Deuxième Bureau said, "because there are no hotels, of course, in Abzug itself."

"Well, how are you going to keep Korsky-Rimsakov and that foul turncoat to France, Jean-Pierre de la Chevaux, from going to the Mamoumian Hotel in Marrakech? Everybody knows where that is."

"*Cher* Boris Alexandrovich is going to be at the Mamoumian in Marrakech?" Petit Chou-Chou asked.

"Possibly," the President said, "possibly."

"What I propose, Mr. President," the man from the Deuxième Bureau said, "is that you, Your Excellency, be at the Mamoumian Hotel when it becomes apparent that Monsieur de la Chevaux and Maestro Korsky-Rimsakov have grossly insulted Sheikh Abdullah ben Abzug by not being there as they have been invited to be."

"You want me to go to the Mamoumian?" M'sieu

le President said, thoughtfully. "Good thinking, Minister!"

"Papa," Petit Chou-Chou said, "my headache is gone. I will go with you!"

"Anything Chou-Chou wants," the President said automatically, "Chou-Chou can have."

"Excuse me, Excellency?" the Minister for Internal-External Security asked.

"I said, I will go to the Mamoumian," the President said. "But you haven't told me how you plan to keep the others away."

"Trust me, M'sieu le President," the Minister said.

"Trust you? I trusted you so far, and look what it got me!" he replied, tartly. "Tell me!"

"We will arrange for the plane carrying M'sieu de la Chevaux to be diverted from Marrakech Airport . . . to Casablanca, probably . . . and then we will see that he stays in Casablanca."

"And what about the singer?"

"No problem at all, Excellency. He is at the moment aboard the Concorde . . ."

"Aboard the Concorde? What is he doing aboard the Concorde? The Minister of the Treasury tells me that the Republic of France cannot afford to transport me, your beloved President and Chief of State, aboard the Concorde, and you tell me that this singer is aboard it?"

"As M'sieu le President knows," the man from the Deuxième Bureau explained, very carefully, *"Cher* Boris Alexandrovich sang tonight at the Paris Opera, a charity performance. The Minister of Culture was forced to make the plane available to him, to bring him from New York, and then to return him to New York. Otherwise, he could not have made an appearance."

"The Minister of Culture," M'sieu le President said, suddenly reversing course, "obviously knows what he's doing. I wish I could say that about some other ministers of this government."

"The Concorde is a French airplane," the Minister from the Deuxième Bureau said, "flown by a French pilot, and will land when and where the government of France tells the pilot to land."

"Anywhere but Marrakech, right?" the President said.

"Yes, Your Excellency," the Minister said, "and I feel sure that someone of Your Excellency's well-known diplomatic skills will be able to exploit the situation to the benefit of our beloved France."

"Quite so," the President said.

"And I feel as sure that Sheikh Abdullah will be so deeply offended when Chevaux and Korsky-Rimsakov fail to show up, that he will be more willing to change his mind and award France exploitation rights—at terms very favorable to France."

"Perhaps I have misjudged you," the President said.

"Thank you, M'sieu le President," the Minister said. "Have I your permission to proceed with the plan?"

"You have my permission," M'sieu le President said, "and the gratitude of our beloved France. Good night, M'sieu le Minister."

"Good night, Excellency. I regret that I had to disturb your rest."

"No sacrifice is too great in the service of France," the President said, and hung up the telephone.

He turned to the Presidential Bed. Petit Chou-Chou was lying on her side, eyes closed.

"Mon Petit Chou-Chou," he said, with infinite tenderness.

"Not tonight, Papa," Petit Chou-Chou said. "If we're going to Marrakech, I'll need my beauty sleep."

The President turned and looked out of the window. A wave of self-pity swept over him, mingled with pride, as he watched late-hour strollers.

"If only," he thought, "the common people knew what sacrifices their leaders have to make for them!"

Penelope Quattlebaum was awakened the next morning at 8:15 by the telephone beside her bed. Her mouth was dry, her temples throbbed, and there was the condition described as "gasidity" by a well-known pharmaceutical manufacturer in her tummy.

She gave off with an unladylike burp and staggered into the rather ornate bathroom of her suite, where she stood for a long time under the shower, trying without complete success to wash the cobwebs from her memory.

The last thing she remembered clearly was being taken by T. Dudley Dulaney to a quaint Paris bistro near the Opera. It was her first Paris bistro, and she had really been impressed with the quaint French artifacts inside the place, as well as the manifestation of Franco-American goodwill in the name: Harry's New York Bar.

Dulaney had fed her something which tasted very much like Papa's hard cider and, from the second glass onward, her memory of what had transpired grew more and more hazy. She remembered only that there had been an unpleasant little scene with T. Dudley Dulaney, who had attempted to press his unwanted attentions on her.

She seemed to remember a Marine and she seemed to remember, quite clearly, a tall, dark stranger with a thick, black mustache; but she was quite sure that what she remembered of what had transpired between her and the tall, dark stranger (the imagery brought a blush of maidenly embarrassment to her pink cheeks) had not really happened.

It must have been a dream. It just didn't seem at all likely that the tall, dark stranger with that *darling* black mustache had really come galloping up on a white stallion to snatch her bodily into the saddle behind him, and to gallop up the Champs-Élysées to ravish her with great skill and wild imagination under the arch of the Arc de Triomphe de l'Étoile, while a detachment of the Garde Républicaine (who had apparently come to the Arc from the Opera, where she had first seen them) urged him on by playing trumpet adagios.

She dwelt on the details for a couple of minutes, decided it really had been a dream and stepped out of the shower. She wrapped herself in a terry-cloth robe and returned to her bedroom.

She heard activity, male voices, in the sitting room and, heart beating rapidly, gathered the courage to open the door a crack and peer out. It wasn't a tall, dark stranger; it was two ancient waiters delivering breakfast. She thought it was really odd that she could remember the face of the tall, dark stranger with such clarity. In her mind's eye, she could count the whiskers in his mustache and feel the warm, overwhelming strength of his hand on her wrist.

She shook her head to clear it. It wasn't such a good idea. Her brain seemed to be rolling around inside her skull. She waited, peering through the crack in the door, until the floor waiters left, and then she went out and sat down at the table they had set up.

She poured herself a cup of coffee. It tasted as though it had been prepared from salt water and discarded ball bearings, but it was obviously just what she needed. The strain, the jet lag and then the excitement of actually being in Gay Paris (plus, of course, the hard cider that miserable twerp, T. Dudley Dulaney, had tricked her into drinking) had simply been too much for her.

The coffee took the lining off the inside of her mouth and throat which, under the circumstances (her mouth and throat felt as if they were lined with floor sweepings), was a decided advantage. She gingerly lifted one of the silver covers off one of the plates. Lying there, obscenely, were two fried eggs. It was obviously true that there was a deep streak of cruelty, of sadism, in these French. She picked up a roll, still warm, in the shape of a half-moon, broke it and then buttered it. And only then did she see the roses, the red roses, the long-stemmed red roses. She went to them and sniffed. *Two* dozen long-stemmed red roses! She counted them and then counted them again, and rage rose in her again. Twenty-two. Somebody had ripped off two of her two dozen roses!

Who were they from? She searched for a card with even more diligence and eager anticipation than she had for the purloined blossoms, and with no more success.

Probably, she thought, they had come from T. Dudley Dulaney, III. That was like him. He would want to send something like flowers after his most undiplomatic, ungentlemanly conduct of the night before (how *dare* he abandon her in the middle of a strange city?); he was just the sort of miserable twerp who would sent twenty-two roses instead of twenty-four, thinking the recipient would never bother to count; and, finally, he was the sort of spineless male-chauvinist sexist pig who would send flowers to make amends for outrageous conduct but would not have the courage to include his card.

The telephone rang.

Penelope answered it. "Good morning," she said, sweetly.

"Good morning, Miss Quattlebaum," T. Dudley Dulaney, III said. "I trust you slept well?"

"What's on your mind, Dulaney?" Penelope snarled.

"Why, I've come to take you to Orly Field," he said. "Your plane leaves at 10:45."

"I'll be right down," she said. If he thought she would ask him to come up to her suite just because he'd sent her twenty-two lousy, long-stemmed, red roses, he had another think coming.

"I'll be waiting," he said.

Penelope dressed. As she began to pull on her panty-hose, she saw that the bottoms of her feet were absolutely black. The French, apparently, felt it was easier to install a special foot-washing bath in each bathroom than to invest in vacuum cleaners for the floors. Penelope carried her pantyhose and her shoes into the bathroom, washed her feet in the porcelain device, dried them and finally completed dressing. She wondered if it would be possible for her to buy one of the foot washers in Morocco and send it to Papa for Christmas. Mama was always complaining that his feet smelled, and she thought they both would really be pleased with something like this.

She summoned a bellboy. Two arrived. Penelope followed them down to the lobby. T. Dudley Dulaney, III, who had been sitting in an armchair, rose when he saw the little procession, marched over to Penelope with a nervous little smile on his face and presented her with a bundle of roses.

Penelope was stunned. "Thank you," she said.

"My pleasure, Miss Quattlebaum," he said, flushing slightly.

Certainly, T. Dudley Dulaney would not send two dozen roses, less two, to her room and then present her with another dozen in the lobby.

Then who had sent the others?

Her mind's eye filled with the image of the tall, dark mustachioed stranger on the white charger who had worked his imaginatively evil ways upon her beneath the Arc de Triomphe. Perhaps it hadn't been a dream. . . .

That was absurd! She forced the imagery from her mind and allowed herself to be led out of the hotel and into an official U.S. Embassy car parked outside.

An hour and ten minutes later, aboard an Air Maroc DC-9, Miss Penelope Quattlebaum, still wondering about the source of the roses, departed Orly Field, Paris, on the last leg of her journey to her first diplomatic post.

Chapter Ten

There is very seldom any waiting to tee up at the Le Club Royal de Golf de Maroc in Rabat, Morocco, for the very simple reason that only the King of Morocco and a few, very carefully selected guests of His Majesty play at the club.

The whole subject of golf in Morocco is a rather
delicate one. Most of His Islamic Majesty's loyal subjects,
for one thing, think there is something a little absurd
in full-grown men swinging a weighted stick at a small,
white ball, and then, with apparent great delight, chasing
the ball several hundred yards to have another whack
at it. A game, the object of which is apparently to nudge
a ball into a gopher hole, is rather alien to the Moroccan
concept of sport.

Moreover, His Islamic Majesty's loyal subjects have
certain prejudices regarding proper attire for their
monarch who is, after all, both King and Keeper of
the Faith. They might begin to ask certain unanswerable
questions if it should become common knowledge that
His Majesty, from time to time, when the press of his
duties permits, could be seen wearing a plaid tam-o'-
shanter, an open-necked, lavender shirt, polka-dot
knickers and argyle socks in the very act of enthusiastically attacking a small, white sphere with a stick. Choos-
ing golfing partners has thus long been one of the major problems weighing heavily upon His Majesty's shoulders. There are, to be sure, many golfers among
the Diplomatic Corps, but His Majesty is understandably
reluctant to play with any of them. He frankly feels that
doing so would give them a chance to blackmail him.

Shortly after His Majesty had learned the Ancient
& Honorable game during a vacation in Switzerland—and
frankly, he became quite infatuated with it—he had
dispatched six wholly trustworthy members of his staff
to the Ancient & Honorable Course at St. Andrew's,
Scotland. They had orders to stay there until they had
learned the rules of the game, had equipped themselves
suitably with equipment and had been able to cover
eighteen holes in no more than ninety strokes.

While they were gone, Le Club Royal de Golf was
constructed at Rabat, ostensibly for the pleasure of the
Diplomatic Corps and other infidel aliens.

This was, of course, a subterfuge. His Majesty had
no intention whatever of allowing *his* links to be trod
down by beet-faced Englishmen, languid Frenchmen

and loudly laughing Americans. When very, very discreet inquiries were made by the Diplomatic Corps to the Royal Chef de Protocol regarding the estimated completion date of the Le Club Royal de Golf, they were put off with observations that building a golf course in the desert was a massive engineering undertaking and that completion was sometime in the future. An announcement would be made.

Sending the six equerries to St. Andrew's had been only a very limited success. One of them had defected, although this story had been effectively kept secret. (What had happened was that Ali ben Baba [Lieut. Col., Cavalry] had been taken, so to speak, under the wing of the Hon. Violet T. MacSporran, spinster daughter and only child of Baron Glenwyddie. Miss MacSporran had turned to golf when it had become patently apparent to her that marriage had become a remote possibility. Her interest in Lieut. Col. Ali ben Baba had been platonic at first, simply the desire of an experienced golfer to help a duffer with his chip shots. When her best efforts to help him failed, she took him home to see what her father could do with him. The Baron, who had been a Cavalry man himself, and the Colonel hit it off immediately. Lieut. Col. Ali ben Baba was invited to participate in the Glenwyddie Hunt and, mounted upon the Baron's personal horse, had immediately endeared himself to the Hunt Club by his spectacular horsemanship. It was the first time that anyone had ever seen the fox run down by a fiercely yelling horseman who then, at full gallop, had leaned out of the saddle to effortlessly snatch the fox up by his tail. A man like that was obviously too valuable to lose and, after a little chat in the library of Castle Glenwyddie about the generous dowry the Baron was prepared to offer, it was announced that the Lieut. Col. Ali ben Baba has asked for, and received, the hand of Miss Violet. He would resign from the Moroccan Cavalry and devote his full time to the Glenwyddie Estates.)

The other five golf scholars did, of course, eventually return to Morocco. But it quickly became apparent that they would not be satisfactory golf partners despite, or perhaps because of, their newly acquired finesse with the tools of the sport. After going around seventeen of the eighteen Royal Links at par, or even two or three strokes under par, leaving His Majesty eight to ten strokes behind them, they all seemed to have extraordinary trouble with the eighteenth hole. Scores of ten and twelve for the last hole alone became common and sometimes ran as high as twenty strokes. The King gradually realized that his loyal subjects were throwing the game his way.

While this was certainly a commendable manifestation of loyalty and subservience to one's monarch, it was not only somewhat patronizing on their part, but made for a lousy golf game. He would never really know when he had won, fair and square.

(Many American golfers, especially those who play with their life-insurance salesmen or stockbrokers, may be able to sympathize with His Majesty's problem.)

The King's problem, therefore, was to find golfing partners who possessed a skill level approximating his own (he shot in the low eighties) and who were, naturally, of suitable noble birth. It was not a problem prone to simple solution, and explains His Majesty's genuine delight to hear from an equerry that His Highness, Sheikh Omar ben Ahmed, grandson of Sheikh Abdullah ben Abzug, was scheduled to arrive at the Rabat Airfield at five that next morning, having flown from Paris.

His Highness would have gone to the airport at five if that had been necessary, but it was still much too dark at that hour to see the ball, much less the fairways. So word was passed to the Rabat Tower to keep Sheikh Omar ben Ahmed's plane in the holding pattern until the first light of day.

The Household Cavalry and the Royal Bodyguard received their marching orders and were assembled, together with crews from Radio et Television Diffusion Maroc, at the airport in plenty of time to greet Sheikh Omar ben Ahmed's plane.

Moroccan televiewers that evening, as the lead story on news of the world, were shown film of their King meeting his friend, and the grandson of his friend, at Rabat International.

There were shots of the Household Cavalry lined up in immaculate array, scimitars drawn and glistening. There were ninety seconds of the Royal Household Band playing the national anthem, and another ninety seconds of His Majesty himself arriving at the airport, in his Mercedes 600 limousine, preceded by jeeps loaded with members of the Royal Bodyguard. His Majesty graciously consented to look in the direction of the camera, smile and wave his hands.

Then the aircraft carrying Sheikh Omar ben Ahmed, a jet Aero Commander, was seen making its approach and landing. There was some delay before Sheikh Ahmed left the airplane. (It was necessary for the Sheikh to put on his robes; he could hardly greet the King, who was wearing his robes, in an open-collared shirt.)

The televiewers saw the King walk up to the aircraft, greet the Sheikh in the formal manner prescribed both by Royal Protocol and the teachings of the Prophet, and then saw them enter the Mercedes 600 and, preceded by the jeeps, race off from the airport.

What the viewers saw next was a shot of the Royal Palace, and the clear implication was that the King and the Sheikh were inside. This was a little technique learned from American television known as conscious deception. The King and the Sheikh were nowhere near the Royal Palace. They were at Le Club Royal de Golf de Maroc.

Sheikh Ahmed did not especially want to play golf with the King. For one thing, the King was a lousy golfer compared to the Sheikh, and playing, as they were, far from prying eyes, the King was not at all above throwing his clubs into water obstacles and snapping putter shafts over his knees when he blew a shot.

But he was so pathetically grateful for a game that the Sheikh would not have the heart to refuse him, even if he dared, under the circumstances, to do so. On the flight from Paris, the Sheikh had made up his mind that he had to talk with the King, so having the King meet him was really good luck.

The Sheikh had a problem. He was heir-apparent to the Sheikhdom itself. (His father had become enarmored of, and run off with, a Bavarian belly dancer he had encountered in a nightclub in Beirut, Lebanon. As a consequence, he and the belly dancer were living together morganatically in Portugal, and the very mention of his name in Abzug was forbidden under penalty of death.)

Frankly, the Sheikh supported his grandfather in the matter. Not only was such conduct clearly unbecoming a Crown Prince, but his father certainly should have been able to see that the belly dancer would (as she indeed had) quickly turn from a female shapely with youth into a typical plump, square Bavarian hausfrau. When he saw his father and his stepmother (which he managed to do about once a year), his stepmother (who insisted that he call her Mama) spent the time forcing Bavarian cream puffs on him, or something equally revolting, like coffee covered with whipped cream; and once, for what she really believed was a treat, she served up a marzipan camel on which a rather good marzipan replica of his father sat somewhat precariously. It had been difficult to force the expected smile while he bit off his father's head.

It was quite obvious to Sheikh Omar ben Ahmed that the status quo in Abzug was, for the immediate future, the best road to follow. The value of the oil beneath Abzug's desert was not going to decline in value, but quite the reverse. The Sheikhdom of Hussid, through Crown Prince Hassan ad Kayam, was perfectly willing to advance the Abzugian treasury whatever money it wanted, at quite favorable interest rates, to meet Abzugian needs. These needs were simple. The agrarian economy supported the population adequately. The only capital expenditure really necessary—which was being made—was for medical and educational purposes. Generally speaking, the health of the tribe—due, the Sheikh believed, to the climate and the healthy diet—was extraordinarily healthy. In the last ten years, illiteracy had practically been eliminated. Furthermore, those tribesmen who showed the ability to absorb education at the college level were sent, on full scholarships, outside the country—mostly to Saudi Arabia's College of Mining and Mineralogy.

When Allah in his wisdom saw fit to take Sheikh Abdullah ben Abzug from his people and Omar ben Ahmed assumed the throne, then, and only then, would it make sense to bring in aliens to begin the exploitation of Abzug oil reserves. Omar ben Ahmed, who had been educated in Germany and had spent a good deal of his life away from the mountains and deserts of Abzug, could lead his people into a closer association with outsiders based on his understanding of the outsiders. He knew, for example, as his grandfather unfortunately did not, that the world community generally frowned on such practices as beheading ambassadors.

Sheikh Omar ben Ahmed had, until just the last few days, placed absolute trust in Sheikh Hassan ad Kayam. They were old friends and, previously, Hassan had done nothing of which Omar had disapproved.

But six days before, Omar had flown in from Zurich to hear that in his absence, Hassan had shown up in Abzug with a helicopter, loaded Skeikh Abdullah ben Abzug aboard it and flown him to Europe. He was prepared to let that pass, at least until Hassan had an opportunity to offer an explanation, but then the business in Paris had transpired. The Sheikh had disappeared for three days and then he had emerged—surrounded by U.S. Marines and a platoon of French doxies—at the Opera to announce that he had decided to go ahead with exploitation of Abzugian oil, and had, indeed, made arrangements with an American firm.

After some thought, Omar ben Ahmed had been forced to conclude that the Americans had somehow found something to hold against Prince Hassan, and that Hassan had led Sheikh Abdullah ben Abzug into a deal which at best was questionable and at worst could be disastrous.

What he must do was separate his grandfather from Hassan long enough for him to explain to his grandfather

his objections to oil exploitation just now. His grandfather, for half a century, had been accustomed to making
announcements, not seeking advice, and to having his
announcements accepted as law. Reasoning with him
was going to be difficult, because he believed sincerely
and quite simply that if Allah had wanted anybody else
to issue orders to the Abzugians, He would have sent
somebody else. And it logically followed that since Allah
had sent him, what he said was obviously the intention
of Allah.

(This *Dieu et mon droit* philosophy is not really that
unusual. It parallels that, for example, of the Hon. Edwards L. Jackson (Farmer—Free Silver, Arkansas) who
had more than once addressed the Congressional Bible
Study & Prayerful Decision Society on the theme that
God had selected them to save the American people
from themselves; and that, therefore, listening to the
contrary opinions of the simple folk back home bordered
on the sinful.)

The King did not prove to be of as much help or encouragement—once Omar ben Ahmed had explained
the problem to him between the fifth and eighth holes—
as Omar had hoped he would be.

"It is a delicate matter, my friend," the King said.
"Your grandfather has a terrible temper, as you well
know. Prince Hassan ad Kayam, to my knowledge, is
a gentleman of impeccable reputation. You must walk
a very narrow path to avoid offending either. I personally
find it impossible to believe that Prince Hassan would
do something dishonorable, or that your grandfather
would change his mind once he had announced a position."

"Then you won't help me?"

"What is it you want me to do?"

"My grandfather has asked these Americans to be
his guests in Marrakech," Omar ben Ahmed said. "If
I could have only three or four hours alone with him
while they are there, I feel I could reason with him."

"That's odd," the King said. "On the way to the airport, my Foreign Minister told me that the President of France is going to Marrakech."

"Do you suppose that the French and the Americans are in on this together?"

"I'd believe it of the French," the King said, after a moment. "However, it seems entirely too subtle for the Americans."

"Perhaps you are right," Omar said. "But we'd better keep an eye on the French, too."

"I have spent my life keeping an eye on the French," His Majesty said, as he drove. It sliced to the right and landed in a grove of palm trees.

"Wrist straight, wrist straight," Omar ben Ahmed said. "Eye on the ball."

"When I want your advice, I'll ask for it," the King snarled. "That was obviously a defective ball." He immediately regretted the blast of anger. "Sorry," he said. Omar pressed his advantage.

"Will you see if you can separate my grandfather from the others, while they are in Marrakech, for just a couple of hours?"

"I will give a party for the French and the Americans. I will serve intoxicants. That way I can invite your grandfather in the sure and certain knowledge that he will not accept."

"Brilliant!" Omar said.

"Naturally," His Majesty said. "I'm a King, you know."

"That doesn't solve the problem of separating Hassan from him, though."

"I will let it be known that there will be blonde women at the party," the King said. "Hassan searches out blonde women like a bird dog."

"I never could understand that," Omar said, aware that he was lying through his teeth. "I have never seen a blonde woman for whom I would cross the street." He bent down and rubbed his shin, where Penelope Quattlebaum had kicked him. Damn, he thought, I don't even know her name. I can hardly call the Crillon on the telephone and ask to speak to the blonde who kicked me in the shin in the lobby.

He had no way of knowing, of course, that Miss Penelope Quattlebaum was approaching him at some 600 miles an hour—she was, in fact, at that moment over central France, where Orleans Area Control had just cleared Air Maroc Flight 102 direct to Rabat—and that at that precise moment, the Teletype was clattering in the Communications Room of the U.S. Embassy in Rabat.

FROM U.S. EMBASSY, PARIS
TO U.S. EMBASSY, RABAT, MOROCCO
    F.S.O. GRADE-SEVEN PENELOPE QUATTLEBAUM DEPARTED PARIS ABOARD AIR MAROC FLIGHT 102 AT 10:45 HOURS THIS MORNING. ESTIMATED TIME OF ARRIVAL—2:15 P.M. MOROCCAN TIME.

                    T. DUDLEY DULANEY III
                    DEPUTY FOURTH-ASSISTANT SECRETARY

The Teletype operator, who had been sleeping when the machine began to clatter, got off his cot, walked to the machine and tore the yellow paper from it. He started out of the room; but before he got to the door, the machine began to make other noises. The bell rang, and then rang two times more. This was known as a three-bell signal, and it signified that a message of the highest importance was about to be transmitted.

The operator returned to the machine.

FROM DEPARTMENT OF STATE, WASHINGTON
TO U.S. EMBASSY, RABAT, MOROCCO

    SENATOR AMOS SCHWARTZ (REPUBLICAN—CONSERVATIVE, PENN.), CHAIRMAN OF THE STATE DEPARTMENT APPROPRIATIONS SUBCOMMITTEE OF THE FOREIGN RELATIONS COMMITTEE, HAS SENT THE FOLLOWING MESSAGE TO THE SECRETARY OF STATE:

    QUOTE DEAR MR. SECRETARY: JUST A SHORT NOTE TO ASSURE YOU OF MY CONFIDENCE THAT

THE STATE DEPARTMENT WILL ASSIGN F.S.O. GRADE-SEVEN PENELOPE QUATTLEBAUM TO SUCH DUTIES AS THE SERVICE MAY REQUIRE, WITHOUT TAKING IN-TO CONSIDERATION THAT THAT DARLING, SWEET CHILD, WHO WILL BE LEAVING HER NATIVE SHORES FOR THE FIRST TIME, HAPPENS TO BE MY ONLY NIECE. PERHAPS YOU WILL BE ABLE TO TELL ME OF HER ASSIGNMENT WHEN WE GET TOGETHER TO DIS-CUSS THE RATHER LARGE BUDGET YOU HAVE RE-QUESTED FOR THE NEXT FISCAL YEAR. MY ASSO-CIATES, AS YOU KNOW, HAVE BEEN TALKING ABOUT MAJOR CUTS. WITH KINDEST PERSONAL REGARDS, AMOS SCHWARTZ, U.S. SENATE UNQUOTE.

THE SECRETARY OF STATE WISHES TO TELL YOU HE HAS EVERY CONFIDENCE IN YOUR ABILITY TO PROPERLY ASSIGN F.S.O. QUATTLEBAUM WITHOUT, OF COURSE, TAKING INTO CONSIDERATION THE FACT THAT HER UNCLE IS THE MAN TO WHOM THE SECRE-TARY MUST JUSTIFY THE STATE DEPARTMENT BUDGET.

FOR THE SECRETARY OF STATE
BY ZENOBIA Q. O'RYAN
SECRETARY TO THE SECRETARY OF STATE

The Teletype operator, whistling tonelessly through his teeth, carried both messages down the corridor of the Embassy to the Ambassador's office.

Chapter Eleven

Although it is generally not common knowledge, few airliner-sized private aircraft "belonging" to major industrial corporations actually belong to the corporation, even though their fuselages are emblazoned with corporate insignia and the aircraft are at the exclusive beck and call of corporate executives. Renting the airplanes, rather than buying them, has several advantages. For one thing, the whole cost of the rental can be written off as a business expense, which has certain obvious pluses. For another, if an airliner is rented from an airline, it has access to regular airline services. The advantages here are obvious, when time is taken to think about them. It is about thirty feet from the door of a 747 to the ground. It is far more convenient, when landing at an airport, to have a set of stairs rolled up to the door of a 747 by airlines personnel (there are reciprocal agreements among airlines) than it is to sit there, thirty feet above the ground, attempting to negotiate for the rental of a set of stairs or, alternatively, to leave the aircraft by means of a knotted rope.

Airplanes of this type are hired out in one of two ways: "dry" and "wet." If a corporation rents a dry airplane, a crew flies it to the agreed point of delivery, debarks and leaves. It is thereafter the responsibility of the company which has rented the dry airplane to find a crew to fly it, a set of stewardi to pass out the coffee, tea and milk, fuel to fill its tanks and mechanics to perform the necessary maintenance. A wet airplane, on the other hand, comes equipped with a full crew, including stewardi. Fueling of the aircraft, filling it with trays full of food, making sure that it is safe to fly and so on is accomplished as for airliners in regular commercial service.

The charges for a wet airplane are so many thousand dollars a day, in the case of a 747, plus so many thousand dollars an hour for each hour actually spent in the air. Most large corporations, such as Chevaux Petroleum International, prefer to charter wet aircraft.

There is an unexpected, and certainly unpublicized, bonus for the charterers of wet 747's. Commercial-aircraft pilots have a union, although, of course, since they are hardly blue-collar employees, they call it an "association." Part of the contractual agreement between the pilots and the airlines deals with seniority. The pilots "bid" for the most desirable flight assignments on the basis of seniority.

In other words, once a man has been designated a captain, he begins his career flying, for example, the midnight flight between Olathe, Kans., and East Saint Louis, Ill. Providing he has been able to remember to lower the wheels each time before landing and other such technical things, he works himself up over the years, as more senior pilots retire, to the more desirable flights —say, an early-morning flight from Los Angeles to New York—and ultimately to the most desirable flights. New York-London-Rome is, for instance, a very desirable flight, and so is Los Angeles-Honolulu-Tokyo.

But what happens, unfortunately, is that after a man has spent twenty years of his flying career working himself up from Olathe-East Saint Louis to Los Angeles-Honolulu-Tokyo and has been flying it for a year or so, he becomes bored with it.

There is, after all, despite what the Honolulu Chamber of Commerce would have you believe, little to occupy the time of a fifty-five-year-old grandfather during a three-day layover in the Hawaiian Islands. Surfboarding is really out of the question; and there is something positively chilling to the masculine ego when a sun-browned, bikini-clad child-of-the-beach at whom you have flashed a broad smile comes trotting up to politely suggest, "Sir, do you think it's wise for someone of your age to be out in the sun like this?"

And, as some wise man once said of Tokyo, "After you've had sukiyaki and watched the sumo wrestlers, what else is there?"

The cold truth is that at this particular point of their careers, many silver-haired, blue-eyed, firm-jawed airline captains begin to think of themselves as airborne bus drivers: Los Angeles one day, Honolulu the next, Tokyo the day after that, followed by two days of dodging Tokyo taxis and then back home. What could be more boring?

Even the flying itself becomes a chore. An airline pilot is not permitted very many decisions. He does not fly from Los Angeles to Honolulu, for example, the way he might like to fly. There is a prescribed flight plan. It tells him when to take off, how high to fly, how fast to fly and in which direction. If he began his career as a military pilot, soaring and zooming amongst the clouds, that rather pleasant sort of flying is nothing but a fond, and increasingly hazy, memory. The airline pilot's credo is straight and level. Soaring and zooming amongst the clouds is a no-no. Not only does it remind the passengers that they are indeed five miles above terra firma, going 600 miles an hour, but it has a tendency to dump filet mignon, creamed peas, Baked Alaska and other items on the airborne menu into their laps, with a consequent rise in letters of complaint to the Customer Relations Department.

For those captains with sufficient seniority to "win" the most desirable flights, there is normally nothing they can do but suffer in silence, taking what little consolation they can from their pay, which runs about $5,000 a month.

But once in a great while (after all, there aren't that many corporations which can justify the full-time use of a 747), there is a little light at the end of the long, dark tunnel. When the notice was posted on the Pilot's Bulletin Board that Chevaux Petroleum International, Inc., had arranged for the semipermanent charter of three wet 747's, which would be engaged in both passenger and cargo operations, worldwide, it caused something of a stir.

There was, at first, some concern in the Personnel Office about the lack of response. Only one senior captain had submitted his name. No other captain, senior or otherwise, seemed interested in assuming command of a 747 which would be required to fly anywhere in the world at a moment's notice, unscheduled, without even a flight plan prescribed by company headquarters.

After waiting a week, another notice was published and, like the first, it attracted only one senior-captain volunteer. A week later, a third notice was posted and it, too, resulted in just one volunteer. At that point, some serious thought was given to the problem, and a spy was discreetly posted at the bulletin board.

The spy reported that the first senior captain who had read the bulletin board had smiled broadly, and then, glancing over his shoulder, had ripped the notice from the board and jammed it into his pocket. He had then submitted his name as a volunteer for what, until that moment, the company had regarded as a very distasteful assignment.

After a notice of the vacancies was sent to each eligible pilot by registered mail, every senior 747 captain but one (who was known to be carrying on in Paris with a blonde stewardess from Air Finland) put his name down to "bid" for one of the eight pilot slots. The final selection of the eight pilots was conducted in the company 300-seat auditorium. A firm of certified public accountants had to be engaged to determine precise seniority. Sixteen international flights had to be delayed or cancelled entirely because their scheduled pilots insisted on being present at the bidding.

There was even a nasty fistfight between Capt. Rollo van Brunt and Capt. Elmo Kildare. Since both Captain van Brunt and Captain Kildare had joined Global

Airways on the same day in 1946, it was necessary
to compare their previous military flying experience to
determine who was most senior. Captain van Brunt had
been an Army Air Corps fighter pilot; Captain Kildare,
a Marine aviator. Words were exchanged, during which
Captain Kildare apparently referred to Captain van Brunt
as a "pimple-faced fly-boy," and Captain van Brunt
responded by referring to Captain Kildare as a "seagoing
bellboy."

They were finally separated and peace was restored.
Both were determined by the C.P.A.'s to have insufficient
seniority to win pilot seats. They did, however, just
barely manage to win co-pilot seats, each one willingly
giving up command of a scheduled 747.

No Global Airways co-pilots (referred to as "first
officers" by everybody in Global but pilots) or flight
engineers were able to successfully bid for the wet-charter
co-pilot and flight-engineer spots. They were filled by
senior captains, the junior of whom was 52 years old
and had 11,000 hours of flight time.

None of them ever had cause to regret giving up the
New York-Paris-Rome or Los Angeles-Honolulu-Tokyo
scheduled runs. They had quickly been accepted as
members of the Chevaux Corporate family. Within
six months, they had been admitted to membership in
the Bayou Perdu Council, K. of C., and quickly came
to prefer the K. of C. uniforms to those of the airline.
(They had all been awarded status as Knight Com-
manders of the Golden Eagle Feather, the regalia for
which included: a three-cornered cap patterned on that
worn by Admiral Lord Nelson at the Battle of Trafalgar;
a uniform tunic with thicker and twice as many golden
stripes around the cuffs as that of Global Airlines; and
navy-blue trousers with a bright-carmine stripe down the
seam. Customs officers and other officials seemed to melt
at the sight.)

But the fight over seniority did not die. The best assignment on the wet charter was flying Mr. Jean-Pierre de
la Chevaux himself. Not only did Mr. de la Chevaux's
flights generally circle the globe as he inspected Chevaux

operations (there was more than enough time to inspect whatever needed inspecting while the huge aircraft was being unloaded of its cargo of oil well supplies), but he liked a little game the pilots had taught him called Bandits at Twelve O'Clock High.

By listening to what are known as "In-Flight Advisories," filed by scheduled-airlines pilots as they made their routine, prescribed way from one airport to another, it was quite easy to locate them in the air. At this point, Mr. de la Chevaux would be summoned to climb the ladder from the main part of the fuselage to cockpit, where he would be installed in the co-pilot's seat.

He would then peer out the window until he saw, for example, Global Airways Flight 304, Miami-Buenos Aires.

"Bandits," he would then call, "at 12 o'clock high."

A bell would then ring in the cabin below, and Chevaux technicians, being flown to or from a distant Chevaux oil field, would dash to the windows. The Chevaux plane, throttles to the fire wall, would then close the distance between them. A fighter-type pass would then be made by the Chevaux 747 against the Global 747. The roaring zoom would not be close enough, of course, to cause any danger whatever of an in-flight collision. However, it would be close enough so that the Global 747 would encounter the turbulence from the Chevaux 747 engines, giving the Global passengers a little thrill and making Global pilots yearn wistfully for the day when they, too, would acquire enough seniority to abandon aerial bus-driving for real flying.

The wet-charter pilots had quickly picked up again an esprit de corps and a certain élan that many of them had last known as nineteen-year-old P-38 fighter pilots in World War II.

They swaggered into Flight Planning Offices around the globe, wearing their Battle of Trafalgar hats at a rakish angle, their half-Wellington boots, and their brilliant-yellow flight jackets, the back of which carried a representation of the Chevaux Petroleum Corporate logotype and the words CAJUN AIR FORCE. On the front was embroidered their personal insignia, golden wings in the center of which were names they hadn't used in thirty years: ACE TIGER THE DETROIT KID ALTOONA AL and the like.

"Any of you kids got the heading from here to Sumatra?" they would ask, or "When was the last time anybody flew into Zamboanga in a 747?" They knew, of course, that the replies would be negative, and that the senior captains of not only Global, but Pan American World Airways, Trans World Airlines, Northwest Orient Airlines and the others were eating their hearts out.

They were, of course, quite cordially loathed and despised by the scheduled-airlines pilots, but they accepted this as a natural reaction of the have-nots toward those who have it made.

When the word came down from Chevaux Corporate Headquarters to the chief pilot that a 747 would be needed to haul Mr. de la Chevaux and a preliminary oil-exploration crew to Abzug, the chief pilot immediately wrote in his own name as pilot on the flight manifest. He had never, in thirty-five years of international flying, ever heard of Abzug and, wherever it was, he wanted the privilege of being the first man to put a 747 down in it. With a little bit of luck, he was soon going to qualify for the *Guinness Book of Records* as the man who had landed more 747's on more obscure and inadequate airfields than anyone else.

The co-pilot and flight-engineer slots were filled from among the other 747 pilots on a strict seniority basis, despite howls of protest from co-pilots and flight engineers (all of whom had been senior captains, pre wet charter) that the old guys got to have all the fun.

It was necessary to park the Chevaux Petroleum 747's at New Orleans's Moisson Airfield. Bayou Perdu International Airport, hailed at the time as an engineering feat of the magnitude of the Aswan Dam in Egypt (it was, in fact, slightly more expensive), had been built to handle the smaller Douglas 707 Intercontinental jets. While the runway would hold up under the far greater weight of the 747's, the taxiways and parking stands would, if 747's parked on them for more than a few hours at a time, sink into the swamp on which the airfield had been built.

As it happened, however, on the Abzug trip, it was not necessary to go into Bayou Perdu International at all. The oil rig available for the exploration, a brand-new, all-electric rig from Tulsa's Unit Rig Company, had already been loaded aboard a 747 in Tulsa for shipment to Borneo. The last-minute decision by Mr. de la Chevaux to go to Abzug fitted in neatly with this; for the fifty-man contingent for Abzug (the seismologists, map men, surveyors, plus the rig crew) was already in Texas, where they had watched a football game between the Dallas Cowboys and the New Orleans Saints. The game had actually been played the day before, and arrangements to have the contingent released on bail from the Dallas County slammer had been nearly completed. (There had been a misunderstanding between the Bayou Perdu fans and some fans of the home team.)

A radio message was sent to Tulsa, ordering the 747 to Dallas. Then, after loading the rest of his crew and the Rev. Mother Emeritus Margaret H.W. Wilson aboard a small Sabreliner (kept around for errand-running of this sort) and stopping briefly at Bayou Perdu International Airport to pick up Mr. de la Chevaux, the chief pilot flew to Dallas.

The original crew of the 747, bitterly complaining about special privilege in high places, was returned to New Orleans in the Sabreliner. The football fans, and their bus, were released by the Dallas County sheriff, who insisted (to insure their departure from Texas) that they be escorted from the county jail to the airfield and seen aboard the aircraft by a sizable contingent of sheriff's deputies under the supervision of three Texas Rangers.

The oil-well-drilling equipment had been loaded aboard the aircraft before, of course, it was known that one of the Bayou Perdu Council, K. of C., flaming-yellow buses would also be going along. It was therefore necessary for the cargo to be unloaded and then reloaded. This action took place in the hot sun, and was performed by the Bayou Perdu Council, K. of C., themselves, most of whom were painfully hung over.

This off-loading, onloading by a half-hundred men in what appeared to be military uniforms was the source of Don Rhotten's report that "fifty uniformed men were leaving the country."

Wesley Greenpaw, editor of the *Love Field Gazette* —an advertising handout intended for free distribution to travelers—whose ambition it was to become a famous television newscaster like his idol, Don Rhotten, had recognized a story when one occurred under his nose. He had sauntered out to the airplane and struck up an acquaintance with one of the Chevaux crew.

"Hi, there!" he said, in his best television-journalist manner. "What's new?"

The first response to his inquiries was a suggestion that he perform a physiologically impossible act of reproduction; but he was diligent and, before he was picked up and carried off the field and stuffed inside a Dempsey Dumpster by several of the ornately uniformed laborers, he had learned that whoever these really *nasty* people were, they were going to someplace called Abzug. It was absolutely apparent that trouble was in the offing. Five minutes after the 747 had zoomed off into the blue, the three Texas Rangers who had been ordered to see them out of Texas and who had mysteriously disappeared, reappeared. They were handcuffed to one another and to a Texas jackass, on which they rode backwards and stark-naked save for their cowboy hats and a large sign reading, "I will never call anyone a Dumb Cajun again," which hung around the neck of the rearmost Ranger. Only real troublemakers, Wesley realized, would *dare* do something like that to three Texas Rangers at once.

There was some talk of having the Texas Air National Guard pursue the Chevaux 747 and shoot it down in flames to restore Texas's honor, but wiser heads prevailed while Wesley Greenpaw was on the telephone to Don

Rhotten's newsroom. It was agreed that throwing the next two hundred and fifty Louisianans who dared cross the border into Texas into the slammer would be enough and probably more profitable.

Wesley was somewhat disappointed to learn that Don Rhotten never ever, as a matter of policy, personally talked to his news sources; but the man on the phone, who assured him he was very close to Mr. Rhotten, promised to keep Wesley in mind for the next slot that opened up on "The Rhotten Report" news staff. That made Wesley feel a lot better.

The flight from Dallas across the Gulf of Mexico and then across the Atlantic was quite pleasant. There was an opportunity to play Bandits at Twelve O'Clock High twice (once over central Florida with an Eastern Air Lines 747 carrying 340 Bronxites to the sun and surf of Miami Beach, and again over the Atlantic with a Pan American 747 en route from Rio de Janeiro). Then there was a Sing Along with Reverend Mother who played popular tunes on the air horns mounted on top of the bus, until the captain sent word that while he liked a jolly song as well as anyone else, he was having Air Traffic Control on the radio.

Mr. de la Chevaux, who always took a personal interest in every detail of operations, was shown the charts of their routes on one of his frequent visits to the flight deck.

"Why?" he asked, pointing to a couple of specks in the Atlantic Ocean off the African coast.

"Why what, Skipper?" the chief pilot asked.

"Why are they called the Canary Islands?"

It was an interesting question, one that had not previously occurred to the chief pilot.

"Maybe," he ventured after a moment's thought, "that's where canaries come from."

"Let's go get some canaries," Mr. de la Chevaux said. "I tink duh Archbishop be happy wit a couple of l'il yellow canaries."

"Roger, Wilco, Skipper," the chief pilot said. He reached for his microphone to inform Central Atlantic

Area Control that Chevaux 747 Three was diverting from direct Dallas International-Abzug International to make a fuel-and-supply stop in the Canary Islands.

"Roger, Chevaux Three," Central Atlantic Area Control came right back. "Understand diverting to Canary Islands. Say again your original destination."

"Abzug International," the chief pilot reported.

"Hold one, Chevaux Three," Central Atlantic Area Control said. Then, three minutes later, "Chevaux Three, where is Abzug International?"

"Right outside the capital of Abzug," the chief pilot replied. The distilled essence of his thirty-odd years of international flying was that every nation in the world had an international airport right outside its capital. The fact that he himself had been able to find such an airport on his own map had struck him simply as one more example of map-making sloppiness. There was bound to be an Abzug International, and he planned to find it by flying to Abzug and then getting on the horn and asking for directions.*

"Chevaux Three," Central Atlantic Area Control said, "we are unable to find Abzug International on our charts. We are unable, as a matter of fact, to find any airfield at all in Abzug. All our charts show is moun-

---

* This is actually how much long-distance aerial navigation is accomplished, airlines public-relations photographs of pilots poring seriously over aerial navigation charts and "shooting the sun" with a sextant to the contrary. The navigation technique is simplicity itself: the plane is flown to within two hundred miles of where it is supposed to be, and then the pilot gets on the horn:

"London Area Control, this is Global 555. Do you have me on radar?" Whereupon the London Area Control Tower replies, "Roger, Global 555. We have you on radar at Three-Zero Thousand feet, One-Five-Zero miles north-northeast of this station."

"Thank you, London Area Control. Just checking to see you're on the job," Global 555 will reply, and then change the radio frequency. "London Approach Control, this is Global 555. I am at 30,000 feet, 150 miles north-northeast of Heathrow. Please furnish approach instructions."

This method of navigation not only does away with the bothersome chore of computing all sorts of confusing figures (distance and airspeed, for example), but obviates the necessity of messing up aerial charts with grease-pencil marks.

tains and desert, both marked 'uninhabited and unexplored.' "

"Ah, Roger, Central Atlantic," the chief pilot said, "close us out in the Canaries, will you?"

"Roger, Chevaux Three," the radio said. "Central Atlantic transfers Chevaux Three to Las Palmas at this time."

The chief pilot turned to the co-pilot. "Did he say where we are?"

The co-pilot shrugged. "No, Ace, he didn't. Maybe you should have asked him."

"Well, what do you expect from an air-traffic controller who can't even find Abzug International Airport?" the chief pilot replied. He spoke to the microphone again. "Canary Islands Area Control, this is Chevaux 747 Three. Do you have us on radar?"

Chapter Twelve

The consulate of the United States of America in Casablanca is a large villa in the Anfa section, on a hill overlooking the Atlantic Ocean. Anfa bears a rather striking resemblance to Southern California generally and to Beverly Hills specifically. There are just as many large houses, about as many glistening Mercedes-Benzes and Rolls-Royces and about as many palm trees and tennis courts. Beverly Hills has slightly more people, however, walking about in the ankle-length Moroccan garments known as caftans than does Anfa, because the residents of Anfa affect Western dress more than Moroccan

dress (except when the King is in town, whereupon
Anfa looks like Beverly Hills in the midst of having an
Arabian masquerade block party).

There really isn't much for the American Consul to
do, diplomacy-wise, since the United States of America
maintains an Ambassador and a full-fledged embassy
in Rabat, which is the city where the Moroccans maintain
a King and a full-fledged palace. An occasional American
will stroll in to have his passport renewed; or the Moroccan authorities will telephone to politely inform the Consul that they have an American sailor in the slammer, and
will the Consul please come get him when it is convenient?

But consulates and consuls are part of the diplomatic
game, and it's nice to have a pleasant place to send
a diplomat not needed at the moment or whose presence
elsewhere is just a wee-bit awkward. No serious thought
has ever been given to closing the American Consulate
in Casablanca.

So it was when Foreign Service Officer Grade-Seven
Penelope Quattlebaum was posted to the Kingdom of
Morocco for such duty the Ambassador might assign.
F.S.O. Quattlebaum had, according to the personnel
records, been graduated from college and, cum laude,
from the Georgetown University School of Foreign
Service. She had completed the basic language course
in Arabic. Her qualifications, in other words, were about
average for a brand-new Foreign Service Officer. But
the cold truth of the matter was that Miss Quattlebaum
was not a welcome addition to the staff of the U.S.
Embassy, Rabat. As a matter of fact, the Ambassador
had worn out two code machines in the process of bitterly
protesting her assignment. His protests had risen as far
in the State Department hierarchy as the desk of the
Secretary himself. The Secretary ruled against him; Miss
Quattlebaum's assignment to Morocco stood. And now,
with the Teletype message from the Secretary's secretary,
the Ambassador knew why.

Faced with, so to speak, the fait accompli, the Ambassador called in his senior staff, swore them to secrecy

and then asked them for solutions to *Le Problème Quat-lebaum,* as it had become known.

The ultimate solution was simplicity itself. The incumbent American Consul in Casablanca was ordered sobered up (forcibly, if necessary) and loaded on a plane home. If Tubby was going to hand him a hot potato and tell him it was his problem to handle, the Ambassador had no compunctions whatever about sending Tubby a lush to keep sober.

The shining ambassadorial Cadillac limousine, curtains drawn, went to the Rabat airport to meet Penelope Quattlebaum's plane. A radio message to her, in the air, had ordered the new diplomat to deplane last on arrival. The Deputy Chief of Mission himself went aboard the plane to make sure Quattlebaum obeyed the order, and she was not permitted to get off until all the others were long gone.

The Ambassador timidly peeked out of the back seat of the Cadillac, pushing the drawn curtains aside no more than half an inch, to get his first look at Miss Quattlebaum as the foreign service officer finally deplaned.

It was worse than he had expected. Penelope Quattlebaum was indeed, as the diplomatic scuttlebutt had phrased it, "stacked like a brick outhouse." Her long legs (almost all of which were visible under the skirt she wore a good eight inches above her knees) were shapely and tanned. Long blonde hair cascaded from her shoulders, framing a tanned face with brilliant-white teeth and sparkling, blue eyes. Her midsection, a good deal of which was not left to the imagination by her low-cut blouse, seemed more than ample for nature's intended purposes. The Deputy Chief of Mission, who had gone aboard the plane to escort her to the limousine, was a dignified gentleman in his middle fifties known behind his back as "Old Lemon Face." Old Lemon Face was now grinning from ear to ear, and his normally pasty skin was flushed red.

The Ambassador got out of the limousine.

"Miss Quattlebaum," he said, "I trust you had a pleasant flight?"

"Very nice, thank you, Mr. Ambassador," she said. "The pilot came back and sat with me most of the flight."

"We have been anxiously awaiting your arrival," the Ambassador said, bowing her into the limousine.

"And I have been anxious to begin my assignment," she said, "to join your team."

The Marine chauffeur, who had just happened to idly, and innocently, drop his eyes in the general direction of Foreign Service Officer Quattlebaum's décolletage as she stooped to enter the limousine, slammed the door on his thumb.

"Oh, you poor boy," she said. "I hope you haven't hurt yourself!"

"Nothing at all," he said, tears streaming down his cheeks.

She patted his cheek. The combination of the thumb-flattening and his reaction to the cheek-patting obviously rendered him unfit to take the wheel, so the Deputy Chief of Mission drove. Before he started off, he carefully adjusted the rear-view mirror to give himself a view of the back seat.

"Mr. Ambassador," Penelope Quattlebaum said, leaning across the seat and innocently laying a hand on his knee, "may I speak to you as one foreign service officer to another?"

"Why, of course you may, my dear," he said.

"I'd like to ask a favor of you, Mr. Ambassador," she said. The rear of the limousine was now filled with the smell of her perfume. The Ambassador wondered if he was about to have a heart attack.

"Certainly, my dear," the Ambassador said. He was staring, rigidly, straight ahead. When he looked at her, his eyes, moving with a will of their own, seemed irresistibly drawn to her décolletage.

"I want you to think of me as just one of the boys," Penelope said. "Can you do that?"

The Marine chauffeur in the front seat groaned.

The Ambassador, who, after all, had long years of

experience in both dealing with delicate situations and controlling himself under stress, managed, not without difficulty, to regain complete control of himself.

"Foreign Service Officer Grade-Seven Quattlebaum," he began, using precisely the same tone with which he had told a Russian counterpart that the next time a MIG-17 buzzed the Pan American flight to Berlin, war would follow, "after some thought and discussions with my staff, I have decided upon an assignment for you, which is in keeping with your experience and education and the cultural mores of the host country."

"Oh," she breathed, "I'm sure I'm going to like it."

"You are herewith and henceforth, from this moment and until further notice," the Ambassador solemnly intoned, "appointed Under Secretary of this embassy for Abzugian Affairs, with duty station and additional duty as Consul at the United States Consulate, Casablanca."

Penelope surprised him. As if she had flipped a switch on a personal computer, she began to recite: "Abzug, Sheikhdom of. Approximately 15,000 square miles of desert and mountainous terrain bordering on the Sahara. Population, estimated 1920 (last estimate), 757,350. Form of government, absolute monarchy. Present head of government, Sheikh Abdullah ben Abzug. Economy, agriculture."

"That's right," the Ambassador said, impressed.

"One teensy-weensy little question, Mr. Ambassador," Penelope said.

"Feel free to ask me anything, my dear," the Ambassador said.

"Am I really to be in charge of Abzugian Affairs, and Consul at Casablanca, or is this some filthy-rotten, male-chauvinist trick to get me out of the way?"

The Marine chauffeur in the front seat groaned again.

"My dear Foreign Service Officer Grade-Seven Quattlebaum," the Ambassador said, "put your mind at rest. You will be in complete charge, reporting only to me.

You will be, in fact, the only foreign service officer with such duties."

"I knew you'd understand how I feel about things," Penelope cooed. "And when am I to assume my duties?"

"Immediately," he said. "The limousine will drop me and the Deputy Chief of Mission at the embassy and then drive you on to Casablanca, immediately."

"And when will I present my credentials to Sheikh Abdullah ben Abzug?"

"Just as soon as His Highness sends the word," the Ambassador said. "His Highness is presently in Europe."

"I see," she said. "I will, of course, notify you of any action I take."

"I would be grateful," the Ambassador said. "And if I may offer a small word of advice, my dear, it would be to suggest that you do not, under any circumstances, attempt to present your credentials until His Highness's Chief of Protocol sends for you. They are sensitive in matters of this nature."

"I understand completely," Penelope said.

After she had left for Casablanca, the Ambassador and the Deputy Chief of Mission revived themselves with a little bourbon and branch to cut the dust, and then congratulated themselves. Once Penelope Quattlebaum was in Casablanca, her major problem would be fighting off the attention of every male between the ages of sixteen and sixty-six. He would drop her a little memo over the teleprinter reminding her that an important part of her duty was socializing with her diplomatic counterparts. She would be so busy with luncheons and *les thés* and *les cocktails* and *les dîners* and the other means by which the diplomatic community whiled away its idle hours on foreign shores that she wouldn't have time to get into trouble.

Keeping her in Rabat, of course, was out of the question. To any Arab, a blonde-headed, blue-eyed infidel dressed in not quite enough clothing to blow her nose was obviously a member of a profession somewhat older but not quite as respectable as diplomacy.

And insofar as the Sheikhdom of Abzug was concerned, that posed no problem at all. He would, of course, notify Sheikh Abdullah ben Abzug's Chef de Protocol that *Miss* Penelope Quattlebaum, a *female-lady* member of the *gentle sex* had been appointed the official United States representative to His Islamic Majesty. There would be a towering forest of Sequoia trees in the middle of the Sahara before the Abzugian Chef de Protocol sent word for a female diplomat to present her credentials.

Le Problème Quattlebaum was neatly solved. The Ambassador's only regret was that he wasn't forty years younger. Foreign Service Officer Grade-Seven Quattlebaum was the most attractive diplomat he had ever seen, as well as the first one in a skirt.

How long the problem would have *remained* solved, however, will never be known.

The Ambassador and the Deputy Chief of Mission barely had time to start their third drink when there was another three-bell signal from the Teletype machine in the message center down the corridor. It announced the arrival of a very important message and roused the message-center clerk from his sleep for the second time.

URGENT
FROM THE DEPARTMENT OF STATE, WASHINGTON
TO U.S. EMBASSY, RABAT, MOROCCO

ATTN.: UNDER SECRETARY FOR ABZUGIAN AFFAIRS
1. THE SECRETARY OF STATE HAS LEARNED FROM UNUSUALLY RELIABLE VATICAN SOURCES THAT THE SHEIKH OF ABZUG HAS GRANTED, IN A SURPRISE MOVE UNANTICIPATED BY THE NORTH AFRICAN DESK, PERMISSION FOR EXPLOITATION OF OIL RIGHTS IN THE SHEIKHDOM OF ABZUG. THE CENTRAL INTELLIGENCE AGENCY ADVISES THAT THE SIZE OF THESE DEPOSITS RIVALS THOSE OF SAUDI ARABIA AND

ARE AS LARGE AS THOSE OF THE SHEIKHDOM OF HUSSID.

2. FROM THE SAME SOURCE, THE SECRETARY OF STATE HAS LEARNED THAT THE ACTUAL EXPLORATION WILL BE CONDUCTED BY THE CHEVAUX PETROLEUM CORPORATION, UNDER THE PERSONAL SUPERVISION OF JEAN-PIERRE DE LA CHEVAUX, CHAIRMAN OF THE BOARD. MR. DE LA CHEVAUX AND HIS ROYAL HIGHNESS PRINCE HASSAN AD KAYAM OF THE HUSSID SHEIKHDOM HAVE HAD PREVIOUS JOINT OIL VENTURES AND ARE BELIEVED TO BE PERSONAL FRIENDS, WHICH TENDS TO INCREASE CREDIBILITY OF VATICAN SOURCE.

3. YOUR ATTENTION IS DIRECTED TO THE ABZUGIAN CODE OF CONDUCT FOR INFIDEL BASTARDS VISITING ABZUG—SPECIFICALLY TO THOSE MAKING REFERENCE TO THE DEATH PENALTY, THE PRESCRIBED MEANS OF EXECUTION, AND THE APPOINTMENT OF A SHEIKH PRO TEMPORE FOR FOREIGNERS WHO WILL BE EXECUTED FIRST SHOULD A VIOLATION BY ANY MEMBER OF A FOREIGN MINORITY TAKE PLACE.

4. THE HON. EDWARDS L. JACKSON, FARMER—FREE SILVER, ARKANSAS, HAS BEEN NAMED SHEIKH PRO TEMPORE BY THE SECRETARY OF STATE EFFECTIVE IMMEDIATELY AND WILL SOON BE EN ROUTE TO ABZUG.

5. NOTWITHSTANDING THE IDENTITY OF THE SHEIKH PRO TEMPORE NAMED IN PARAGRAPH THREE ABOVE, EVERY EFFORT WILL BE MADE TO PRESERVE AMERICAN LIFE. THE FOLLOWING PRIORITIES ARE ESTABLISHED:

    A. COMPLETION OF A FIRM AGREEMENT BETWEEN THE ABZUGIAN AND UNITED STATES GOVERNMENTS PROVIDING DELIVERY OF ABZUGIAN OIL PRODUCTS TO THE UNITED STATES

    B. PRESERVATION OF THE LIFE OF EMPLOYEES OF THE CHEVAUX PETROLEUM CORPORATION

    C. PRESERVATION OF THE LIFE OF SHEIKH PRO TEMPORE EDWARDS L. JACKSON

6. THE FOLLOWING FACTS BEARING ON THE PROBLEM ARE FURNISHED FOR YOUR PLANNING PURPOSES:

A. PRELIMINARY EXPLORATION CREW OF CHEVAUX PETROLEUM TECHNICIANS AND CERTAIN BASIC EQUIPMENT ARE EXPECTED TO DEPART FOR ABZUG VIA CHEVAUX DOUGLAS 747 AIRCRAFT FROM THE UNITED STATES WITHIN HOURS.

B. JEAN-PIERRE DE LA CHEVAUX WILL BE ABOARD AIRCRAFT. ACCOMPANYING THEM AS SPIRITUAL ADVISER IS THE REV. MOTHER EMERITUS MARGARET HOULIHAN WACHAUF WILSON, R.N., LIEUT. COL., U.S. ARMY, RETIRED, OF THE GOD IS LOVE IN ALL FORMS CHRISTIAN CHURCH, INC.

C. IT IS TO BE ANTICIPATED THAT HIS HIGHNESS SHEIKH ABDULLAH BEN ABZUG WILL RETURN FROM EUROPE PRIOR TO ARRIVAL OF CHEVAUX AIRCRAFT. HE WILL PROBABLY BE ACCOMPANIED BY HIS HIGHNESS PRINCE HASSAN AD KAYAM OF HUSSID.

D. PRINCE HASSAN AD KAYAM IS FREQUENTLY IN THE COMPANY OF BORIS ALEXANDROVICH KORSKY-RIMSAKOV, THE OPERA SINGER. MR. KORSKY-RIMSAKOV IS PRESENTLY IN NEW YORK, BUT THE POSSIBILITY THAT HE MAY TURN UP IN MOROCCO AND/OR ABZUG CANNOT BE IGNORED. THIS MESSAGE IS PERMISSION FOR YOU TO REVOKE HIS PASSPORT AND TAKE WHATEVER OTHER MEASURES ARE NECESSARY TO KEEP HIM OUT OF ABZUG.

E. THE SECRETARY OF STATE HAS SECURED THE SERVICES OF THE ONLY TWO PEOPLE IN THE WORLD WHO ARE ABLE TO OFFER ADVICE TO MR. CHEVAUX WHICH HE WILL FOLLOW AGAINST HIS WISHES. DRS. BENJAMIN FRANKLIN PIERCE AND JOHN FRANCIS XAVIER MCINTYRE WILL DEPART NEW YORK THIS AFTERNOON ABOARD A SPECIAL AIR FORCE AIRCRAFT FOR CASABLANCA. THEY WILL BE ACCOMPANIED BY Q. ELWOOD POTTER, III,

DEPUTY ASSISTANT UNDER SECRETARY OF
STATE FOR NORTH AFRICAN AFFAIRS, WHO WILL
ASSUME COMMAND OF THIS OPERATION, WHICH
HAS BEEN DESIGNATED "OPERATION LATENT
VESUVIUS," ON HIS ARRIVAL. UNFORTUNATELY,
DRS. PIERCE AND MCINTYRE MAY NOT BE CON-
SIDERED WILLING PARTICIPANTS ON THE TEAM,
AND SHOULD BE WATCHED ACCORDINGLY. IN
THIS CONNECTION, THEY ARE SOMETIMES, BUT
NOT ALWAYS, RECEPTIVE TO SUGGESTIONS
FROM THE REVEREND MOTHER EMERITUS.
FURTHER, IN THIS CONNECTION, DO NOT, RE-
PEAT DO NOT, EVER REFER OR PERMIT OTHERS
TO REFER TO THE REVEREND MOTHER EMERI-
TUS AS QUOTE HOT LIPS UNQUOTE.

7. WHILE THE SECRETARY OF STATE PERSONALLY
HAS THE HIGHEST POSSIBLE CONFIDENCE IN THE
ABILITY OF THE AMERICAN EMBASSY IN MOROCCO TO
DEAL WITH THIS PROBLEM EFFECTIVELY, IT SHOULD
BE KEPT IN MIND THAT THE DEPARTMENT OF STATE
PERIODICALLY REVIEWS AFTER ACTION REPORTS WITH
AN EYE TO CUTTING THE DEADWOOD.

END MESSAGE. DESTROY AFTER READING.

And while they were reading that rather lengthy epistle
from the nation's capital, the Teletypewriter bell rang
again, this time only twice, signifying a message of more
than unusual importance but not a real wall shaker.

FROM DEPT. OF PUBLIC RELATIONS
    STATE DEPARTMENT, WASHINGTON

TO: U.S. EMBASSY, RABAT

1. DON RHOTTEN, AMALGAMATED BROADCASTING
SYSTEM TELEVISION JOURNALIST, ANNOUNCED ON
HIS PROGRAM LAST EVENING THAT HE WAS IMME-
DIATELY FLYING DIRECTLY TO ABZUG TO INVES-
TIGATE REPORTS OF SECRET U.S. AID TO SHEIKH
OF ABZUG.

2. SINCE THE OPERATIONS DIVISION OF THE STATE DEPARTMENT ASSURE US THAT THE UNITED STATES IS NOT AIDING ABZUG, SECRETLY OR OTHERWISE, THE PUBLIC-RELATIONS DEPARTMENT BELIEVES THAT MR. RHOTTEN IS, IN THE SLANG OF THE TRADE, QUOTE CHASING ANOTHER WILD GOOSE UNQUOTE. IT WILL BE RECALLED THAT LAST MONTH MR. RHOTTEN ANNOUNCED EXCLUSIVELY THAT THE SECRETARY OF STATE HAD SOLD ALASKA TO JAPANESE INTERESTS. FURTHERMORE, THE CENTRAL INTELLIGENCE AGENCY ADVISES THAT THERE IS NO AIRFIELD IN ABZUG.

3. IT IS POSSIBLE, HOWEVER, THAT MR. RHOTTEN AND HIS STAFF WILL APPEAR IN MOROCCO. IN THIS EVENTUALITY, YOU ARE DIRECTED TO PROVIDE HIM WITH ALL COURTESIES, BEARING IN MIND THAT MR. RHOTTEN, WHO HAS SOME 11,345,213 VIEWERS, HAS BEEN KNOWN IN THE PAST TO MAKE UP HIS OWN STORIES WHEN HIS JOURNALISTIC EFFORTS TO FIND A SUITABLE STORY HAVE BEEN UNSUCCESSFUL.

4. THE DEPARTMENT OF PUBLIC RELATIONS IS TO BE KEPT FULLY ADVISED OF DEVELOPMENTS.

HARRY J. WHELAN
DEPUTY ASSISTANT UNDER SECRETARY
OF STATE FOR PUBLIC RELATIONS

The Deputy Chief of Mission was rather upset by the Teletype messages—not so the Ambassador. He had labored long years on alien shores in his nation's service, and he had long ago evolved a strategy for dealing with imminent diplomatic disasters.

The basic principle of this strategy was to separate oneself just as far as possible from the site of a disaster.

"As I understand all this," he said to the Deputy Chief of the Mission, "the Deputy Assistant Under Secretary of State for North African Affairs and the two doctors with him are going to Casablanca. Congressman Jackson will come here, as will this Rhotten television person . . . "

"I believe that's pronounced Row-ten, Mr. Ambassador," the Deputy Chief of Mission said.

"*Row-ten,* then," the Ambassador went on impatiently, "and the oil exploration team. Once they find there is no airfield in Abzug, they will naturally seek out their embassy and their Ambassador for guidance, advice and assistance."

"Naturally," the Deputy Chief of Mission said.

"And so far as I can see," the Ambassador went on, "no one involved in all this is going to Marrakech."

"No one at all, Mr. Ambassador," the Deputy Chief of Mission said.

"Since the Deputy Assistant Under Secretary of State for North African Affairs," the Ambassador said, solemnly, "who will certainly be able to control this situation, is coming, this seems to me to be a splendid time to visit Marrakech. Don't you agree?"

"Are you planning to go alone?" the Deputy Chief of Mission asked.

"I was thinking of taking you," the Ambassador said.

"In that case, Mr. Ambassador, I am in full agreement."

"See if you can get rooms at the Mamoumian Hotel overlooking the pool and the garden," the Ambassador said.

Chapter Thirteen

"Air Force V.I.P. Flight Sixteen," the radio crackled, "this is Air Force Central Atlantic Area Control."

"Go ahead, Central Atlantic."

"Air Force Central Atlantic has two messages for you. Are you ready to copy?"

"V.I.P. Sixteen ready to copy."

"Message one follows—you ain't gonna believe this—Pan American Four-Oh-Nine, Rio de Janeiro-Paris reports that they were attacked in mid-ocean by a 747 aircraft which made three threatening, fighter-type passes. Air Force V.I.P. Sixteen is advised to be on the alert for a menacing 747 aircraft."

"Central Atlantic, say again the type of menacing aircraft."

"I say again, seven-four-seven, repeat, seven-four-seven. I told you you weren't going to believe it."

"V.I.P. Sixteen understands 747," the pilot of the Sabreliner carrying Q. Elwood Potter and Drs. Benjamin Franklin Pierce and John Francis Xavier McIntyre from New York to Morocco said. "Is that 747 as in Boeing 747 jumbo jet?"

"Affirmative, V.I.P. Sixteen, that is 747 Boeing jumbo jet."

"V.I.P. Sixteen suggests pilot of Pan American Four-Oh-Nine be given a little balloon to blow up on landing."

"Central Atlantic advises V.I.P. Sixteen that Pan American Four-Oh-Nine was intercepted 800 miles north-northeast of Gibraltar by U.S. Navy Interceptor aircraft from carrier *Forrestal*. Navy pilots escorting Pan American Four-Oh-Nine to Paris report plane is being flown in normal manner, and pilot seems perfectly sober."

"Central Atlantic, you say there are two messages?"

"V.I.P. Sixteen, second message follows: 'Quote from Department of State, Washington, to Q. Elwood Potter aboard U.S.A.F. V.I.P. Flight Sixteen. Intelligence confirms Chevaux Petroleum Aircraft departed Love Field, Dallas, for Abzug. Intelligence advises further that nearest airfield to Abzug capable of handling Chevaux 747 aircraft is Marrakech International. You are directed to divert from Casablanca to Marrakech in attempt to join up with Chevaux party. Unquote end message.' Did you copy, V.I.P. Sixteen?"

"Central Atlantic, V.I.P. Sixteen understands divert from Casablanca to Marrakech to rendezvous with Chevaux aircraft."

"Roger, V.I.P. Sixteen, Central Atlantic out."

"Jesus H. Christ!"

"V.I.P. Sixteen, this is Central Atlantic, say again your last transmission."

"Operational Immediate message to any U.S. Forces within radio range. U.S.A.F. V.I.P. Flight Sixteen, a Sabreliner aircraft, is currently under aerial attack. Altitude—28,500 feet; coordinates—Four Niner Three-Seven Baker Two-Two-Zero-Zero Fox-trot. Attacking aircraft is a 747 Boeing jumbo jet. I say again, a 747 Boeing jumbo jet."

Another voice came immediately over the radio.

"V.I.P. Sixteen, this is U.S. Navy F-104 Two-Seven. I am thirty minutes from your present position. Please say again description of attacking aircraft."

"V.I.P. Sixteen has just been attacked by a 747 jumbo jet. No apparent damage. Attacking aircraft made a pass from below, passing 100 yards in front of this aircraft, and is now departing this area on a heading of 050 degrees true."

Navy F-104 Two-Seven didn't believe a word of

it, of course. The Bus Drivers in Blue, as their Air Force counterparts are fondly known to Naval aviators, had apparently been at the sauce again. But he had nothing better to do at the moment, so he wheeled the fighter over on its wing, took up a course which would permit him to intercept an aircraft on the course given by V.I.P. Sixteen and flicked on his radar.

At the extreme range of the radar, there *was* a blip on the course given. His heart began to beat a little faster.

"Navy Two-Seven to Navy Mediterranean," he said to his radio. "I am in pursuit of an aircraft which allegedly attacked U.S.A.F. V.I.P. Sixteen. I have him on radar and am kicking in the afterburners at this time." As he did so, he threw the switch that increased the power of his engines manifold (at the expense of greatly increased fuel consumption), and felt himself being pressed against the cushions of his seat by the acceleration. The Mach gauge, which is sort of a high-speed speedometer, indicated when he accelerated past the speed of sound; and he was approaching maximum speed, which was well over twice the speed of sound.

"Navy Two-Seven, this is Navy Mediterranean. Have you a description of the aircraft you are chasing?"

"Air Force V.I.P. Sixteen . . . you're not gonna believe this . . . identifies the attacking aircraft as a Boeing 747 jumbo jet."

"Navy Two-Seven, you say you have it on radar?"

"Affirmative," Navy Two-Seven reported. "Radar indicates aircraft is at a distance of 300 miles, just off the Moroccan coast; estimated airspeed is 650 knots. I am closing at Mach Two."

"Navy Two-Seven, keep us posted," Navy Mediterranean said.

Another strange voice came over the emergency frequency:

"Operational Immediate to any U.S. Forces within radio range. This is Air Force V.I.P. Eleven, a Sabreliner aircraft, at 30,500 feet, 100 miles due west of Casablanca. This aircraft is under attack. This aircraft is under attack."

Navy Two-Seven pointed his radar in the direction given. There were two blips now on the screen, one moving in close to the other. For a moment, the blips merged, and then they separated again.

"Air Force V.I.P. Eleven, this is Navy Two-Seven. I have you on radar. Please identify attacking aircraft."

"Navy Two-Seven, this is Air Force V.I.P. Eleven. The attacking aircraft is a Boeing 747."

"Is everybody in the Air Force plastered?" Navy Two-Seven asked himself aloud, forgetting that his microphone was hot.

"Air Force V.I.P. Eleven advises Navy Two-Seven that this aircraft is carrying Congressman Edwards L. Jackson on a diplomatic mission and deeply resents the suggestion that the pilot has been drinking. I know a 747 when I see one."

Navy Two-Seven watched the blip representing the attacking aircraft move off the edge of his radar screen. When he changed radar direction to follow it, he put it back where he had originally had it pointed, and there were now two blips on the screen, one obviously heading for the other.

"Navy Two-Seven advises Navy Mediterranean that he has what it believed to be attacking aircraft and another unidentified aircraft on radar within fifty miles of Moroccan coast. Am closing at Mach Two-Point-Five."

He watched his screen with rapt fascination (there is, in fact, nothing much else to look at at those speeds and altitudes) as one blip approached the other. They appeared to merge, and then they separated again. He was not at all surprised to hear still another hitherto-unheard voice come on the air.

"Jesus Christ!" a voice said, then: "Mayday, Mayday, this is Charter Flight Thirty-Two, approximately forty miles off the Moroccan coast. We have just experienced a near mid-air collision with a Boeing 747 aircraft."

"Charter Thirty-Two, this is Navy Two-Seven. Now you just take it easy, the Navy's here."

"Take it easy? Take it easy? Have you ever had a 747 pop up from nowhere and wag its tail at you? It threw Don Rhotten and two girls out of the round bed, that's what it did."

"Charter Thirty-Two, this is Navy Two-Seven. I am approaching you at Mach Two. The Navy will handle the attacking aircraft."

"Well, you better hurry up, Sailor-Boy. The last we saw, the 747 was diving straight for the ground."

"Charter Thirty-Two, are you an all-black 707?"

"Roger, we're all black. There's a rabbit painted on the tail."

"Say again, you were garbled. I thought you said you had a rabbit painted on the tail."

"That's what I said, that's what I said," Charter Thirty-Two snapped.

"I think I have you in visual contact," Navy Two-Seven said.

"Navy Two-Seven, this is Air Force V.I.P. Eleven. Congressman Jackson says that while he's sorry about those other airplanes, the over-all interests of the United States Government and the United Nations must be first and foremost in all our minds in this time of trial. He orders you to fly back to him immediately and provide him with a protective escort."

"Navy Two-Seven," another voice said, immediately, "we have a Deputy Assistant Under Secretary of State aboard. You come back here and guard us. The Congressman is expendable."

"Navy Two-Seven, this is Navy Mediterranean," the radio said.

"Go ahead, Navy Mediterranean."

"We have scrambled eighteen fighter aircraft from carrier *Franklin Delano Roosevelt.* You will provide escort service to U.S.A.F. V.I.P. aircraft until further notice."

"Roger, Navy Mediterranean, Two-Seven turning. Which V.I.P. aircraft gets the escort?" There was a silence. "I'll be damned, it does have a rabbit painted on the tail," Navy Two-Seven said, as he zoomed up in front of the black 707, and then flew back in the direction from which he had come.

"Mayday, Mayday, this is Charter Thirty-Two. I just had a near mid-air collision with a Navy fighter with Two-Seven painted on its tail."

"Navy Two-Seven, this is the *Franklin Delano Roosevelt* Navy Fighter Force. You say the attacking aircraft has two-seven rabbits painted on its tail?"

"The *attacked* aircraft has *one* damn bunny, you dummy!" the pilot of the 707 carrying Don Rhotten and his crew screamed into his microphone.

"Attention, Navy Fighter Force. The attacking aircraft is a black 707 with a rabbit painted on its tail."

"I've heard of some damn fool operations," an unidentified voice said, "but this sure takes the cake."

And another voice: "I have a black 707 in sight."

"See if it has a bunny rabbit on its tail, Charley," another voice said.

"Roger, this aircraft has a bunny rabbit on its tail."

"*F.D. Roosevelt* Fighter Force, fire a rocket across his nose and signal him to follow you to nearest airfield. That will be Casablanca."

"Mayday, Mayday," the voice screamed hysterically, "this is Charter Thirty-Two, ten miles off the Moroccan coast. We are under attack again, this time by Navy fighters . . . from *our* own Navy, damnit . . . firing rockets."

"This is Congressman Edwards L. Jackson," another voice said. "In the name of the Congress of the United States, I demand that I be protected with all the might of the American Armed Forces while I am traveling on matters of state."

"Black 707 with white figure of *Lepus cuniculus* on vertical stabilizer, this is Commander J.C. Armstrong, of the *Franklin Delano Roosevelt* Fighter Force, U.S. Navy. Acting under the provisions of the 1862 Act against Piracy & Other Warlike Acts, I am placing you under arrest on the high seas. You are ordered to follow me."

"Good evening, ladies and gentlemen," the very

familiar voice said, "this is Don Rhotten, and this may well be the last 'Rhotten Report.' I have long known of the feelings, the petty feelings, I may say, of others who call themselves broadcast journalists, but I never thought they would stoop to aerial piracy to keep me from bringing you the news." His voice broke, and there came the unmistakable sound of weeping.

"Casablanca Approach Control, this is Navy Two-Seven. Request priority landing permission. I am out of fuel."

About the only aircraft in a 500-mile area which hadn't heard all this was a Boeing 747 with the familiar Chevaux Petroleum Corporation logotype painted on its tail. There were, of course, radios aboard the plane, but the pilots weren't listening to them; the headsets were hung neatly on their hangers.

There was no control tower (because there was no airport) in Abzug, and there was just no need to wear headphones because there would be no one to talk to. While Horsey and Hot Lips and the others had spread out from Las Palmas the night before, in search of canaries, the pilot had gotten on the telephone with the Geographic, Geologic and Seismologic Department of Chevaux Petroleum.

In a matter of fifteen minutes, the computer reported that while there was no airfield in Abzug, there was a dried salt lake, some 4 miles long and 300 yards wide, with a perfectly level surface compacted over the ages, so that it was more than strong enough to take a 747.

The only problem was that the precise location of the lake was not accurately reflected on the available maps.

"What you're going to have to do, I suppose," the geographic specialist told the pilot, "is fly back and forth looking for it. It's only 300 yards wide, so look for a couple of mountain ranges close together."

"No problem," the pilot replied. "Thanks a lot."

In the morning, they had refueled the airplane, loaded the canaries and the passengers aboard, counted noses and then wasted an hour finding and getting one

seismologist and two drillers out of a local massage
parlor and onto the plane, and then taken off.

The flight to Morocco was a genuine joy and pleasure.
They played Bandits at Twelve O'Clock High the way
it had been played in the old days, that is, before the
days of long-distance radio communication and radar.
They just got the ones they found on their route, two
tiny little Sabreliners and a funny-looking 707 with
a large white rabbit painted on the tail. Since he had
done so well in finding the Sabreliners, the pilot permitted
Mr. Chevaux to make the pass at the black 707, and
then to power-dive toward the ground. That was a lot
of fun, with the wind screaming so loud you could barely
hear the Reverend Mother playing "Off We Go into the
Wild Blue Yonder" on the bus air horns.

Once they leveled off at sea level and crossed the
coast, of course, the pilot resumed command of the
aircraft from Mr. de la Chevaux and began a methodical
search of the mountainous range where Abzug was supposed to be.

It took more than an hour to find what they were
looking for but, suddenly, there it was, just to their left,
ahead.

"Ladies and gentlemen," the pilot said into his microphone, "we are about to land in Abzug. Please fasten
your seat belts and observe the No Smoking sign. Please
remain in your seats until the aircraft has stopped rolling.
We hope you have enjoyed your flight and we thank
you very kindly for flying Chevaux."

The 747 which appeared at the end of the valley
between the mountains was not the first aircraft that
the men of First Platoon, Second Cavalry Squadron
("Omar ben Ahmed's Own") had ever seen, but it was
unquestionably the largest, possibly because the only
other aircraft they had seen had been passing overhead
at 30,000 feet.

Lieut. Ali Mohammed turned in his saddle and reached
for his Collins Radio Corporation Single Sideband short-
wave radio, which was stored in the prescribed position,
centered immediately behind the second camel hump.

"Long Range Patrol Commander to Patrol Headquarters," he said.

"Go ahead."

"We are in the Valley of the Dead River between the Mountains of Atlas and the Mountains of Sidi ben Kulmg."

"That's that long salty place, right, Ali?"

"That's it. An airplane . . . a *large* airplane . . . looks like it's going to land here."

"Now look carefully, Ali, and then tell me: is it on fire? Or is it coming in like it wants to—on purpose?"

"It looks like it's coming in on purpose. The wings are straight and level, and it's not on fire."

"Damn, for a minute there, I thought we were in luck. If it's coming in on purpose, it's probably the Americans the Sheikh invited."

"The Sheikh invited? *Americans?*"

"Yours not to reason why, Ali," Patrol Headquarters said. "Try to keep that in mind. I got the word from Omar ben Ahmed himself. He called from Rabat yesterday. These people are the personal guests of His Highness himself."

"You mean we let them land and don't even get to shoot at them?"

"You got it, kid. You just go up there and lay the charm on them. Be discreet. Ask them who they are. If they're the Americans His Highness invited, get back to me, and I'll send out a camel caravan for them."

"And if they're not?"

"You know the rules as well as I do, Ali," Patrol Headquarters replied. "Treat it just like a regular truck convoy. Behead the men, and we split the women and the cargo twenty-five percent to you, twenty-five percent to the squadron and fifty percent to His Most Merciful Majesty, Abdullah ben Abzug, Keeper of the Peace."

"Yes, sir." He replaced the mircophone and the headset, and put his flowing headdress back on.

"No one fires except on my order," he shouted to his men. Then he stood up in his saddle, raised his right arm over his head and gave the command. "Foooorward, Ho!"

The twenty-six camels of the First Platoon, with Lieut. Ali Mohammed in the van, started down the long, narrow expanse of salt flat, in the direction of the huge, silver bird which had just descended from the heavens.

As they approached, it seemed to grow larger and larger. The troopers nervously fingered their weapons. Swords slid out of scabbards and back in, with a bone-chilling sound of metal scraping on metal. There was the sound of rounds of ammunition being loaded into submachine guns and automatic rifles.

"Anyone who fires without my order gets slit," Lieut. Ali Mohammed said, making reference to Abzug's jumbo-size guillotine.

He kicked his camel in the ribs, and the animal picked up speed, moving him perhaps ten yards ahead of his men as he approached the airplane.

As he watched, a small door opened in the side of the huge, silver bird, and a rope came sailing downward. Lieutenant Mohammed admitted to himself he was impressed with both the man who came rappelling down from the airplane and the rappelling itself. The man, who was bare-chested and enormous, was François Mulligan. He was both Knight Commander of the Peace of Bayou Perdu Council, K. of C. (a position corresponding to sergeant-at-arms, to which was naturally appointed the largest Knight), and Rig Boss of Chevaux Petroleum Rig Number seventy-five.

Lieutenant Mohammed looked at François Mulligan and François Mulligan looked back at him.

"How y'all?" François Mulligan inquired politely, formed as much of a smile as he was capable of, and walked up toward Lieutenant Mohammed. The only camel which François Mulligan had previously seen was printed on a cigarette package; and it is not, therefore, surprising that he was unaware that camels not only spit but do so frequently and with great accuracy.

"There is but one God, and Mohammed is His Prophet," Lieutenant Mohammed said, in the traditional

Islamic greeting. He spoke, of course, in Arabic, and François Mulligan didn't understand what he said, of course. Actually, it wouldn't have mattered much for, even as the lieutenant spoke, his camel let fly with what was known in Bayou Perdu as a "goober," which "goober" struck François Mulligan in the forehead.

François Mulligan, who had been many places and done many things and was generally unflappable, was now, as they say, shocked to the quick. His mouth fell open, closed long enough for him to say, *"Merde!"* (which is an impolite term in French, to which language, the mother tongue of the Bayous, Mulligan in his shock and surprise reverted) and then fell open again. Then, as if he had suddenly regained complete control of himself, he took four steps forward, cocked his fist, swung it in a brief arc and connected with the camel's temple.

He moved with such surprising grace and speed for someone of his bulk that Lieutenant Mohammed, who had his finger on the trigger of the submachine gun beneath his flowing robes, did not have time to react. One moment, a smile was forming on his face at the sight of an infidel bastard with a camel "goober" dripping down his face; and the next moment, his camel was collapsing, unconscious, under him.

He had the presence of mind, however, to yell to his platoon that all was right, and that they should not fire. He scrambled off the collapsing camel onto his feet and, for lack of something better to do, bowed deeply, remembering that he had been ordered to lay the charm upon the infidel bastards.

"It's all right, Jack," François Mulligan said, magnanimously. "Just don't let it happen again."

He turned his back to Lieutenant Mohammed, put his fingers to his mouth, emitted a shrill, piercing whistle, and then, raising his hands above the level of his shoulders, made circling motions with his index fingers.

Lieutenant Mohammed, after a moment's thought, decided this was an infidel-bastard religious rite of some sort, probably a prayer of thanksgiving for having been returned to earth safely. He bowed his head reverently to show his goodwill.

A whining noise came from within the great, silver bird. Lieutenant Mohammed raised his eyes. The great, silver bird was coming apart. Just behind the enormous wheels, part of the skin was separating from the body. For a moment, until he saw the shining-steel cables along the edges, he thought that it was magic, for the piece of airplane moved very slowly downward to the ground.

Then a vehicle, a large, bright-yellow bus, came into sight—first the wheels, then the body itself, on the top of which sat seven enormous chrome-plated horns. When the platform on which the bus was riding reached the ground, the bus engines started, and the bus rolled off the platform. Immediately, the platform rose again into the aircraft.

The bus pulled up in front of the airplane, stopping where François Mulligan and Lieutenant Mohammed stood side by side. The door opened. A very tall, very blonde, quite amply endowed female wearing her vestments as the Reverend Mother Emeritus of the God Is Love in All Forms Christian Church, Inc., stepped from the bus.

"I come in peace!" she said, raising both arms dramatically over her head.

That was the cue for thê bus driver, with whom she had rehearsed her entrance, to hit the keys. The air horns on the roof of the bus sounded off, and the familiar hymn "Onward, Christian Soldiers" boomed out, reverberating and echoing against the canyon walls.

It was at this point that Lieutenant Mohammed's command disintegrated. Approximately half of his force were scattered down the valley, aboard hysterical, quite uncontrollable camels. The other half were thrown off their camels and found themselves on the salt lake's dry surface. They naturally looked to their leader for guidance. Lieutenant Mohammed, his eyes focused on the blonde goddess in the off-pink vestments, was obviously in rapture, as if he had seen a vision of Heaven as promised by the Prophet to the faithful.

First one, and then another, and finally all the troopers of the First Platoon of "Omar ben Ahmed's Own" Second Cavalry Squadron who had not been carried off on their camels dropped to their knees in the Islamic fashion, touching their foreheads thrice to the ground in reverent humility.

"Watch out for the camels, Hot Lips," François Mulligan said. "One of 'em just spit at me!"

Chapter Fourteen

At five-fifteen the previous evening, Miss Penelope Quattlebaum, riding with dignity if some discomfort in the rear seat of an official U.S. Embassy Pinto, an American flag flapping from the front fender and CORPS DIPLOMATIQUE stickers seriously impairing the driver's front-and-rear views out the windows, had rolled up to the rather elegant villa housing the United States Consulate General, Casablanca.

After some initial confusion (the embassy staff, not quite willing to believe that a well-stacked blonde with light-blue eyes was actually a bona fide member of the Diplomatic Corps, had mistakenly gotten the idea that she was simply one more well-stacked blonde in a long line of well-stacked blondes summoned to the consulate for "consulatation" by the previous Consul, and that she had not, so to speak, gotten the word that the Consul had been forcibly sobered up and loaded on a plane for the States), she gained admission to the building.

She located her personal quarters and, after examining them and ordering the staff to immediately clean out the three months' accumulation of beer and spirits bottles, went through the rest of the consulate.

It was quite a facility, and she was thrilled with the prospect that it was hers alone (in the name of the American taxpayer, of course) over which to reign. There was a large dining room, a library, and a reception room (complete with photographs of the President, the Secretary of State and, for a nice touch, of Uncle Amos in, of course, his official, rather than familial position). There were two bars, one in the house proper, and one by the tennis courts to quench the thirst of those too fatigued from diplomatic tennis to make it inside. There was also a large official office, complete with American flag, another picture of Uncle Amos, a solid-mahogany desk, telephones, couches and the like. She also found the Code Room, a bank-vault-like affair in which the consulate Teletype and code machines were located.

Penelope was thrilled as she opened the Code Room door with the interim combination provided her by the Ambassador, and then reset the combination with a series of numbers which would be known only to her. She had been taught at the Foreign Service School that when selecting a safe combination, it was best to use numbers which were familiar (and thus would not be forgotten when it came time to open the safe) and yet of a quite personal nature, not known to others.

The numbers Penelope set on the combination lock fit those criteria: 38-24-36. Those figures were known only to Penelope and to a middle-aged lady of impeccable reputation who earned her living as a foundation-garment consultant and who would be very unlikely to think of using them to crack the Code Room safe of the U.S. Consulate in Casablanca, Morocco.

The telephone rang as Penelope was about to climb the wide stairs to her second-floor living quarters to see how the housekeeper and gardener were doing with regard to the removal of the empty bottles.

She answered it herself, taking a deep breath as she savored the very words.

"This is the Consulate of the United States," she said.

"Is the Consul sober?" a rather tough male voice asked, in French.

"I am Miss Penelope Quattlebaum," Penelope said, icily, "Consul of the United States of America, and I am quite sober."

"Zut alors!" her caller said. "So it is true!"

"So what is true?"

"They have replaced Lushwell with a female."

"If you are referring to my predecessor, the Honorable C.T. *Lash*well, that is so. How may I be of service?"

"This is Inspector Gregoire de la Mouton, mademoiselle, of the Gendarmerie Nationale. We have one of your compatriots, one Matthew Z. Gonzales, under arrest."

"Is that so?"

"He is charged with an assault against the peace and dignity of the Kingdom of Morocco, mademoiselle, a very serious charge."

"What, precisely, did this countryman of mine allegedly do?" Penelope asked.

"He became involved in an altercation, mademoiselle, with some British seamen."

"Can you be more specific, Monsieur L'inspecteur?"

"Specifically, Mademoiselle, he sang along with the British as they sang their national anthem. When it came to the line, "God save the Queen," your countryman, mademoiselle, substituted certain words which a gentleman cannot repeat over the telephone. The altercation followed."

"How much is his bail?"

"Twenty dollars in American money."

"And what is the usual fine in a case of this nature?"

"Twenty dollars in American money."

"I shall be down directly, Monsieur L'inspecteur, with the money. Is Mr. Gonzales a tourist?"

"No, mademoiselle, he is an oiler from the tanker S.S. *Hoboken,* which arrived from New York today."

"To remove any possibility of further difficulty with Mr. Gonzales, Monsieur L'inspecteur, could you furnish me with an escort so that I may take my countryman back to his ship and place him in the custody of his captain?"

"With the greatest pleasure, mademoiselle."

Penelope's fears were groundless. Once Mr. Gonzales laid eyes upon her, he became as tame as a lamb. He allowed himself to be led docilely back to his ship, where Penelope placed him in the custody of his captain, to whom she gave a little lecture concerning the absolute necessity for Americans on foreign shores to comport themselves in a manner to bring credit upon their homeland.

The captain was so taken by her speech that he insisted she repeat it for the ship's company, which Penelope did, quite touched and flattered by the wild applause and cheers that followed. She was then forced, by protocol, to join the captain and his officers in a series of toasts to the United States of America, Morocco, the U.S. merchant marine, the Diplomatic Corps and a long list of other toastable subjects. It could quite possibly have gone on all night, had not one of the officers, a tall, blond-headed first engineer of Scandinavian ancestry, made what Penelope considered an improper advance toward her.

What he said, in all innocence, was that he had the midnight-to-eight-in-the-morning shift, but would consider it a deep personal honor if he might be permitted to buy the Consul General breakfast after that hour. Unfortunately, he made this suggestion after the eleventh toast ("to Christopher Columbus, and other distinguished navigators"), by which time Miss Quattlebaum had again fallen victim to her unsuspected malady. The first engineer received a kick in the shin and a small, bony fist in the eye for his invitation. But he was a sturdy son of the sea, who passed it off with a smile and waved cheerfully at Miss Quattlebaum as she made her way somewhat unsteadily down the ship's ladder and to her Pinto.

A Rolls-Royce was sitting in the consulate driveway when Penelope (after some difficulty finding her way home) rolled in. It bore CD plates, and the British flag hung limply from a small pole on the right front fender.

Her caller was Sir Desmond Farquaite, O.B.E., Her Britannic Majesty's Consul General in Casablanca. Sir Desmond's announced purpose at the American Consulate was twofold, he told her. (Actually, he had been put onto the well-stacked blonde by M'sieu L'inspecteur Gregoire de la Mouton when he had called at the local bastille to spring from durance vile the British seamen with whom Mr. Gonzales had been involved.)

"I am here, my dear Consul General," he said, stroking his guardsman's mustache, "both to accept the pro forma apologies of your government to my government about Mr. Gonzales's unfortunate choice of words . . ."

"You may," Penelope said, hiccuped, and then went on, "assume our apologies to your gracious Queen."

"And also, my dear Consul General," Sir Desmond said, "to offer whatever services I may to help you get started in your new post."

"As a matter of fact, Sir Desmond," Penelope said, "I do need a little information."

"If I don't have the answer, my dear, I will find the answer."

"How do I get from here to Abzug?"

"What in the world do you want to go to Abzug for?" he asked, his surprise destroying his normal savoir-faire. "They're nothing but a bunch of cutthroat savages!"

"Be that as it may," Penelope said, severely, "I have been appointed Deputy Assistant Secretary of my Embassy for Abzugian Affairs, and I wish to present my credentials to the Abzugian Chef de Protocol as soon as possible."

The last declaration was interrupted several times by Penelope's unsuccessful attempts to stifle hiccups, and Sir Desmond had sufficient time to consider the options open to him, diplomatically speaking.

"I applaud your devotion to duty, Madame Consul General."

"That's *Mademoiselle* Consul General, Sir Desmond," Penelope corrected him, but she was pleased.

"My Land-Rover and my services as guide, Mademoiselle Consul General," Sir Desmond said, "are at your disposal. Hands across the sea and that sort of thing, don't you know?"

"That's very good of you," Penelope said. "When could you fit taking me to Abzug into your busy schedule, Sir Desmond?"

"How about right now?" Sir Desmond replied. "We could pop by the British Consulate, pick up the Land-Rover and leave immediately."

"How far is it? How long a trip?" Penelope asked.

Sir Desmond had no idea whatever. He had never been to Abzug and, from what he'd heard of those bloody savages, had no intention of going.

"Some distance, I fear," he said, solemnly.

"In that case, Sir Desmond," Penelope said, "I think it would be best if we scheduled our departure for first thing in the morning. Would oh-six-hundred hours be too early for you?"

He was disappointed, of course; but, on reflection, it wasn't so bad an idea after all. Certain preparations would have to be made.

"Not at all," Sir Desmond said. "Until that hour, Mademoiselle Consul General." He bowed from the waist, clicked his heels and, taking Penelope's hand in his, raised it to be kissed. Something went wrong. Either he had bowed too deeply, or Mademoiselle Consul General had raised her hand too quickly in anticipation of the courtly gesture (which Sir Desmond had used with success ever since he had watched Helmut Dantine, playing an SS officer in a World War II movie, do it to Bette Davis), for, instead of contacting her fingers with his lips, he contacted her somewhat-bony knuckles with his eye.

Keeping a stiff upper lip, Sir Desmond made his exit from the American Consulate General, pausing at the door to wave gaily and call out, "Until oh-six-hundred, my dear!"

Penelope then retired to her private living quarters. The bottles were all gone, and that struck her as a good omen. She found that her luggage had been unpacked, and that the maid had turned down the bed and laid her peignoir and dressing gown on it. She carried these garments to the bathroom, and took a long shower. She noted with pleasure that the official Consulate General's bathroom was equipped with the same special footbath she had found in her hotel in Paris. Her feet didn't need washing after the shower, of course, but it was nice to know that it was there in case she needed it in the future; and it seemed logical that if one was in the bathroom, she would probably be able to find one in a store to send home to Daddy. She thought a moment about that, and decided she would buy two footbaths—one for Daddy and one for Uncle Amos. She owed Uncle Amos something for living up to his promise not to use political influence in her behalf. One of the special footbaths would be just the thing for Uncle Amos. Aunt Gertrude had complained more than once (in the intimate family circle only, of course) that Uncle Amos's feet stank.

Then she went to bed, rather savoring the notion that this was her first official, diplomatic bed. She fell asleep almost immediately, but her sleep was disturbed by dreams, more precisely three dream vignettes, each merging into the next, as in television soap opera. In the first segment, Matthew Z. Gonzales pressed his unwanted attentions upon her. At the last moment, before her pearl of great price was about to be lost forever, the tall, blond, handsome first engineer from the S.S. *Hoboken* rushed up, clasped Penelope to his massive chest (he was not, in her dream, for some reason, wearing a shirt—just his uniform cap with the gold braid, and a tight pair of pants, like a ballet dancer) with his left and dispatched Matthew Z. Gonzales with a right cross to the jaw.

There was sort of a station break, and then she found herself alone with the first engineer in his cabin. He kept trying to shove waffles, bacon and scrambled eggs at her with his left hand, crying "everybody eats break-fast," as he tried to work his wicked way with her with his right hand.

Virtue was about to go down to defeat again, when Sir Desmond Farquaite, O.B.E., crashed through the cabin door on a horse, wearing a full suit of armor and skewering the first engineer with a long, sharp-pointed lance.

There was another station break, and then Penelope found herself with Sir Desmond. Sir Desmond was chasing her around an ancient castle, having, in the interim, divested himself of his armor. He was now wearing only a kilt and a T-shirt on which was lettered precisely what Matthew Z. Gonzales had sung and which had so annoyed the British seamen—IN HER SLEEP, PENELOPE BLUSHED.

After running down an apparently bottomless flight of stairs, with Sir Desmond breathing hotly on her neck, Penelope found herself in the castle courtyard. Sir Desmond, leering wickedly at her, cornered her.

At that point (without a station break) the door of the castle was suddenly flung open, and a bare-chested man, wearing a flowing headdress and mounted atop an enormous white horse, came galloping in, waving a curved sword. One swipe, and Sir Desmond's head went rolling across the castle floor.

Penelope looked up at her savior to thank him with a smile. He threw his headdress back, for the first time exposing his face. It was the tall, dark stranger whose shin she had kicked at the Crillon Hotel in Paris. He stroked his mustache, a gesture Penelope found strangely attractive; a faint smile crossed his face, exposing his pearl-white teeth; and then he gently spurred his large, white horse. The horse whinnied (Penelope, who, after all, had been raised on a quarter-horse ranch, recognized the significance of the whinny, which was odd, because there were no mares in her dream) and then advanced on her. It reared backward onto its hind legs and then came down again. Penelope felt herself snatched up by the tall, dark stranger. She realized that she was being carried out of the castle by the tall, dark stranger, who was laughing wickedly.

Her position was precarious. Having many times fallen off a horse, Penelope naturally did not want to fall off again. It was, therefore, logically necessary for her to swing into the saddle behind him and wrap her arms around his massive chest. No matter that he, too, was carrying her off somewhere to work his wicked way with her; it was not an entirely unpleasant sensation.

"Mademoiselle," he said.

"Yes?" Penelope asked.

"Mademoiselle?" he asked again, as if he hadn't heard her reply.

"Yes?" Penelope asked, more loudly this time.

"Mademoiselle," he said a third time, and this time, strangely, his voice had lost its rather enchanting, masculine tone. He sounded, in fact, like a woman.

"Mademoiselle!" the female voice said again. "The British Consul General is downstairs with his Land-Rover."

Penelope opened her eyes and was suddenly wide-awake. It must have been something she ate, she decided, for she seldom slept with her arms wrapped around her pillow. She looked up at the consulate's maid.

"Please inform Her Majesty's Consul General," Penelope said, formally, "that the Consul General of the United States of America will join him shortly."

Penelope dressed quickly, brushed her hair and went downstairs.

Sir Desmond Farquaite, O.B.E., wearing a sun helmet, a khaki shirt and breeches, gleaming riding boots, and a silk foulard knotted around his neck, waited for her.

"Are you ready for the desert, my dear?" he asked.

"Just don't get any ideas about getting me into your castle," Penelope replied.

"I beg your pardon?" Sir Desmond said.

"Forget it," Penelope said. "Let's get this show on the road."

There are Land-Rovers and then there are Land-Rovers. Some of them are really not much different than a Jeep, which was the model Penelope expected. What she got was the large, deluxe model, which came equipped with: air-conditioning, a stereo tape player, on which Sir Desmond was playing Montovani; a refrigerator, filled with champagne and pâté de foie gras; and bunk beds complete with air mattresses, onto which Sir Desmond tried to entice Penelope (his ploy was the straight-faced announcement that rest and relaxation in the desert was as important as water) when they were no more than an hour out of Casablanca.

She managed to elude his clutches and escape from the Land-Rover. A firm believer in the principle that being burned once is enough, Penelope refused to re-enter the Land-Rover, even though Sir Desmond promised on his word of honor as a gentleman, a member of the Order of the British Empire and a fellow member of the Diplomatic Corps that he wouldn't try any further hanky-panky.

The result of this was that two hours later, a jeep patrol of the Royal Moroccan Desert Patrol, on their regular rounds, came upon a rather well-stacked blonde striding purposefully through the desert, trailed by a Land-Rover in low gear.

The corporal in charge raced up to her in his jeep.

"May I be of assistance, mademoiselle?" he asked, smiling.

"I am Miss Penelope Quattlebaum, Consul General of the United States of America," Penelope announced. "I call upon you, under the established provisions of international law regarding diplomatic privilege, to carry me to the United States Consulate."

"I understand, sweetie," the corporal said. "You're having trouble with Lover-Boy, right? Hop in!"

Penelope got in and laughed bitterly as she remembered her dream. She had been rescued by a son of the desert, all right, a five-foot-five son of the desert, weighing 250 pounds and reeking of garlic.

An hour later, shortly before noon, the Royal Moroccan Desert Patrol jeep deposited Penelope back at the consulate. Her once neatly brushed hair was now in tangles; the crisp seersucker suit and white blouse in which she had intended to present her official credentials were no longer either crisp or white. Her shoes were full of sand from her trek across the desert, and the only cheerful thought she could come up with was a mental vision of how good it would feel to put her feet into the special foot-washing device in her private bath.

There was a man standing impatiently before the consulate door. Feminine curiosity as to his purpose was overridden by feminine pride. She could hardly reflect credit upon the Diplomatic Corps of the United States of America sweat-soaked, hair mussed, and with her shoes full of sand.

She strode purposefully past the man and started to push open the door. A thin, bony, if rather hairy, arm barred her way.

"Just a minute, baby," the bald man in thick, horn-rimmed spectacles said to her, "the line forms to the rear."

"I beg your pardon?" Penelope said, icily.

"You heard me," he said. His voice was somehow familiar. "You ain't the only outraged citizen wanting to see the Consul."

"Get out of my way!" Penelope said. "Who do you think you are, anyway?"

"I'm Don Rhotten," he said, "internationally famed television journalist and sage, *that's* who I am."

"You are *not*," Penelope Quattlebaum said, shocked to the quick. "I don't know who you are, and it wouldn't surprise me at all to learn that you have been imbibing, but you're not Don Rhotten. Don Rhotten has the most *darling* head of curly, black hair and pearly white teeth, and he doesn't wear thick glasses. You should be ashamed of yourself!"

A rage, which had nothing whatever to do with her reaction to a combination of handsome men and stimulants, swelled up in her. "Don Rhotten indeed!" she said, kicking him in the shin. "How dare you take the name of a great American in vain?"

Rhotten bent over to grasp his injured shin. He said

a word that, had he said it over the airwaves, would have seen him paying a large fine to the Federal Communications Commission for offending public morals. It offended Miss Penelope Quattlebaum's sense of private morals. She let him have it in the other shin.

While it is possible to hop up and down on one leg while clutching the other, in-pain leg, it is not possible to hop up and down clutching two in-pain legs at once. Mr. Rhotten solved this problem by sitting down on the consulate steps and howling in pain and rage as he tenderly massaged both shins.

"I don't know who you are, you dumb broad," he screamed, "but Don Rhotten will get you for this!"

Penelope pushed open the door and entered the embassy. Another man was waiting inside, wearing a half-head of silvery locks and a wide, somewhat-vacant smile.

"I regret that the Consul of the United States is not here," he said. "A situation, madame . . . "

"Miss," Penelope corrected him, automatically.

"Miss," he corrected himself, "which I assure you will be brought up at the highest levels of the State Department, to the Secretary himself."

"Who are you?"

"I am the Honorable Edwards L. Jackson, member of Congress, as well as Sheikh pro tempore to the Sheikhdom of Abzug. I don't suppose you're from Arkansas, by any chance?"

"And what brings you to the consulate, sir?" Penelope said, suddenly remembering a course she'd had at the Foreign Service School which dealt with the "Overseas Kook Problem."

The "Overseas Kook Problem" had been explained to Penelope as a by-product of the high cost of providing what is known as "domiciliary care" for those individuals who, while posing no threat to themselves or to others, are somewhat embarrassing to have around high-rise apartments and split-levels in the better suburbs, possessed as they are of the notion that they are Napoleon,

Clark Gable, John F. Kennedy or, in a few cases, God Himself.

It is far less embarrassing and much cheaper to send Uncle Henry, who believes he is Gen. George Patton, off on "an extended European trip" than it is to have him bundled off to the Happy Valley Home for the Harmlessly Insane.

Since few Americans speak any foreign language, Aunt Martha is far less liable to cause a stir, say in Ankara, Turkey, with her announcement in English that she is Marilyn Monroe waiting for a call from Cecil B. DeMille to star in the greatest Biblical epic of all time than she would cause making the same announcement in the lobby of the Grosse Pointe Hills Country Club.

Penelope had been warned to expect these people at embassy and consulate doors, firmly convinced that they were high-ranking politicians or celebrities, or divinities of one faith or another.

There was no question in her mind that she had two of them on her hands right now: one ugly, middle-aged, balding man with the pathetic notion that he was young-and-handsome Don Rhotten; and another whose sadly twisted mind made him believe he was not only a Congressman but a Congressman about to be slit down the middle by an Abzugian guillotine as Sheikh pro tempore.

The standard procedure for dealing with them was to treat them, insofar as possible, as gently and as understandingly as possible. When their dementia, however, was of such a magnitude that it appeared likely to get out of hand, it was official State Department policy that the host country be asked to lock them up for their own protection until arrangements could be made for them to be shipped home to the next of kin.

"Congressman," Penelope Quattlebaum said, 'if you will wait outside the door with Don Rhotten, I'll have you taken care of in just a few minutes."

She then went into her office, sat down at her official desk under the portrait of her Uncle Amos and called

Inspector Gregoire de la Mouton of the Gendarmerie Nationale. Inspector de la Mouton was sympathy itself. He was quite familiar with what he called "Le Problème des Américaines Bananes" and assured her that a squad of his police would leave immediately to place the poor unfortunates under protective custody.

He was as good as his word. Within five minutes of her telephone call, Penelope watched, a tear of sympathy running down her cheeks, as the middle-aged balding man who thought he was Don Rhotten and the "Congressman" were taken away, fighting every step of the way, by the gendarmes.

Just as soon as Inspector de la Mouton was able to determine their real identities, Penelope would send Teletype messages to the states arranging for their return home to their loved ones.

Chapter Fifteen

"Marrakech International, this is U.S.A.F. V.I.P. Sixteen, about thirty minutes from your field. Request landing instructions," the pilot of the plane carrying Deputy Assistant Under Secretary of State Q. Elwood Potter and Drs. Benjamin Franklin Pierce and John Francis Xavier McIntyre said.

Ali ben Khan (who was actually Maj. Pierre St. Fondue of the Deuxième Bureau), the Air-Traffic Controller at Marrakech International, paused thoughtfully before replying. His orders were to divert an American aircraft carrying a French traitor named De la Chevaux from

Marrakech. The instructions had said it was a civilian aircraft, a Boeing 747; but Ali ben Khan had been around long enough to have learned, sometimes painfully, that the Americans were clever scoundrels, not above trying to fool people to get their way.

"U.S.A.F V.I.P. Sixteen," he said, making up his mind, "this is Marrakech International. You are directed to divert to another airfield. This airfield is closed temporarily."

"Marrakech International, this is U.S.A.F. V.I.P. Sixteen. We have aboard a high-ranking American diplomat, the Deputy Assistant Under Secretary of State."

"U.S.A.F. V.I.P. Sixteen," Ali ben Kahn repeated, sure now that he had cleverly seen through one more example of shameless American chicanery, "I repeat, this airfield is closed. Sorry about that."

"U.S.A.F. V.I.P. Sixteen," the pilot said, resignedly, "advises Marrakech International it is diverting to Rabat International."

As the plane changed course, the co-pilot went to the passenger compartment to inform Deputy Assistant Under Secretary Potter of the change in destination. Mr. Potter ordered the pilot to get on the radio and arrange for a car to meet the plane on landing. Rabat was within driving distance of Marrakech, and no lasting harm had been done. Mr. Potter then went farther aft in the aircraft to break the news to his passengers.

"I'm glad you're here, Potter," Hawkeye Pierce said, raising his head to look at him. He was about to putt a golf ball down the aisle toward a paper cup lying on its side. "I want you to have a word with the driver. I find it very difficult to practice my putting back here when the green keeps tilting. Would you please ask him to stop slanting the airplane?"

"There has been a change in our plans, gentlemen," he said. "We are about to land at Rabat. A car will meet us there and drive us to Marrakech."

"If you think," Trapper John said, "that these in-flight bulletins are going to make the kidnappees forgive the kidnappers, forget it!"

"You are not a kidnappee, Doctor," Q. Elwood Potter said. "Your situation is more analogous to that of a draftee."

"That thought," Hawkeye said, raising his putter over his head in what Mr. Potter recognized to be a threatening gesture, "has already occurred to me."

"Gentlemen," Potter said, "I give you my word. If there is any possibility at all for you to do so, I will make every effort to see that you have an opportunity to play golf—once the Chevaux situation has been stabilized."

"Huh!" Hawkeye snorted. He waved the putter even more menacingly. Naturally wishing to avoid a nose-to-nose confrontation, Mr. Potter hurriedly left the compartment. Dr. Pierce glowered at the closed door a moment and then bent over the ball again. At the precise moment he swung the putter, the pilot lowered the nose of the aircraft to begin the descent to Rabat International Airfield.

The ball, following the laws of gravity, rolled downhill in the direction of the cup.

"No fair," Trapper John said, snatching up the cup just as the ball reached it. "It doesn't count unless you hit the ball first!"

"If at first you don't succeed," Hawkeye said, "quit!" He put the putter back into the golf bag and slumped into a seat. Trapper John joined him. They looked out the window as the aircraft approached the field. They saw the desert, the mountains, the ancient buildings and a strangely familiar-appearing, green area.

"Do you see what I see?" Trapper John asked.

"It must be a whatchamacallit, you know, a miracle," Hawkeye said.

"Mirage, dummy," Trapper John replied. "But I don't think so. I see little numbered flags on poles. That's a golf course!"

"That doesn't mean we'll get to play on it," Hawkeye said, "or even get near it. You heard what he said about playing golf *after* the 'Chevaux situation is stabilized.' If we have to wait for that to happen, the game will take place immediately after the last roll is called up yonder." He raised his eyes, semi-reverently, toward Heaven.

"Well, at least we know that Horsey's still alive," Trapper John said. "I saw him waving from the cockpit window as that 747 went by."

"Unless, of course," Hawkeye went on thoughtfully, ignoring him, "by some unfortunate happenstance, we should happen to become separated from dear Mr. Potter."

"How are you going to work that? There is only one way off the airplane, and that Air Force Amazon is guarding it."

"The trouble with you, Doctor," Hawkeye said, "is that you don't read enough."

"What did I miss in Captain Marvel that could possibly be of help to us now?" Trapper John asked.

Instead of replying, Hawkeye made a pointing motion in front of Trapper John's nose.

"What am I supposed to be looking at?" Trapper John asked. "The sign that says WELCOME TO RABAT?"

"No, dummy," Hawkeye said. "What does that little sign say?"

" 'Caution,' " Trapper John dutifully read.

"What else?"

" 'This lever controls the emergency egress from the aircraft. When pulled, a canvas chute will be automatically released from the fuselage wall. Egress may be effected via the chute in times of emergency,' " Trapper John read. "I understand everything but 'egress,' " he said. "I thought an egress was a white bird which hops around on one leg."

"It was Phineas T. Barnum's favorite feathered friend," Hawkeye replied. "He used it to get the suckers out of his museum in New York. He put up a large sign reading THIS WAY TO THE EGRESS, and thousands of people with your mental capacity pushed eagerly through the door and found themselves outside on the street."

"I knew what it meant all the time," Trapper John

said. "I was just checking to see if you did. When do I pull the lever?"

"Right now seems like a good time," Hawkeye said. "The airplane has stopped moving."

As a purely routine precaution, the Rabat Airport Authority had dispatched a security guard in a jeep to the arriving U.S.A.F. aircraft. Purely by coincidence, he had stopped his jeep precisely at the spot where the emergency egress chute unfolded and, from which, moments afterward, two golf bags and two doctors emerged.

"What's going on here?" the security guard demanded.

"Thank God you're here, officer," Trapper John said. "There's a wild egress loose inside that airplane."

"A wild egress?" the security guard asked.

Simultaneously shaking his head sadly and making a circular motion with his index finger in the vicinity of his temple, Hawkeye said, "Tragic case. He thinks he's an American diplomat named Potter."

"Who is Potter?" the guard asked.

"I am," Trapper John said. "And if you will let us borrow your jeep while you keep the poor, tragic egress aboard the airplane, we will arrange with the U.S. Embassy for the men in white coats to come for him."

At that moment, Q. Elwood Potter appeared at the now-open aircraft window.

"You can't use this egress," he screamed.

"Who are you?" the security guard screamed back.

"I am Q. Elwood Potter of the United States Department of State," Potter announced.

"What did I tell you?" Trapper John said. "A classic case."

"I would hate to think what would happen if an egress like that one," Hawkeye said, "should somehow manage to get off the plane and be allowed to run loose around this fine airport."

"Fear not," the security guard said, jumping out of the jeep and pointing his rifle at Q. Elwood Potter, "Mustapha ben Ali is in command." Hawkeye jumped behind the wheel as Trapper John threw the golf bags into the back seat. "Tell the embassy to hurry," Mustapha ben Ali added.

Q. Elwood Potter let out a scream of rage as he saw the jeep carrying Hawkeye and Trapper John race off. Mustapha ben Ali made menacing gestures with his rifle. Suddenly, the face of Airwoman Betty-Lou Williams appeared at the window beside his. She immediately saw what was going on and nimbly hopped into the egress chute. Moments later she was nose-to-nose with Mustapha ben Ali.

*"Au secours, au secours!"** Mustapha ben Ali screamed. "I am being attacked by two American egresses, one of them female." He pointed his rifle at Airwoman Betty-Lou Williams. She snatched it from his hands with a smile of disdain and broke it over her knee. Then she started running after the jeep.

Hawkeye, of course, really had no idea where he was going. He drove aimlessly, if rather rapidly, away from the airport and, ten minutes later, found himself in downtown Rabat.

"Now what?" Trapper John asked, looking around at burnoosed natives, small-sized jackasses and other native fauna. "This doesn't look like a golf course to me."

"When in doubt, take a taxi," Hawkeye replied, slamming on the brakes and pulling to the curb behind a line of one-horse fiacres, each bearing little signs reading TAXI.

The driver unfortunately did not speak English, and the distinguished surgeons did not unfortunately speak Arabic; so there was something of a communications problem until Trapper John, in desperation, snatched his driver from his golf bag and addressed an imaginary ball.

"A-ha-ha," the fiacre driver said, recognition dawning. *"Le Golf."*

---

* *Au secours* is how the naturally loquacious French say "Help."

Trapper John and Hawkeye smiled broadly and nodded enthusiastically.

"But, gentlemen," the fiacre driver said, "there is but one place where full-grown men beat upon small white balls with sticks such as yours." He said this in Arabic, of course, and although they hadn't the foggiest idea of what he said, Trapper and Hawkeye nodded even more enthusiastically in agreement.

"That is Le Club Royal de Golf de Maroc," the driver went on. Since the phrase "Royal Golf Club of Morocco" does not readily translate into Arabic, he used the French words. They were close enough to English so that Hawkeye and Trapper understood them, which caused them to smile at each other triumphantly and nod their heads even more enthusiastically.

"Only the King of Morocco and his guests are permitted to play at Le Club Royal de Golf de Maroc," the fiacre driver went on. "It is absolutely forbidden on pain of imprisonment for anyone else to play there."

"You got it, pal," Trapper John said. "Le Club Royal de Golf de Maroc—that's for us."

These two strangers did not look like royalty, the fiacre driver thought. But then again, they had arrived in an official jeep, and they seemed to know where they wanted to go. He would give them the benefit of the doubt. He bowed deeply, a gesture he reserved only for royalty and, with great dignity, climbed into the driver's seat.

After some prodding, the horse started to move, very slowly. It wasn't very far to the club but, at the speed they were going, the fiacre driver had plenty of time for second thoughts. He decided that discretion was the better part of valor. Instead of taking them to the clubhouse proper, where there were bound to be all sorts of police and other officials, he decided that he would drive them along the road which ran beside the golf course and discharge them there.

Five minutes later, the fiacre creaked to a halt. The driver stood up in his seat, turned around, bowed deeply

in the direction of what turned out to be the sixth tee
and held out his hand for his fare.

Trapper put dollar bills into his hand, one at a time,
until the fiacre driver's face changed from outrage through
hurt to reluctant acceptance. And then, their bags over
their shoulders, Hawkeye and Trapper John marched
onto Le Club Royal de Golf de Maroc.

They liked what they saw. It was a well-tended course,
and there was no one else, so far as they could see,
playing on it. They played, in fact, five holes before
they even saw anyone else on the links, another twosome,
two holes ahead of them. One seemed to be a pretty
decent golfer; the other, while enthusiastic, was not likely
to be asked to play in the Masters.

"Probably the pro and a student," Trapper John suggested, and Hawkeye nodded his agreement.

"The pro's got his work cut out for him," Hawkeye
said. "Look at that! The duffer just broke his club—probably the number-three iron—over his knee."

"Temper," Trapper John said solemnly, "has no place
on the fairway." Then he missed his putt and threw
his putter high into the air.

Two holes later, as they began to tee up, they saw
that they had caught up with the pro and his student,
mainly because the student had played his ball into the
largest sand trap (it had dunes) that either Hawkeye
or Trapper had ever seen.

"Fore!" Hawkeye called, the traditional warning of
a ball about to be driven in the direction of other players
on the course.

The duffer looked back in their direction in apparent
shock and surprise.

"Well, what did he expect?" Hawkeye said. "As slow
as he's playing, he'd need the whole course to himself,
if he expected to complete a round without letting anybody play through." He addressed the ball again, called
"Fore!" again and swung. It was a good drive, landing
about twenty yards from the duffer.

"I never saw such bad manners," Trapper said, as

he teed up. "Look at him! Screaming and shouting and waving his arms around like that!"

"If the membership committee sees him behave like that," Hawkeye agreed, "they'll never let him join."

They caught up with the duo ahead, two strokes later.

"Nice little course you've got here," Trapper John said.

The man they assumed to be the pro smiled at them. "Are you gentlemen members? I don't recall seeing you on the links before."

"Pierce is my name," Hawkeye said. "Call me Hawkeye." He put out his hand and the pro shook it. The student did not. Hawkeye interpreted this as bashfulness, the beginner meeting two experienced golfers. "Don't worry, slim," he said. "you'll catch on after a while. We all looked pretty bad when we started off."

His little attempt to cheer up the duffer apparently failed. If anything, the poor guy's face got even redder with embarrassment.

"You're guests, then?" the pro said. Hawkeye and Trapper exchanged significant glances. They were right: this guy was the pro, and he was checking to see whose guests they were.

"Right," Trapper John said. A light clicked on, so to speak, simultaneously, in their brains.

"I'm sure you know," Hawkeye began, and Trapper interrupted him.

"Good ol' Hassan ad Kayam?"

"Ol' Lard-Belly?" Hawkeye added.

"You are guests of His Royal Highness Prince Hassan ad Kayam of Hussid?" the pro said.

"Ol' Lard-Belly himself," Trapper John repeated. "You know him, I guess?"

"I have that privilege," the pro said.

"What is that you called him?" the duffer asked. "Old Lard-Belly?" A smile crossed his face, which broadened. A delighted laugh came out of him. "How delightful. I shall have to remember that!"

"And is Prince Hassan coming here today?" the pro asked.

"He told us if he wasn't here when we got here," Hawkeye said, "that we should start without him."

"And where is he coming from?" the pro asked.

"Either from New York or Paris," Trapper said. "Just between us, fellas, Ol' Lard-Belly's out on a toot."

"A toot? What is a toot?" the duffer asked.

"Well . . . I didn't get your name?"

"I am the King," the King said. His Majesty's English, while, of course fluent, was understandably accented. Phonetically, what he said sounded like this: "I am zee Kink." Understandably, Trapper John heard this as Zeekink which, to his alien ears, sounded like a perfectly ordinary Moroccan name.

"How are you, Zeekink?" he said. "My name's Trapper John McIntyre, and this is my pal, Hawkeye Pierce."

This time His Majesty shook hands. "And this is my pal," he said, glad to have learned another English word, "Omar ben Ahmed. You were telling me about a 'toot,' Trapper John."

"Well, Zeekink," Trapper John said, "I don't know how it is here, of course, but where I come from, every once in a while, a man just has to get away from the job, and the wife and kids, you know what I mean? Nothing against the job or wife and kids, of course. Just a little too much of a good thing."

"I find that very interesting," the King said. "I've never heard it expressed quite that way before, but I certainly know what you mean. And when a man does find the opportunity to get away from his job, as you put it, and his wife and children, and has a little party, this is called a 'toot'? Do I understand the term correctly?"

"Right on, Zeekink," Trapper said.

"And that is what Hassan is doing at the moment?" Omar ben Ahmed asked.

"Right," Hawkeye said. "He's having a toot with another Arab fella—Abdullah something."

"Abdullah ben Abzug, by any chance?" Omar ben Ahmed offered, icily.

"That's right. Hassan, Abdullah and another friend of ours."

"Let me guess," Omar ben Ahmed said. "Boris Alexandrovich Korsky-Rimsakov?"

"Well, I see we're among friends," Hawkeye said. "You know old Foghorn, too, do you?"

"The Mr. Korsky-Rimsakov of whom I speak is an opera singer," Omar said.

"Finest kind," Hawkeye said.

"And old Bull-Bellow really knows how to throw a toot, too," Trapper John said, helpfully.

"And they are coming here on their toot?" the King asked.

"That's the way we understand it," Trapper John said.

"I don't know the singer, unfortunately," the King said. "But I do know Abdullah ben Abzug and Hassan ad Kayam very well. Do you think that they would permit me to join them on their toot?"

"Any pal of Hassan's is a friend of ours, Zeekink," Trapper John said, clapping His Majesty on the back.

"Tell me, Trapper John," His Majesty asked, "is it necessary for a man to have a wife and children from whom to get away in order to go on a toot?"

"Not at all," Trapper replied. "You appreciate it more if there is a wife, children and a job to get away from, but I have been on some perfectly satisfactory toots in my life before I had any of those things."

"In that case," His Majesty said, "with your permission, I will ask Omar ben Ahmed to join us as well."

"Glad to have him, Zeekink," Hawkeye said. "The more the merrier."

"That's very nice of you," Omar ben Ahmed said, "but as I was saying just before we met you gentlemen, as much as I like a good game of golf, I must meet my responsibilities. I have an important errand to run for my father. He is expecting guests, and I have to go prepare for them."

"You know, Omar," His Majesty said, "there's a

streak of party-pooper in you that I never noticed before."

"Perhaps I'll be able to join you in Marrakech," Omar said. "You haven't forgotten about the party you're going to give for the President of France and my father's guests, have you?"

"It slipped my mind," His Majesty said. "But my word, as you know, is my bond. I will give a party. I probably won't be able to make it myself, as I will be tooting with these gentlemen, but you will have your party."

"It won't be the same thing if you're not there," Omar ben Ahmed said.

"Gentlemen," His Majesty began.

"Call me Hawkeye, Zeekink," Hawkeye said.

"Hawkeye, then," the King said. "I don't suppose that you and Trapper John could possibly see your way clear to tooting with me in Marrakech?"

"Is there a golf course in Marrakech?" Trapper John asked.

"Yes, there is," the King said.

"In that case, Zeekink," Hawkeye said, "fine. Just between you and me, this course here isn't the finest course I've ever played."

"You don't think so?" the King asked, disappointed. "You tell me what you don't like about it, and it will be corrected. I am, after all, the King."

"You told us that before," Trapper said. "Me Trapper, you Zeekink!"

"You may go, Omar," the King said. "We shall see you in Marrakech."

Chapter Sixteen

There was a considerable degree of embarrassment in the Moroccan Foreign Ministry in Rabat concerning the unfortunate incident at Rabat International Airport. There had been a misunderstanding during which the airfield security-guard detachment, not without effort, had placed under protective custody two Americans: an Amazon who insisted she was a master sergeant in the United States Air Force; and a small, semi-hysterical male who insisted he was the United States Deputy Assistant Under Secretary of State for North African Affairs.

After an unfortunately rather lengthy period of detention in the Rabat Home for Mentally Disturbed Nomads, it turned out that the strange pair were, in fact, who they represented themselves to be. Not all of the delay, to be sure, was the fault of the Moroccan Foreign Ministry. If the American Ambassador had not chosen this precise time to take a vacation from his duties, a vacation under an assumed name, it would have been much easier to establish the identity of Master Sergeant Williams and Deputy Assistant Under Secretary Potter.

As it was, it had been necessary to contact the individual who was apparently the only American diplomat on duty in the whole country. This functionary turned out to be in Casablanca. A long telephone conversation, during which Mademoiselle Le Consul Général insisted that the Deputy Assistant Under Secretary prove who he was by describing in detail the interior of the Secretary of State's office and giving the nickname ("Schatzie") of the Secretary's secretary, finally cleared the matter up.

By the time that had been accomplished, however, and an official apology offered and accepted, the two men (described by the Hon. Mr. Potter as "two maniacs masquerading as doctors") who had arrived on the aircraft and escaped from it by use of the egress chute had vanished in Rabat. Most probably, the police felt, they had disappeared into the maze of narrow corridors in the souk (or bazaar) of the Ancient City itself. The stolen jeep had been found nearby.

All exits to the souk were immediately barred, of course; and, against the improbable chance that the two maniacs might be elsewhere within the capital, road-blocks on all other routes of possible departure were set up.

The Foreign Minister, who had passed this information onto the Deputy Assistant Under Secretary, was rather surprised at his response. "My dear Mr. Potter," he said, "I wish to assure you that egress from Rabat is now impossible."

"If I thought for one moment," Mr. Potter had replied, "that you were mocking me with the use of the word 'egress,' I would recommend to my government that we institute a state of war."

In the belief that he had been misunderstood, the Foreign Minister had rephrased his statement.

"At the moment, my dear Mr. Deputy Assistant Under Secretary," he said, "the only way the men you seek could possibly get out of Rabat would be, ha-ha, in the back seat of His Majesty's Rolls-Royce, and even then, His Majesty would have to vouch for them, personally."

"You may take this whole affair as something of a joke, Mr. Foreign Minister," Q. Elwood Potter said, "but I do not. How would your government react if you landed in Washington and we threw you in the booby hatch while we aided and abetted two Moroccan maniacs to escape?"

"It could not happen, my dear Mr. Deputy Assistant Under Secretary," the Foreign Minister said, "for the very good reason that the Government of Morocco does not conduct wholesale exportations of those . . . of . . ." Unable to find the proper words, he paused, visibly frustrated, and then described circles with his index finger at his temple. "You know what I mean."

"I do not know what you mean," Potter replied tartly. "It is only when their services are required in matters of the gravest diplomatic importance that we send madmen outside our country's borders."

"Hah!" the Foreign Minister replied. It was a diplomatic "Hah!" signifying that he disbelieved, rather intensely, the last remark.

"'Hah'? What do you mean, 'Hah!'" Potter replied, sternly.

"At this very moment, my dear Mr. Deputy Assistant Under Secretary," the Foreign Minister said with infinite relish, his trap having slammed shut on his prey, "we have two more of your expatriate maniacs in one of our mental institutions. Don't try to tell me that you aren't shipping them out of the country in wholesale lots!"

"I don't believe it," Potter said. "I refuse to believe it!" Potter said. "I cannot recall ever having seen such a shameless bluff! You should be ashamed of yourself!"

"Hah!" the Foreign Minister said. This, too, was a diplomatic "Hah!"; but it differed from the first "Hah!" in both tone of delivery and meaning. This had sort of a triumphal tone to it, and meant, "I'll show you, wise guy!"

The Foreign Minister picked up his red (urgent, official business) telephone and snapped, "Get me the Casablanca Funny Farm on the line. I want to speak to one, either one, of the crazy Americans."

He dropped the phone back into its cradle, and he and the Deputy Assistant Under Secretary glowered at each other silently for a full five minutes until the telephone rang again.

"This is the Foreign Minister," he said. "Which crazy American are you?"

There was a pause, during which the rather attractive darkness drained almost completely from the Foreign Minister's face. Then he said, "My dear Monsieur le President, I fear there has been a ghastly mistake."

Deputy Under Assistant Secretary Potter brightened visibly.

"Hah!" he said.

"I was expecting a call from a crazy American," the Foreign Minister said. Then he chuckled warmly. "Oh, I wouldn't go so far as to say that. Here and there, maybe, there may be one, or two who . . ." He suddenly remembered the nationality of the official guest in his office. "What I mean to say, Monsieur le President, is that I have something of a crisis on my hands in my office and, for that reason, I was unable to be at the airport in Marrakech to meet you and Madame le President."

Monsieur le President apparently responded to that, although Potter, straining mightily, could not make out what he had said.

"I look forward to seeing you, Monsieur le President, at His Majesty's party," the Foreign Minister said, "and to paying my respects to your charming and delightful wife." There was a pause. "No, Monsieur le President, as of this minute, no Americans have been invited, so far as I know."

"Hah!" Potter snapped again.

"There may be some last-minute developments of which I am not aware, however," the Foreign Minister went on. "It is His Royal Majesty's personal party, you know, and I am but a lowly toiler in the diplomatic vineyard."

"Hah!" Potter said, with still another diplomatic change of intonation.

"Good-bye, Monsieur le President," the Foreign Minister said. He put the phone back into its cradle. "And what exactly is that supposed to mean?" he said to Potter.

"Is what supposed to mean?"

"Hah!"

"I 'Hah!'ed three times," Potter said. "To which specific 'Hah!' do you make reference?"

"Hah!" the Foreign Minister said.

"That one, huh? Well, you may be assured, Mr. Foreign Minister, that the Moroccan Ambassador to Washington will have moss growing on his patent-leather shoes before he gets invited to another of *our* parties now that I know how I rank *vis-à-vis* parties for some lousy European President."

"As a matter of protocol, of course," the Foreign Minister said, "the American Ambassador has been invited to His Majesty's party. But since the Ambassador is unfortunately unable to be with us . . ."

"In the absence of the American Ambassador, I am the ranking American diplomat in Morocco," Q. Elwood Potter said. "As a matter of fact, I'm the ranking diplomat in Morocco, period. A Deputy Assistant Under Secretary of State is *de facto* and *de jure* far more important than an Ambassador. There are only eleven Deputy Assistant Under Secretaries of State. We don't even know how many Ambassadors we have. What about that?"

"In that case, Mr. Deputy Assistant Under Secretary of State, the Government of Morocco hopes to have the pleasure of your company at His Majesty's party."

"I should hope so," Potter said.

The red telephone rang again.

"Hello?" the Foreign Minister said. "Am I by chance speaking with one of the crazy Americans at the Casablanca Mental Sanitarium?" He listened to the reply; a smile crossed his face. "Well, Mr. Congressman, if you will just hold the line a moment, I will put one of your diplomats on the line." He handed the phone to Potter. "This one thinks he is a Congressman," he said. "Hah!"

"Hello," Potter said, "this is Q. Elwood Potter, Deputy Assistant Under Secretary of State. With whom am I speaking?" There was a pause. "Of the United States

of America, of course," he said. There was another
pause. "You *say* you are Edwards L. Jackson, third-rank-
ing member of the House Committee on Sewers, Subways
and Sidewalks, but how do I know that?"

While the Foreign Minister could not hear what was
being said at the other end, he did pick up what sounded
like a muted explosion.

"Well, Mr. Congressman," Q. Elwood Potter said,
"how is it that you have been confined?" Another pause.
"The American Consul had you locked up? You and
Don Rhotten? That wouldn't be the world-famous television journalist Don Rhotten by any chance? Oh, it
would, eh? Well, Mr. Congressman, you just stay where
you are, and I'll get to the bottom of this." He took
the telephone from his ear and laid it back into the
cradle.

"Mr. Foreign Minister," he said, sonorously, "it appears that a ghastly error has been made."

"Hah!" the Foreign Minister said.

"It appears that the Honorable Edwards L. Jackson,
member of Congress, and the distinguished, world-
famous television journalist, Don Rhotten, are being
detained in your Casablanca funny farm."

"Hah!" the Foreign Minister said.

"And what is that 'Hah!' supposed to mean?"

"And which American diplomat asked that they be
locked up?" the Foreign Minister replied. "We just didn't
snatch them off the street, you know."

Deputy Assistant Under Secretary of State Potter
looked thoughtful for a moment. "Now look," he said,
"speaking as one career diplomat to another, Mustapha.
I can call you Mustapha, can't I?"

"As one career diplomat to another, Elwood, you can
call me Mustapha," the Foreign Minister said.

"The way I see it, we both have a little problem,"
Q. Elwood Potter said. "On one hand, I would frankly
be just a little embarrassed to have it get out that a
fellow diplomat on our team had a U.S. Congressman
and a famous TV guy tossed in the booby hatch."

"Hah!" the Foreign Minister said.

"And, on the other hand, I don't think you'd really want the word to get around that the way you greeted a United States Deputy Assistant Under Secretary of State arriving in your capital on an official mission was by wrapping him up in a long-sleeved white coat and throwing him—that is, me—into the booby hatch here. Right?"

"It might be misunderstood in some quarters," Mustapha said. "What are you thinking, Elwood—just off the top of your head?"

"Now, far be it from me to suggest that women aren't just as smart as men," Elwood said, "but, when you get down to the nitty-gritty, can you imagine a male diplomat doing something like this?"

"Just between you and me, Elwood, I'm not too big on lady diplomats, period," Mustapha agreed.

"And you yourself heard her on the telephone making me describe the Secretary's office, and then, violating every standard of executive secrecy, forcing me to tell her what the Secretary of State calls his private secretary in private."

"I was a little shocked at that," Mustapha admitted. "What a man calls his secretary in private is nobody's business but theirs."

"Exactly," Elwood said. "Now I would call that conduct unbecoming a diplomat, wouldn't you?"

"There's no other way to describe it," Mustapha agreed. "But what's the bottom line?"

"Simplicity itself," Elwood said. "We hang the whole thing on her."

"How?"

"You declare her Persona Non Grata, for Conduct Unbecoming a Diplomat."

"There's bound to be an investigation if I should do something like that. I mean, it's not the usual sort of thing. She's a woman, and unlikely to have been . . . shall we say 'playing around' . . . with another diplomat's wife."

"There is always an investigation," Potter said, "con-

ducted by the senior diplomat in the area. Guess who
is the senior diplomat in the area, Mustapha?"

"I knew you were my kind of guy the minute I laid
eyes on you, Elwood," the Foreign Minister said.

"It takes one to know one, as I always say," Q. Elwood
Potter said. He rose and bent over the Foreign Minister's
desk, hand extended. The Foreign Minister rose and
shook Potter's hand in both of his.

"And I'll tell you what else I'll do," Mustapha said,
"to sweeten the pot. I'll send someone to spring your
people from the funny farm, and give them invitations
to the King's party."

"If you don't mind my saying so, Mustapha," Elwood
said, "you're my kind of guy, too."

"Elwood," Mustapha said, "as you are doubtless
aware, it is against the teachings of the Prophet for the
faithful to partake of intoxicants. However, we realize
that there are times and places when it is diplomatically
necessary to offer intoxicants to diplomatic personnel,
and that at such times, it may be necessary to put aside
one's religious principles in the name of hospitality."

"I understand your problem," Elwood said.

The Foreign Minister picked up his telephone.
"Chérie," he said to his secretary, "have somebody type
up a Persona Non Grata notice for the American Consul
General in Casablanca, to be delivered immediately.
And while it's being typed up, how 'bout mixing up
a batch of martini-er-oonies—very dry and with a twist
of lemon? And bring a glass for yourself, *chérie.* I want
you to meet a pal of mine."

"And while all this is going on," Potter mused, "I
have every confidence that your gendarmerie will be
so kind and keep my two crazies on ice."

"Put your mind at rest, Elwood," Mustapha said.
"They'll never get out of Rabat."

Monsieur L'inspecteur Gregoire de la Mouton of the
Casablanca Gendarmerie genuinely liked Mademoiselle
Le Consul Général Penelope Quattlebaum, and not only
because she was a well-stacked, blue-eyed blonde. She

kindled in his somewhat-slipped but still-massive chest a sense of gallantry he hadn't felt in twenty years.

Penelope was the sort of female for whom doors should be opened, whose hand should be kissed and who should receive floral tributes every hour on the hour. He had no idea why anyone with the charm and physical attributes of Penelope Quattlebaum should wish to spend her life as a diplomat; but since she obviously did, he automatically decided that he would do whatever he could to assist her.

Even before the business about two crazies beating at her consulate door had come up, word had been passed from Gendarmerie Headquarters, for example, that any vendors attempting to sell hand-woven rugs and brass trays to the new American Consul General had better be selling rugs that were indeed woven by hand, and trays that were indeed brass. A word in the ear of the Deputy Inspector of the Gendarmerie for Traffic Affairs had insured that Penelope could park her automobile anywhere in Casablanca and return later to find all its tires, wheels and other accessories still bolted in place. He had personally called the president of the Beggars Union and told him that he would consider it a personal favor if the boys would ply their trade elsewhere than in front of the American Consulate. And the word went out all over to the effect that if anything happened having anything at all to do with regard to Mademoiselle Quattlebaum, he was to be the first to know.

Inspector de la Mouton was, therefore, rather concerned when he learned from the attendants at the funny farm that the two American crazies he had locked up for Penelope were either the most advanced cases of schizophrenia ever to grace the Casablanca Mental Sanitarium or were indeed what they said they were: an American politician and an American television journalist.

He said nothing then, but when he was informed that the Foreign Minister himself had telephoned to speak to one of the crazies, and that during the conversation, a senior American diplomat had come on the phone and apparently been convinced that the man who said he was Congressman Jackson was indeed Congressman Jackson, he decided that he had better let Penelope know of this latest development.

He found Penelope sitting by the side of the consulate pool, looking at once ravishing and disconsolate. When she looked up at him and smiled, Monsieur de la Mouton's heart melted. He would defend this delightful female against all enemies, foreign and domestic, so help him, Allah.

"My dear Mademoiselle Penelope," he said, bowing from the waist, "you look so forlorn and disconsolate. How may I be of assistance?"

"It's nothing," Penelope said bravely, but even as she said it, a tear ran down her cheek. "Oh, Inspector de la Mouton!" she said. "I can't seem to do anything right!"

That, Inspector de la Mouton thought, seemed a rather accurate analysis of the situation.

"What seems to be the major problem?" he asked.

"I'm supposed to be the American representative to the Sheikhdom of Abzug," she said, "and I can't even find it!"

A flood of rage against those cold, cruel and heartless officials who would appoint a defenseless female like this to deal with the Abzugians welled up within Inspector de la Mouton.

"Many have sought," he said, "and few have found."

"But I must find it," she said. "Otherwise, my superiors are going to get the idea that I can't do my job."

"Mademoiselle Penelope," Mouton said, "I fear that I must be the bearer of bad tidings."

"What now?"

"You know those two crazies, the ones you described as 'overseas kooks' whom I took off your hands?"

"Oh, I feel so sorry for them," Penelope said. "That funny little man with the flowing, silver locks who thinks he's a Congressman, and that ugly, bald-headed man with the bad teeth who thinks he is young-and-handsome

Don Rhotten. Compared with their problems, my problems don't seem nearly as bad—disastrous, but not as bad."

"Mademoiselle Penelope," he went on, as gently as he could, "I fear your problems are worse than theirs."

"How could they be?" she asked.

"I have just learned that the little man with the long hair is indeed the Honorable "Smiling Jack" Jackson, member of Congress."

"Oh, no!" she said, horror in her voice.

"And that the other one carries with him a small bag containing a wig, contact lenses, and caps for his teeth. When he puts these items on, he bears such a strong resemblance to an advertising poster he carries with him with a likeness of Mr. Rhotten on it that I am forced to conclude he is indeed Rhotten."

"That's pronounced Row-ten, Inspector," Penelope said, and then she broke down and began to weep. "That does it," she said. "My diplomatic career is finished! I'm a ruined woman at twenty-three!"

He stood it as long as he could, and then he wrapped his massive arms around her, paternally.

"If it will help any," he said, as he patted her back, paternally, "I will officially state that I saw them wandering around Casablanca acting crazy."

"That would be dishonest," Penelope said, nobly. "No, I had them locked up and I will accept the responsibility."

"What can I do?" he asked, helplessly.

"You can help me find Abzug, so that I can present my credentials," she said, looking up at him with tear-filled blue eyes.

"That will help?"

"It's the only thing," she sobbed, "that could possibly help."

"Then I, my dear Mademoiselle Penelope, Gregoire de la Mouton, will personally take you to Abzug!" he said.

What the hell, he thought, we all have to die sometime.

Chapter Seventeen

Omar ben Ahmed, in full costume (that is to say, a headdress with three golden ropes running around it, signifying royalty; and a white, ornately embroidered robe), examined himself in the mirror with satisfaction. With the cartridge belt around his shoulders, the pistol and two-foot-long dagger in his belt, and wearing what he thought was a really fine sneer, he looked enough, he was sure, like Rudolph Valentino to scare hell out of the only American the First Platoon of the Second Squadron Abzugian Cavalry had succeeded in placing under arrest in the Royal Abzugian Palace. The others were, he had learned, already drilling for oil.

He regretted, as a gentleman, that the American he would momentarily scare hell out of happened to be a female, but that was the fortune of war. It was not yet time for Abzug to be dragged kicking and screaming into the Twentieth Century. He frankly doubted his ability to get his grandfather to change his mind about permitting oil exploitation. The Old Boy was rather set in his ways and, although he intended to give it the Old School (Marburg University, class of '73) try at the party that night in Marrakech, it simply made sense to hedge his bet.

Omar ben Ahmed was more than a little embarrassed about the behavior of "Omar ben Ahmed's Own" Second Cavalry Squadron. The Third Cavalry Squadron was still running down some of the Second Squadron troopers,

who had been quite literally scattered to the winds by
the sound of a couple of air horns. And the cold truth
of the matter was that the Second Squadron hadn't actually "arrested" the one American now in the palace.
She had come of her own free will, he had been told,
because it had afforded her the opportunity to take a
ride on a camel.

The odds against the other Americans finding oil
(he had seen the oil-well-drilling rig on the helicopter
flight over Rabat) with the first hole were about 14
to 1, so that didn't pose any immediate problem. He
would throw a scare first into the woman, and then
into the rest of the American oil people, a scare that
would keep them out of Abzug no matter what his
grandfather wanted.

"Bring in the infidel woman!" he shouted, as fiercely
as he could, taking one last glance at himself in the
mirror and, as he took satisfaction in this, framing a
mental image of the terrified female he would in a moment
face.

He would not, he thought, be too menacing, just menacing enough to accomplish his purpose. He looked ex-
pectantly toward the door. No one was entering.

"Bring in the infidel woman!" he shouted again.

A head of one of the palace servants peered nervously
around the door frame.

"The infidel woman is not coming," the servant said.

"What do you mean, she's not coming? I have summoned her."

"She said she is busy, Your Highness."

"I gave explicit orders to the guards that she was
to be brought to me, by force, if necessary," Omar ben
Ahmed said.

"Yes, Your Highness," the servant said, "I remember
you saying that."

"Well, what happened?"

"She threw the guards out of the harem, Your
Highness," the servant said.

"What was she doing in the harem?" he asked, angrily.

"Delivering a baby, Your Highness," the servant said.

"Who told her she could do that?" Omar ben Ahmed said.

"No one, Your Highness," the servant said. "She just walked in, threw the midwife out and took over."

"Where's the Captain of the Guard?" Omar ben Ahmed asked.

"Boiling water, Your Highness," the servant replied.

"Why is this woman delivering her baby in the harem?" Omar asked. "In the name of my grandfather, I issued specific orders that women in . . . er, that condition . . . were to be taken to the hospital in Marrakech."

"Her condition came on unexpectedly, Your Highness," the servant said. "We would have sent her in the helicopter, except, forgive me, Your Highness, you were flying it."

"How is she?" Omar asked.

"The mother or the infidel woman, Your Highness?"

"The woman, you moron!"

"Making a lot of noise, Your Highness."

"I believe that's customary," Omar said. "Who is she?"

"Captain Kalih's wife, Your Highness."

At that moment, the unmistakable wail of a newborn baby filled the high-vaulted rooms of the palace.

"Shall I have the infidel woman dragged in now, Your Highness?" the servant asked.

Putting his sneer back on, Omar ben Ahmed strode off furiously in the direction of the baby's crying. As he approached the harem, the door suddenly flung open, and a woman in white medical costume emerged. Blonde hair peeked out of her headdress.

Omar steeled himself. While he appreciated what she had done, she still had to be frightened.

"You're the one I'm looking for!" Hot Lips said, pointing a finger at him.

"You are searching for me, mademoiselle?" Omar heard himself ask.

"Nurse Wilson to you, buster," she said. "I saw a

chopper land from the harem window. That was you, right?"

"Why, yes, it was," Omar said.

"I thought so," she said. "O.K., Hotshot Charlie, get out of that Rudolph Valentino suit and crank up the chopper. You're running a medical-evacuation mission to the nearest hospital. I've seen some sloppy lash-ups in my time, but this pile of stones takes the cake."

"Do I understand you to say you wish me to fly you . . . and perhaps the baby and the mother . . . to a hospital?" Omar asked

"What's the matter with you? Can't you speak English? Get cracking!"

The Captain of the Guard appeared, carrying a bucket of steaming water in each hand.

"Where do you want the water, Reverend Mother?" he asked.

"I told you to get moving!" Hot Lips said to His Highness. "You wouldn't be the first chopper jockey I've booted in the tail!"

His Royal Highness Omar ben Ahmed turned on his heel and ran toward the helicopter landing pad. He told himself that he was motivated by humanity; his primary duty lay certainly in doing whatever was necessary to see that Captain Kalih's wife and newborn child received the best possible medical attention. He could deal with the infidel woman later.

By the time he had started up the helicopter, as the blades began to rotate, Captain Kalih's wife, the baby in her arms, was brought to the helicopter on a stretcher. She was loaded into the rear seat, and the infidel woman got in beside her.

"O.K., Hotshot Charlie," the infidel woman screamed at him, "scramble!"

His Royal Highness devoted the next couple of minutes to the business of flying. He radioed ahead to Marrakech Approach Control, and received permission to land on the hospital roof. Helicopter transport of patients was a fairly standard procedure. It was an hour and ten minutes by chopper from the palace to Marrakech, and six-and-a-half days, presuming nothing went wrong, by ground transport.

"What exactly is wrong with her?" he finally asked, over his shoulder.

"Don't tell me you still believe in the stork?" Hot Lips replied.

"I mean is there something specifically wrong with her?"

"She just had a baby," Hot Lips replied, with barely concealed impatience. "Women who have babies, and the baby, belong in the hospital. Kabish?"

"Madame . . . " Omar said.

"Nurse Wilson, to you. I told you that!"

"Nurse Wilson, I am Sheikh Omar ben Ahmed," he said, flashing what he had been told by other infidel women was a smile dazzling in its menace. Once the infidel woman, realizing now who he was, had a moment to reflect on her outrageous treatment of his royal personage, once she literally shook in her boots, he would graciously forgive her, because of her obviously valuable contribution to the welfare of one of his subjects.

"Well, Sheikh," Hot Lips said, flushing just a little, "I'm flattered and all that, but . . . though I may not look it . . . I'm almost old enough to be your mother. You just fly the chopper and behave yourself."

"What did you think I had in mind?" Omar asked.

"I know what you had in mind, sweetie," Hot Lips said, and reached up and pinched his cheek. "And I told you I was flattered. If I was twenty years younger, I'd probably take you up on it. I always had a thing for tall, dark strangers. But, like I said, I'm almost old enough to be your mother. Besides, how would it look? The Reverend Mother Emeritus running around with some chopper jockey still wet behind the ears? People would talk, sweetie. You can see that!"

His Royal Highness peered out the window of the helicopter. He could not think of one word to say.

His eye caught, a thousand feet below him, just off to the right, four small, black specks. This was the heart of the desert. He gently changed course, remembering his passengers, to get closer. Then he picked up the microphone.

"This is Abzug Chopper One to Desert Patrol."

"Go ahead, Chopper One."

"I've got two people and two jackasses at coordinates Seventeen Twelve, Fifteen Six," he said. "What are they doing there? That whole area of desert is off-limits."

"Hold One, Chopper One," Desert Patrol said, and then, a moment later, came back on the radio. "Nobody has been cleared through our checkpoints, Chopper One. It must be somebody trying to sneak into the country."

"Don't be absurd! Who would want to sneak into Abzug?"

"I don't know. Just who do you think you're talking to, anyway?"

"I don't know who I'm talking to," he replied. "But *you're* talking to Sheikh Omar ben Ahmed."

"Forgive me, Your Highness," the voice replied contritely, "I had no way of knowing."

"You should have been able to figure it out," Omar said. "We have one chopper, and one pilot—your beloved heir-apparent to the Sheikhdom."

"Well, now that you put it that way, Your Highness, I suppose I should have figured that out."

"Well, you better send somebody out to get those jackasses out of there," Omar ben Ahmed said.

"Just the jackasses, Your Highness?"

"Rescue the whole party, stupid," Omar said.

"Right away, Your Highness. I'll send out a camel patrol right away."

"Let me know who they are," Omar said. "Chopper One out."

Thirty minutes later, the chopper fluttered down onto the roof of Marrakech General Hospital, and Mrs. Kalih and her baby were off-loaded.

"That's a handsome child," Omar ben Ahmed said as he watched the procedure. He felt it was his royal obligation to do so, even if it meant lying. Like all other newborn babies he had ever seen, this one was, viewed objectively, an object of rather spectacular ugliness.

"Thank you, Your Highness," Mrs. Kalih said, beaming. Having gone this far, Omar went the rest of the way.

"And have you thought of a name for the little fellow?"

"Oh, yes, Your Highness," Mrs. Kalih giggled shyly. Omar ben Ahmed was pleased. The child would obviously be named after him. " 'Hot Lips,' Your Highness, after the infidel lady who brought him into the world."

"An appropriate choice, I'm sure," His Highness said.

"Don't go anywhere, sweetie," Hot Lips said to him. "Just as soon as I check her in, I want to go back with you."

"Madame, I don't have time to waste waiting around here!" His Highness said.

"Now don't be a sorehead, sweetie," Hot Lips said. "A gentleman takes a 'no' graciously." She pinched his cheek again and marched into the hospital.

In five minutes, she was back. "They seem to know what they're doing in there," she said, approvingly. "Now are you going to behave, or am I going to have to ride in the back seat, out of reach?"

"Madame," Omar ben Ahmed said, "please accept my assurances that I have no interest whatever in you or in any other infidel woman."

"What do you mean, infidel woman? I'll have you know, you mustachioed heathen, that you're addressing the Reverend Mother Emeritus of the God Is Love in All Forms Christian Church, Inc."

Omar didn't reply for, even as he spoke the words 'any other infidel woman,' his mind was full of the delightful, soft, sweetly smelling infidel woman who had kicked his shin in the lobby of the Crillon Hotel.

He raised the helicopter on its skids, lowered the nose and took off.

"Watch it, Hotshot Charlie," Hot Lips said, "your rotor r.p.m.'s dropping into the red. Let's not bend the bird with the Reverend Mother in it."

Omar's mouth opened in shock, but automatically

his eyes dropped to the rotor revolutions gauge; the needle showed that he was indeed on the edge of a hazardous flight condition. He hastily made the necessary adjustments to correct the situation.

"You want me to drive awhile, sweetie?" Hot Lips asked. "You look kind of shook."

"You can fly a helicopter?" he asked.

"Oh, sure," Hot Lips said, putting her hands on the controls. "I got it, sweetie," she said. "You just sit back, relax and enjoy. What's the heading, anyway?"

After a long moment, His Highness, a touch of respect in his voice, asked, "May I ask how it is that you can fly?"

"Well, sweetie," Hot Lips said, "it's none of that women's lib nonsense, if that's what you're thinking. I personally like the idea of having men take care of helpless and feminine little me. It's just that I had . . . a good friend . . . who taught me to fly one of these when I was in the Army in Korea."

"You were a soldier in Korea?" he asked.

"I told you I was a little older than I look," Hot Lips said. "I retired as a lieutenant colonel. And I asked, what's our heading?"

"On the way here," Omar said, regaining some composure, "I saw two men, two fools, leading two jackasses across the desert. I think we'd better have a look at them. Fly Two-One Nine True."

"Two-One Nine True," Hot Lips repeated, and the helicopter banked as she took up that heading.

"I didn't have," Omar said, biting the bullet, and admitting to himself that he really felt a sense of camaraderie with this amazing blonde woman, "a chance to thank you for what you did for Mrs. Kalih. Permit me to express, on behalf of Sheikh Abdullah ben Abzug, the appreciation of the Abzugian people."

"What's the matter with him, anyway?" Hot Lips responded.

"I beg your pardon?"

"I asked what's wrong with him? How come he doesn't have a hospital back at that so-called palace of his?"

"When our people need hospitalization, we take them to Morocco," Omar said.

"Like now, huh?" Hot Lips said, sarcastically. "Don't try to hand me that. Sheikh Whatsisname is blowing his job, and you know it."

"Hospitals cost money," Omar said, loyally.

"With the dough the old boy's going to get from his oil, money won't be an excuse."

"You seem supremely confident that oil will be found," he said.

"It's been found," Hot Lips said with certainty. "Horsey told me he smelled it the minute he got off the plane."

"And who," Omar sniffed sarcastically, "is Horsey?"

"Horsey is the world's greatest oil sniffer," Hot Lips replied. "He's infallible. If he says he sniffs oil, you can bet your a . . . Arabian heart on it, there's oil."

His Highness, of course, regarded this as highly unlikely. At the University of Marburg, he had taken courses in geology; and what he had learned was that finding oil was a science, not something you did with your nose.

But there was no time to argue. To the left of the helicopter, perhaps a mile away, he spotted the people and animals he had seen earlier, on the way to Marrakech.

"There they are!" he said, and pointed, and Hot Lips banked the chopper in that direction. Omar's worse fears were realized. The jackasses were no longer moving. They were standing, heads down, beside two prone forms on the sandy dunes.

"Were they moving the last time you saw them?" Hot Lips asked, all business.

"Slowly," Omar replied, "but moving."

"Then we may be in luck," Hot Lips said, as she dipped the nose of the chopper toward the ground. "If you get to them within an hour or so of the time they lose consciousness, you can sometimes save them. You got some water aboard this thing?"

"Yes, of course," Omar said.

"Well, if you think you're all right to fly, I'll take care of them. You think you can find Horsey and the boys?"

"Why?" he asked.

"We brought a field hospital in the plane," Hot Lips said, "and they're closer than either Marrakech or that so-called palace."

"Right," Omar said. "They're right over that next range of mountains."

"Landing one of these things in blowing sand is hairy," Hot Lips said, professionally. "Stick your head out the window and sing out when you see the ground."

"Don't you think I'd better fly?" Omar asked.

"Don't be ridiculous," Hot Lips snapped. "This is an emergency. No time for amateurs."

His Royal Highness did as he was told and, thirty seconds later, the skids of the helicopter touched down on the sand dunes. Omar rushed out of the machine and ran to the first fallen figure. He was a short, fat Arab, and when Omar pushed aside his caftan to put his hand on his heart, he was surprised to see he was wearing the uniform of a high-ranking officer—an Inspector, of the Moroccan Gendarmerie Nationale. The heart was still beating. Omar then rushed to the other fallen figure and pushed its caftan aside so that he could put his hand on the chest to feel for a heartbeat.

At precisely the moment he realized tactilely that the Inspector's comrade was of the other sex, the second figure opened its eyes (light-blue eyes, which produced a very strange physio-chemical reaction in His Highness) and spoke.

"I knew I'd see you again, my darling, if only in Heaven," the fallen figure said, and then lapsed into unconsciousness again. Sheikh Omar ben Ahmed moaned loudly, and then scooped up Miss Penelope Quattlebaum and ran with her in his arms toward the helicopter. As he gently placed her in the back seat, Hot Lips ran up, with Inspector Gregoire de la Mouton over her shoulder.

"How come I got to carry the fat one?" she asked,

as she dumped him unceremoniously beside Penelope. "O.K., sweetie, get this show on the road!"

Alerted by radio, the personnel of Chevaux Petroleum International's Rig Number seventy-five were waiting when the helicopter fluttered to the ground fifteen minutes later.

Even before the rotors had stopped spinning, two huge, bare-chested men had carried Penelope Quattlebaum off on a stretcher toward a prefabricated building which bore the sign: FIELD HOSPITAL AND EXPLOSIVES WAREHOUSE.

Once he had seen the short, fat man loaded onto another stretcher, Omar ran toward the hospital, but was barred at the door by the shorter of the two men.

"Hot Lips says nobody goes in there," he said.

"Will she live?"

"Hot Lips said all she needs is some water," the man said.

"Thank God!" Omar said.

"Friend of yours, is she?"

"In a manner of speaking," Omar said, and then realized the time had come for him to face facts. "Actually," he said, "I fear it's a bit more than that."

"Horsey's my name," the man said. "What's yours?"

"You're the oil sniffer?" Omar asked. "The Reverend Mother told me about you."

"I didn't catch the name."

"My name is Omar," he said.

"Come on, Omar, I know what you need," Horsey said, taking Omar's arm and leading him to another prefabricated building, this one with a sign reading: ANNEX NUMBER SEVEN, BAYOU PERDU COUNCIL, KNIGHTS OF COLUMBUS, LOUNGE.

It was dark in the building, and Omar was so momentarily confused that he thought he was perhaps suffering from heat exhaustion himself. He was in a bar. He had, purely as an educational experience, of course, visited several bars while a student in Germany, and he knew a bar when he saw one. There was a line of beer taps, serving a line of beer drinkers. At one end of the bar, one man wept bitterly as another man tried to comfort him. Two other men were enthusiastically playing an electronic tennis game. There was a picture of a rather plump lady, au naturel, over the bar. And there was a jukebox in the corner playing country music.

A glass was thrust in his hand.

"Chug-a-lug," Horsey ordered.

"I don't drink intoxicants," Omar said, somewhat stiffly.

"Hot Lips said to get a couple of belts into you," Horsey replied. "Think of it as medicine."

Omar obediently tossed it down. It burned his throat and he coughed. Horsey slapped him on the back. "Atta-boy, Omar," he said. "Now one more."

"I am forbidden by the Prophet to partake of fermented grapes," Omar said.

"That's not fermented grapes; that's distilled Kentucky corn," Horsey said.

"I suppose that's something quite different," Omar said, and tossed another belt down. A warm glow spread through his stomach. He took a deep breath and realized he felt much better. As a matter of fact, he could not recall ever feeling quite so good.

"Horsey," he asked, "that man singing on the phonograph—who is he?"

"One of the Knights," Horsey said. "He had those records made special for us."

"Remarkable voice," Omar said. "If he wasn't singing "The Wabash Cannonball," I'd swear it was Boris Alexandrovich Korsky-Rimsakov, the world's greatest opera singer."

"That's ol' Bull-Bellow, all right," Horsey said, grasping his hand. "It's a real pleasure, Omar, to meet a fellow music lover."

Chapter Eighteen

There were six members of the Gendarmerie Nationale, backed up by an armored car and a light tank of the Royal Moroccan Cavalry, blocking the Rabat-Marrakech road. Their search of the cars was detailed and thorough, and the cars-to-be-searched were backed up along the road for half a mile when the first sounds of the sirens on the motorcycles were heard.

There was a good deal of hectic activity, whistle-blowing and shouting, as a path was cleared for the Royal Motorcade. In a moment, it appeared over a rise in the road: four motorcycles, sirens screaming; a Land-Rover filled with four heavily armed members of the Royal Bodyguard; a second Land-Rover carrying only a driver and three golf bags; the Royal Mercedes-Benz 600, His Majesty's personal flag flying from both front fenders; and, bringing up the rear, still another Land-Rover filled with heavily armed, ornately uniformed members of the Royal Bodyguard.

The personnel manning the roadblock snapped to attention and saluted. The Royal Rolls skidded to a halt. His Majesty himself, in full robes, jumped nimbly from the car, followed by two other regal gentlemen, similarly attired.

"What's going on here?" His Majesty demanded.

"Captain Belli ben Khan, Your Majesty," the officer in charge said, "officer in charge of the roadblock."

"What is the purpose of the roadblock?" His Majesty asked, returning the salute.

"There are two crazy Americans in Rabat, Your Majesty," Captain Belli ben Khan said. "We have orders from the Foreign Minister himself to insure they do not leave the city."

"Two crazy Americans? How do you know they're crazy?"

"The Foreign Minister himself, Your Majesty, has told me," the captain said. "He said they believe they are doctors, and they are not, no matter what the cost, to be permitted to go to Marrakech."

"I see," His Majesty said. "Well, carry on, Captain!" He turned back to the Mercedes and made a little bow. "After you, Hawkeye," he said.

His Majesty turned. "Captain, you don't have any idea where the Foreign Minister is at the moment, do you?"

"Yes, Sir, Your Majesty," the captain replied. "He passed through here not fifteen minutes ago, together with an American diplomat. He said he was going to Marrakech."

"Well, we'll catch up with him there, I suppose," His Majesty said. He turned again and bowed to Trapper John. "After you, Trapper," he said, graciously.

"I get sick to my stomach if I have to ride in the middle," Trapper said.

"Well," His Majesty said generously, "in that case, I'll ride in the middle." Golfing partners like these, he realized, were hard to come by. He got in, Trapper John followed him, the door closed and, with screaming sirens, the Royal Motorcade resumed its journey toward Marrakech.

"Instruct the pilot to divert to Mecca," His Royal Highness Sheikh Abdullah ben Abzug said, upon wakening. "I am dying, and I wish to die in Mecca."

"You ain't dying, buddy," Boris Alexandrovich Korsky-Rimsakov said, with sympathy born of his own condition, "you're just a little hung over, is all."

"My teeth itch," His Highness announced, "my eardrums are ringing and I have sand in my mouth. I will shortly be greeting Allah."

"All you need is a little of the hair of the dog what bit you," Boris said.

"You drank it last night," His Royal Highness Prince Hassan ad Kayam said.

"Both cases?" Boris asked, incredulously.

"Both cases," Hassan reported, just a trifle smugly. "The last of it as you sang 'Aloha Oh!' to your assembled fans at the airport."

"My only regret," Sheikh Abdullah announced, "is that I am being called up yonder before I have had a chance to see my great-grandchildren."

"I didn't know you had any great-grandchildren," Hassan said. "I didn't know Omar was even married."

"He's not," Abdullah said. "But the time comes to all men, including Omar, and I would have been perfectly willing to wait, so to speak, until the time had come to him becoming leaving."

"You'll have plenty of time to see your great-grandchildren," Hassan said, soothingly.

"A lot you know!" the Sheikh snapped back. "You don't know how I feel."

"Hassan, are you trying to tell me there's not a drop of anything on this airplane?" Boris asked.

"There *was* a case of champagne," Hassan said, "Dom Perignon '54, as you requested."

"That, too?" Boris asked. Hassan nodded. "Every last drop?"

Hassan nodded again. "You and the Sheikh worked up quite a thirst chasing the Rockettes up and down the aisle," he said.

"My God, I forgot about them!" Boris said. "I even forgot about going to Radio City Music Hall. How many did we bring?"

"Six," Hassan said. "The others had a midnight show and couldn't make it. You promised to send the plane back for them."

"My God!" Boris said. "Hassan, why did you do this to me?"

"Tell the pilot to hurry," Sheikh Abdullah groaned. "I feel the very presence of the Grim Reaper on my brow!"

"That's not the Grim Reaper, stupid," Boris said. "That's that little air whatchamacallit." He turned it off. "Where are the Rockettes now?"

"In the back cabin asleep," Hassan said. "They're not used to that much exercise. They're all pooped out."

Boris groaned. "Hey, Abdullah," he said, "can I ask you something about your religion?"

"Anything," Abdullah said. "But ask quickly, before it's too late."

"How do they feel about last-minute converts?"

The pilot chose that minute to make his little announcement.

"Gentlemen," he said, "there has been a change in our destination."

"I know that, you simpleton," Sheikh Abdullah said. "I gave orders to be taken to Mecca."

"I don't know anything about Mecca," he said. "But I just received orders to land at Casablanca, rather than Marrakech."

"I don't want to go to Casablanca, you idiot," Sheikh Abdullah said. "I want to go to Mecca. I demand that I be taken to Mecca."

"I regret, Your Highness," the pilot said, "that I have my orders, and they are to land at Casablanca. I regret any inconvenience this may cause."

"Orders, schmorders," the Sheikh said. "I am Sheikh Abdullah ben Abzug. I give the orders. Allah willed it that way. If He wanted you to give orders, He would have made *you* Sheikh instead of a lousy flying Frog."

"You tell 'em," Boris said, admiringly. "That goes twice for me, buddy, if you want to make anything out of it."

"Gentlemen," the pilot said, his standard French savoir-faire stretched beyond the breaking point, "the

President of France has ordered me to take you to Casablanca, and I am going to take you to Casablanca."

"The President of France himself?" Boris asked.

"The President of France himself," the pilot said, with dignity.

"Well, it'll be a long time before I do another benefit for *his* unwed mothers, I'll tell you that," Boris said. "It's a good thing I'm dying, or this wouldn't be the end of this."

"You are ill, monsieur?" the pilot asked, with concern. The word had come down from the public-relations department of the firm which had built the Concorde that, officially, no one would ever get sick aboard the Concorde.

"We are both dying. Me before him, but still, both of us," the Sheikh said. "Look at me!"

The pilot looked. The Sheikh's skin was a deathly grey; he appeared to be bleeding to death through the eyeballs, and when he breathed, there was a foul odor which could only be the smell of death. The other one didn't look much better.

"I'll have ambulances meet the plane," he said, and ran from the cabin back to the cockpit.

"I'm holding you personally responsible for this whole affair, Hassan," Boris said. He slumped back in his seat and could be heard murmuring something about the infidelity of those you trust.

The Foreign Minister of the Kingdom of Morocco, just before he and Q. Elwood Potter had left for Marrakech by limousine, had dispatched the Deputy Foreign Minister on a special airplane to Casablanca on a triple mission: he was to arrange for the release of Mr. Rhotten and Congressman Jackson from the Casablanca Mental Sanitarium; to explain that their predicament was solely the responsibility of Miss Penelope Quattlebaum, who had been declared Persona Non Grata; and to convey Mr. Rhotten and Congressman Jackson to Marrakech in the special plane so they could attend His Majesty's party.

The plane had the highest priority, of course, in keeping with the diplomatic delicacy of the situation, to insure that the honored guests would arrive in Marrakech in time for the party. The schedule encountered a snag, however, when it came out that a large mongrel dog belonging to one of the attendants at the Casablanca Mental Sanitarium had become strongly attached to Mr. Rhotten's hairpiece. Apparently in the belief that it was a miniature possum, the dog had carried the hairpiece to his kennel where, for two hours, fangs bared, growling steadily, he waited for the wig to stop pretending it was dead and ferociously resisted all attempts by Mr. Rhotten to reclaim it.

By the time the rug, so to speak, had been rescued, liberally doused with flea powder and reset in the familiar Rhotten curly coiffure, and Rhotten and Smiling Jack had been taken to the airport, the Air France Concorde was in the pattern, second to land behind a glistening DC-4 of Yugo-Air, the Yugoslavian Tourist Airline.

"The Rhotten Report's" film crew had set up their camera at the foot of the stairway to the Air Maroc airliner sent to carry Rhotten and Smiling Jack to Marrakech. Rhotten was going to a thirty-second color bit. He was going to tell all the folks out there in television land of his illegal imprisonment, the result of either gross stupidity or personal vindictiveness (and probably both) of the American Consul General, one Miss Penelope Quattlebaum. He was also going to assure them they had nothing to worry about. Don Rhotten was about to resume his relentless pursuit of his story. They would soon have all the facts.

He got as far as saying, "This is Don Rhotten . . ." when the Yugo-Air DC-4 landed, the sound of its engines effectively drowning him out. Mr. Rhotten was understandably miffed, but he waited until the Yugo-Air aircraft had turned off the runway, taxied to the terminal and shut down its engines. Then he opened his mouth again, and got as far as "This is . . ." when the air was filled with the rather awesome whistling scream of the Concorde coming in to land.

"It's a conspiracy!" Rhotten screamed against the

noise. "That's what it is! If they can't knock me out of the rating one way, Cronkite and Smith'll stoop to anything!"

"Now, just take it easy, Don-Baby," Seymour said. "Whatsisname, that diplomat guy, told me just now that he's closed the airport until after we leave. It'll only be a minute."

As the Concorde, engines whistling, taxied up to the terminal, stairs were rolled up to the Yugo-Air aircraft, and the forty-eight passengers began to debark. The aircraft was carrying forty-eight Croatian trade unionists, steelworkers given Seven Days in the Sun of Merry Morocco as a token of the appreciation of the state for their faithful labor in the steel mills.

Since they had been the subject of much official attention in their homeland, they quite naturally assumed that the television camera was there to record their arrival in Morocco. They headed directly for it, several of them waving, two of them holding up signs and all of them smiling broadly.

A small melee resulted. Mr. Rhotten, after first furiously waving his arms in an attempt to drive them away, finally resorted to physical force and tried to push them out of camera range. This was mistaken (Rhotten was unable to push very hard; his most furious efforts were regarded as polite pushes) as an attempt to arrange them before the camera, as they had been arranged before cameras in Zagreb. Those who had been pushed to the rear in Zagreb were now, of course, determined to be in the front line.

As this was going on, the door to the Concorde opened and Boris Alexandrovich Korsky-Rimsakov, blinking in the harsh sunlight, appeared at the head of the stairs.

He looked over at the melee and at the Yugo-Air aircraft, and immediately came to the very logical conclusion that both Sheikh Abdullah ben Abzug's and his own prayers had been answered. Where there were Yugoslavians, there was bound to be slivovitz.

Brushing aside four stretcher bearers who were trying

to make their way up the steps to the Concorde, he walked quickly toward the Yugoslavians.

"Good afternoon, brothers," he said in Croatian. "Which of you is going to offer a thirsty traveler a little snort of slivovitz?"

"What's in it for me?"

"What did you have in mind?" Boris asked.

"How about this?" a Yugoslavian trade unionist asked, holding up a four-color brochure published by the *Bienvenu à Merry Morocco* Tourist Agency, showing a bikini-clad blonde on one of Morocco's glistening beaches.

Boris looked back to the Concorde. Sheikh Abdullah ben Abzug was, somewhat shakily, making his way down the stairs. Behind him, the first of the six Rockettes had appeared in the door for her first view of Morocco.

"The price," Boris said, gesturing, "is six bottles a broad, payable in advance."

"Four," said the first Croatian.

"Five, and you got yourself a deal," Boris said.

The Deputy Foreign Minister of the Kingdom of Morocco, who had been waiting inside the terminal with Congressman Jackson, had seen the Concorde landing, and then he had watched as the door opened and Boris debarked. His eyes had widened when he saw His Royal Highness Sheikh Abdullah ben Abzug make his appearance. He ran as fast as diplomatic dignity would permit to the foot of the stairway.

"Good afternoon, Your Highness," he said.

"Who are you?" Sheikh Abdullah ben Abzug demanded.

"I am the Deputy Foreign Minister, Your Highness."

"I have come to Mecca to die," His Highness said. "You may make the necessary arrangements for me to do so."

"This isn't Mecca, Your Highness," the Deputy Foreign Minister replied.

"Why not?" His Highness said. "I distinctly gave orders that we were to go to Mecca."

By now the Rockettes had come down the stairs,

to be immediately surrounded by Yugoslavian trade unionists, who smiled and took their arms possessively.

Boris, holding a bottle of slivovitz in each hand, elbowed his way through the crowd.

"Here you are, Abdullah," he said, "elixir!"

"My prayers have been answered," the Sheikh said, reaching for one of the bottles. "I should have known that I was too young and too good to die." He took a deep pull at the bottle neck, quivered a little, took another pull then smiled. "Mud in your eye," he said to the Deputy Foreign Minister.

"Your Highness," the Deputy Foreign Minister said, after a moment, "may I take the liberty of inquiring what Your Highness is doing in Casablanca?"

"I don't really know," His Highness said. "I was en route to Marrakech when I suffered my attack."

"The plane wouldn't land at Marrakech," Boris said. "The pilot came back and said that the President of France said we couldn't land at Marrakech."

"That's right!" the Sheikh said.

"I'm sure there's some mistake, Your Highness," the Deputy Foreign Minister said. "Why would the President of France say something like that?"

"No problem," the Sheikh said, after another pull at the bottle. "Your King has told me, many times, that what is his is mine."

"I'm afraid I don't follow you, Your Highness," the Deputy Foreign Minister said.

"You doubt my word? The word of Sheikh Abdullah ben Abzug?"

"No, of course not, Your Highness. If the King said that what is his is yours, then what is his is yours."

"Now that we understand that," the Sheikh said, "we will take that plane," he said, pointing at the Air Maroc aircraft, "which is your King's, and therefore mine, to Marrakech."

"That poses a certain, small problem, Your Highness," the Deputy Foreign Minister said.

"Which is?"

"Could I infringe on Your Majesty's well-known

generosity?" the Deputy Foreign Minister asked, thinking quickly.

"To what extent?"

"It is a large aircraft," the Deputy Foreign Minister said, "with first-class and tourist accommodations. Would Your Highness graciously permit some stranded Americans to go with you to Marrakech?"

"On *my* airplane?" the Sheikh asked, disbelieving what he had heard. "You are bereft of your senses!"

"Come on, Abdullah," Boris said, "be a sport. They'll be in tourist, and you won't even know they're there."

"My friend has spoken," the Sheikh said. "The stranded Americans may come with us, providing I don't have to look at the infidel bastards."

"Hey, Hassan," Boris said, raising his voice, "I'm sorry, little buddy, but I swapped the broads to the Yugoslavs. Let go of the redhead's hand and come on!"

With the Deputy Foreign Minister trailing respectfully behind them, Boris and Abdullah marched over to the Air Maroc Caravelle. They reached the stairway just as Don Rhotten, for the third time, pressed his caps in place and faced the camera.

"This is Don Rhotten . . ." he said.

At that point, Boris dealt with him. He disliked granting interviews under any circumstances, and he despised suddenly finding himself before an uninvited television camera. He attempted to deal with Mr. Rhotten in the manner which, over the years, had proved most effective. He had formed the habit of holding would-be interviewers two feet off the ground by their hair while he informed them, sternly, that he granted interviews only by appointment. When he grabbed Mr. Rhotten's locks now, however, they came off in his hand.

"I'll be damned!" Boris said, in surprise, holding the wig in his fingers at arm's length for a moment before dropping it.

Mr. Rhotten was so stunned by this outrageous violation of his person that it took him a moment to react. He was, however, on the verge of assaulting his assaulter when Boris dropped the rug. Remembering the difficulty he had had only hours before finding someone to reset his wig after that damned dog had mauled it, he naturally decided to put off the assault until a more appropriate time and save the rug now. He quickly dropped to his knees and scurried after it as a gust of wind picked it up and blew it under the airplane.

When he returned to the airplane, Boris and the Sheikh were already inside, and Hassan ad Kayam was about to board the stairs.

"Who was that big ape that just got on the plane?" Don Rhotten asked.

"I believe," Hassan said, rather coldly, "that you refer to His Highness Sheikh Abdullah ben Abzug."

"The big guy with the beard," Rhotten asked, forgetting momentarily that that description fit both Boris and the Sheikh, "is the Sheikh of Abzug?"

"That is correct," Hassan said, and boarded the airplane.

The Deputy Foreign Minister came running up with the honorable Edwards L. "Smiling Jack" Jackson in tow. They followed Don Rhotten up the stairs, went up it themselves, and were, in turn, followed by the camera crew. The door closed, the engines were started, and the Air Maroc Caravelle moved to the end of the runway and took off.

Chapter Nineteen

Thirty minutes after Omar ben Ahmed had entered Annex Number Seven to the Bayou Perdu Council, K. of C., Lounge, Inspector Gregoire de la Mouton, accompanied by Hot Lips, entered. The Inspector seemed no worse for his close call on the burning desert, except for an apparently insatiable thirst, which he attempted to satisfy at the beer taps.

"Come over here, Hotshot Charlie," Hot Lips ordered, beckoning him over to where they stood at the bar. "We have a problem, and you can help us with it."

Omar had a little trouble negotiating the twenty feet which separated them, something which he ascribed to the mysterious malady which seemed to be in possession of him. He could not force the tactile memory of the blonde from his mind, no matter what he did.

"Easy does it," Hot Lips said, propping him up on a barstool. "Never knew a chopper jockey who could hold his sauce."

"How may I be of assistance, madame?" Omar said, rather thickly. At Horsey-the-Oil-Sniffer's insistence, he had taken eight drinks of the fermented corn.

"You're a native, right?" Hot Lips asked. "Of this . . . wherever we are?"

"Abzug," Omar said.

"O.K. Do you happen to know somebody called the Chef de Protocol?"

"As a matter of fact, I do," Omar said.

"You get along with him all right?" Hot Lips pursued.

"I think that adequately describes our relationship," Omar said.

"How much did you give him, Horsey?" Hot Lips asked.

"Not even half a quart," Horsey replied, disapprovingly.

Omar began to sing along with the jukebox, which was playing the Boris Alexandrovich Korsky-Rimsakov version of "It Ain't God Who Makes Honky-Tonk Angels."

"Knock that off," Hot Lips said sharply. "We've got a problem on our hands with that sweet little Penelope."

"And who," Omar said, icily, "if I may be so bold to inquire, is Penelope?"

"The one," Hot Lips said, rather nastily, "you copped a feel from, you lecherous good Samaritan."

"I beg your pardon?" Omar asked, not quite comprehending.

"The beautiful little blonde," Inspector de la Mouton said.

"She told me what you did to her," Hot Lips said. "And it seems to me, the least you can do, Romeo, is try to make it up to her."

"As soon as I regain my health, monsieur," Inspector de la Mouton said, "I will deal with you myself. In the meantime, you would be well advised to stay out of my police jurisdiction!"

"How may I help the beautiful little blonde?" Omar asked.

"Penny," Hot Lips said, "is a diplomat."

"Madame," Omar said, "you jest!"

"Mademoiselle Penelope," De la Mouton said, in Arabic, "is the American Consul General, or was, in Casablanca."

"Which?" Omar asked. "Is or was?"

"What are they talking about?" the Reverend Mother asked. "Sounds like the Holy Rollers talking in tongues."

"She has just been declared Persona Non Grata by the Moroccan Government," Inspector de la Mouton went on, this time in English. "She will be sent home in disgrace."

"She will be sent home over my dead body!" Omar said furiously.

"How are you going to stop it?" Hot Lips asked.

"I'll speak to Bernie personally," Omar said.

"Who's Bernie?"

"The King," Omar said.

"You know the King?"

"Of course, I know the King," Omar said.

"He's crazy-drunk all right," Horsey said, "on eight, lousy little drinks."

"I am not drunk!" Omar said. "I don't even drink!"

"Humor him," Hot Lips whispered, "we're desperate."

"Putting aside for a moment your great first-name friendship with the King," Inspector de la Mouton, who, after all, had extensive experience in dealing with drunks, said, "you say you know the Abzugian Chef de Protocol?"

"Of course, I know him. I grew up with him!"

"Can you arrange it so that Penny can present her credentials to him?"

"I thought you said she had been declared Persona Non Grata?"

"She doesn't know that yet," De la Mouton said. "I haven't had the heart to tell her."

"What was the reason, anyway?" Horsey asked.

"She made an unfortunate mistake in judgment," De la Mouton said. "She had an American Congressman locked up as a crazy."

"Which Congressman? We've got 400 and some, and a 50-50 chance she was right," Horsey said.

"His name is Edwards L. Jackson," De la Mouton said.

"We're in luck," Hot Lips said. "He's one of the real crazies. You remember him, Horsey? The one the cops chained to the airport fence in London?"

"Sure," Horsey said. "Smiling Jack. Hell, if having Smiling Jack put in a padded cell is all she did, there's no problem at all. I'll get on the horn to Chubby in Washington and tell him she was just doing her duty."

"Unfortunately, there was another one," De la Mouton said. "A television news journalist named Don Rhotten."

"They pronounce that Row-ten," Hot Lips said. "She had him tossed in the funny farm too, huh? What did he do, get fresh like Romeo here?"

"Madame, I resent the insinuation that my conduct with regard to Mademoiselle Penelope has been anything but proper," Omar said. "As a matter of fact, the first time I saw her, she kicked me in the shin."

"She was probably reading your mind," Hot Lips said. "I know how easy that is.

"What is it you wish me to do for Mademoiselle Penelope?" Omar asked, desperately.

"If we can fix it so that she can present her credentials to the Chef de Protocol," Hot Lips said, "maybe we can get her off the hook. Can you really fix that?"

"You tell me when and where, Hot Lips," Omar said, "and I will have the Chef de Protocol crawl into Mademoiselle Penelope's presence on all fours."

"He exaggerates a lot," Horsey said, "but I like his spirit!"

"There is a condition," Omar said.

"Which is?" Hot Lips asked, suspiciously.

"That I be permitted to see Mademoiselle Penelope, so that I may both inquire after her state of health and offer what apologies are necessary for any misunderstanding that may have arisen between us."

"What did he say?" Horsey asked.

"He wants to tell her he's sorry," Hot Lips said. "O.K., Hotshot, you fix it so that Penny can see this Chef de Protocol, and I'll let you tell her yourself."

"There is a radio in the chopper," Omar said. "I'll radio the palace immediately!"

They all marched out to the helicopter and Omar picked up the microphone. The sudden blast of heat plus the knowledge that the blonde was in trouble had sobered him up completely. He looked at Inspector Gre-

goire de la Mouton. "Believe me, my dear Inspector,"
he said in Arabic, "I deeply appreciate your interest
in Mademoiselle Penelope. I recall quite clearly your
advice to me to stay out of your police jurisdiction."

"You fix things for Mademoiselle Penelope, you dirty
young man, and I'll forget the whole thing," De la Mouton
said, "providing you keep your hands off her!"

"Do you know what the penalty is in Abzug's police
jurisdiction for raising your voice above a discreet whisper
when addressing the nobility?" Omar asked.

"Certainly," De la Mouton said. "Two slices with the
guillotine—one vertical, one horizontal."

"Correct," Omar said. He pushed the microphone
switch. "Abzug Palace, this is Omar ben Ahmed. Put
the Chef de Protocol on the radio."

"Immediately, Your Royal Highness," the radio
replied.

Inspector Gregoire de la Mouton collapsed where
he stood, in a dead faint.

Horsey looked down at him. "Eight drinks," he said,
disdainfully, "and this one gets plastered out of his skull.
A lousy six beers, and this one passes out."

"Your Highness," the radio said, "I must regretfully
inform you that the Chef de Protocol is not in the
palace."

"Where is he?"

"In Marrakech, Your Highness."

"Oh, yes," Omar said, "I'd quite forgotten—the King's
party. What's the word on my grandfather?"

"He is due in Marrakech momentarily, Your Highness."

"Please get word to the Chef de Protocol," Omar
said, "that I am on my way to Marrakech and wish
to see him immediately on my arrival."

He replaced the microphone in its holder and took
off the earphones. Hot Lips and Horsey were bent over
Inspector de la Mouton. Hot Lips slapped his face, and
one eye opened. It saw Omar standing over him, and
promptly shut again.

"Inspector," Omar said, still in Arabic, "I would

consider it a personal service if you would not, just yet, let these people know who I am."

"Whatever you say, Your Highness," De la Mouton said.

"Hey, he's coming around."

"For the present, I don't want you calling me 'Your Highness,' either," Omar said.

"What should I call you, Your Highness?"

"Call me what Madame Hot Lips calls me," Omar said. "Hotshot Charlie."

"Yes, Your Highness," De la Mouton said, "Hotshot Charlie it is."

Horsey pulled De la Mouton to his feet.

"What now?" he asked.

"I will now go to pay my respects to Mademoiselle Penelope," Omar said, "and then we are all going to see the Chef de Protocol."

Omar marched off toward the Field Hospital and Explosives Warehouse. Hot Lips started after him. Horsey stopped her.

"Butt out, Hot Lips," he said. "Let him go."

"Why, Horsey," Hot Lips said, "you're a romantic!"

"I'm a pretty good judge of character, is all," Horsey said. "Besides, if we're going to the party, we'll have to get washed up."

"What are you talking about? What party?"

"Hotshot Charlie's taking us to a party his friend Bernie is giving," Horsey said. "I heard him say so on the radio."

"But he was talking in Arabic."

"You sink as many holes as I have in Arabian countries," Horsey said, looking directly at Inspector de la Mouton, "you can't help picking up some of the lingo."

Omar ben Ahmed knocked politely at Penelope's door.

"Who is there?" Penelope called.

"Omar ben Ahmed."

There was a long pause before he was given permission to enter; but finally, Penelope told him to come in, and he walked inside the small room.

Penelope was out of bed, dressed in her desert-crossing clothing: blue jeans, desert boots, and a sweat shirt reading SLIPPERY ROCK STATE TEACHER'S COLLEGE.

"I believe, mademoiselle, that I have had the great pleasure of making your acquaintance, briefly, in Paris," Omar said formally.

"I seem to recall, vaguely," Penelope said, flushing furiously, for some unknown reason.

"My name, mademoiselle, is Omar ben Ahmed."

"So you said," Penelope said. "I am Miss Penelope Quattlebaum, Consul General of the United States of America."

"Charmed, mademoiselle," Omar said, taking her hand, bowing, and kissing it.

Penelope thought she would faint.

"And, then, of course, we met just awhile ago, again, on the desert."

"Yes, we did, and you should be ashamed of yourself!"

"My interest, mademoiselle, I assure you, was purely medical," Omar said.

"Well, I like that!" Penelope said. "That's what's known as adding insult to injury!"

It was time, Omar realized, to change the subject.

"I gather that Mademoiselle is what is known as a career woman?"

"Yes, of course, I am."

"And there is certainly no room in mademoiselle's life for romance?"

"Absolutely none," she said.

"Mademoiselle will then doubtless be pleased to hear that it has been arranged for her to present her credentials to the Abzugian Chef de Protocol."

"I am, of course, pleased," Penelope said.

"And I am, of course, pleased that Mademoiselle is pleased," Omar said.

"If you can really arrange for me to present my credentials," Penelope said, "I will accept your apologies for the . . . . incident . . . on the desert."

"Mademoiselle is most gracious," Omar said, bowing again and taking her hand and kissing it again. Her right foot, with a mind of its own, suddenly kicked Omar in the shin. He didn't flinch. He just looked at her. The rage welled up again within her. She kicked him again.

"Mademoiselle would be well advised not to repeat that a third time," Omar said.

She rose to the challenge and kicked him in the other shin.

"Mademoiselle was warned," Omar said. He reached out for her, pulled her off the floor and to him, and kissed her. He kissed her a long time, until her hands stopped beating at his face. Then he let her go, setting her, out of kicking distance, on the floor, and keeping her there with a hand planted firmly on each shoulder.

"There remains but one question, mademoiselle," Omar said.

"And what is that, you filthy-rotten, male-chauvinist sexist-pig and cheap feel stealer?"

"How soon do you think we can be married?" Omar asked.

Penelope stared at him in utter disbelief. Her eyes widened and her mouth dropped open.

"What makes you think I would marry you?" she asked. "That would mean giving up my diplomatic career, just when it's finally taken a turn for the better."

"The question, mademoiselle," Omar said, "was not whether, but when?"

Omar pulled her to him and kissed her again. This time she did not beat on him.

"I wonder," Penelope said, when he had turned her loose again, "if diplomatic immunity extends to waiving the usual three-day waiting period?"

There is a large pool in the garden of the Mamoumian Hotel in Marrakech, in which blissfully floated the United States Ambassador to the Kingdom of Morocco and his Chief of Mission, the former on an air mattress and the latter inside an inner tube.

"I have carefully considered the problem from both an ethical and a practical standpoint," the Ambassador said.

"And what decision did you reach, Chief?"

"If the King of Morocco is throwing a party, it is clearly my duty to attend. Paddle over to the side, Homer; get on the telephone, and telephone to His Majesty's Chef de Protocol that I am here in Marrakech."

"Just you, Chief?"

"You, too, of course," the Ambassador said. "Where would I be without you?"

By the time the Chief of Mission had paddled to the poolside telephone, it was in use. It was in use by a rather attractive French female, and it was only after a moment that the Chief of Mission became aware of what she was saying, rather than what she looked like.

"Now don't give me that," she said sharply. "I know he's in the hotel. I know Boris Alexandrovich Korsky-Rimsakov when I see him! Now you connect me immediately!"

There was a pause. Now the Chief of Mission's every sense was alerted. The word had come from the Secretary of State himself that Korsky-Rimsakov's passport was to be picked up, and that, at all costs, he was to be kept out of Morocco.

"*Cher* Boris Alexandrovich!" the woman went on, "I recognized your voice immediately. This is Chou-Chou!" Another pause. "What do you mean, Chou-Chou who? Who did you just give a benefit for in Paris?"

The Chief of Mission waved furiously for the Ambassador to paddle over, so that he, too, could hear what was being said, proof that this man had somehow sneaked into the country against the express prohibition of the Secretary of State himself. The Ambassador's attention, unfortunately, was directed toward an amply bosomed young woman about to make a swan dive from the high diving board.

"Well, *Cher* Boris Alexandrovich," the blonde said,

"if Papa did something like that, I give you my word he'll be sorry he did. He knew the only reason I came along with him was so that I could thank you personally. I can't imagine why he would forbid your plane to land here."

The diver made her splash and, for a moment, the Chief of Mission thought he would now be able to get the Ambassador's attention. But another young woman took up a place on the high diving board. The Ambassador's concentration was complete.

"If you want to know how I look in a bathing suit," the blonde on the telephone said, "look out your window. I'm using the poolside telephone." She raised her free hand and waved in the direction of the hotel.

"Oh, you can fit me in at six o'clock? I'm so glad!" the blonde said. "Until then, *Cher* Boris Alexandrovich!" She made little kissing noises and then hung up the telephone.

The Chief of Mission watched her walk away, and then picked up the telephone. He telephoned the Royal Chef de Protocol and got another bad bit of news. Not only was the Chef de Protocol rather reluctant to issue an invitation to the King's party at all, but he made it plain that the Ambassador could not expect to sit at the head table. The King was bringing two personal guests, and the Foreign Minister was bringing the United States Deputy Assistant Under Secretary of State, who was going to officially apologize for the conduct of the Consul General in Casablanca. With the Sheikh of Abzug, the Sheikh of Hussid, and their guests, plus the Sheikh of Abzug's grandson and his special guest, there was barely room for the President of France and his wife. The Ambassador and the Chief of Mission were welcome, of course, to enjoy the King's hospitality if they clearly understood that they would be in the category of super-numeraries, along with the King's golf professional and his chauffeur.

The Chief of Mission paddled furiously back to where the Ambassador was floating around.

"The balloon has gone up, Chief," he said. "We're in trouble."

"Look at the . . . form . . . of that diver," the Ambassador said. He waited until the diver had entered the water and then turned to the Chief of Mission. "What are you spluttering about? Try to remember you're a diplomat."

"Well, for one thing, that Korsky-Rimsakov person is here."

"Impossible!" the Ambassador said. "They revoked his passport, and the Foreign Minister himself assured me, before we left Rabat, that if he did show up in Morocco, he would send him out of the country on the same plane."

"He's here, Chief," the Chief of Mission said. "I just saw him waving to a blonde from his hotel room."

"Waving to a blonde?"

"Yeah, she was making a date to meet him at six o'clock."

"I'll check into it," the Ambassador said. "What else?"

"The Deputy Assistant Under Secretary of State, Potter, is here."

"You don't say?"

"He's going to be sitting at the King's table. The Chef de Protocol said he's going to offer the King official apologies for the American Consul in Casablanca."

"Well, that can be hardly called bad news, now can it?" the Ambassador said. "*He* can tell her Uncle Amos why she got fired."

"That's the good news," the Chief of Mission said. "The bad news is that we don't get to sit at the head table!"

"I'm the United States Ambassador," the Ambassador said. "I don't know about, you, Homer, but I *always* get to sit at the head table."

"We get to sit with the golf pro and the chauffeur," the Chief of Mission reported. "The head table is full."

"I'll protest this directly to the Foreign Minister

himself," the Ambassador said. "It's an absolute outrage!"

"Speak of the devil, Chief," the Chief of Mission said, pointing toward the end of the pool where Deputy Assistant Under Secretary Potter and the Moroccan Foreign Minister were standing watching the girls climb the ladder to the high diving board.

"You get back on the phone, Homer," the Ambassador said. "Call the Gendarmerie Nationale and have them arrest this Korsky-Rimsakov chap at precisely six-fifteen. It'll look much better if they catch him with some blonde bimbo."

With that, the Ambassador rolled off the air mattress and, looking something like a drunken whale, paddled toward where Potter and the Foreign Minister were watching the girls.

Chapter Twenty

The Deputy Assistant Under Secretary of State for North African Affairs was about as glad to see the Ambassador to Morocco (once he recognized the dripping-wet swimmer to *be* the Ambassador) as the Ambassador was to see the Deputy Assistant Under Secretary of State.

This feeling of euphoria lasted no more than sixty seconds, however, until they began to compare notes and realized that things were worse collectively than they had been separately.

The C.I.A.'s man on the Abzugian border (there was no agent, of course, within Abzug) had reported, top-priority, that the first reaction to the American presence in Abzug had been revealed. Orders had gone out to all border patrols and troop installations to arrest on sight and immediately guillotine in six slices, vertically, the American television-news journalist Don Rhotten and the Hon. Edwards L. "Smiling Jack" Jackson. The Abzugian security forces furnished a very professional description of the wanted men, including the information that while Jackson's silver locks were real, Rhotten wore a toupee, contact lenses, and caps on his teeth. The order had come personally from Omar ben Ahmed, heir-apparent to the Sheikhdom. The offense was against paragraph seventeen of the Abzugian Code: "interfering with the love life of a member of the royal family."

The Fleet Marine Force, Mediterranean, was standing by to rescue, by force if necessary, the Chevaux Oil Corporation personnel. They would helicopter into action the moment the guillotine dropped on either Mr. Rhotten or Mr. Jackson.

The emissary sent to deliver the notification that she was now Persona Non Grata to Miss Penelope Quattlebaum had not been able to locate the lady. Furthermore, there was a pronounced lack of cooperation on the part of the Casablanca Gendarmerie; the officer in charge, Inspector Gregoire de la Mouton, had even refused to see him.

There was, peripherally, the same emissary reported, evidence that slavery was not dead in Casablanca. A bearded giant had sold six American girls to a group of Yugoslavian tourists. Full details on the transaction were a little fuzzy, but an investigation was under way.

"You don't think, Mr. Deputy Assistant Under Secretary, that this Quattlebaum female would show up here?"

"She wouldn't dare!" Potter said.

The Moroccan Foreign Minister reported, with some chagrin, that the Gendarmerie Nationale operating in the Rabat area was, so far, unsuccessful in locating the crazy Americans who had escaped from Deputy Assistant Under Secretary Potter's control. The authorities had turned up a fiacre driver, however, who informed them that he had taken two men meeting the description to a point near Le Club Royal de Golf de Maroc and, while Potter discounted the suggestion, the gendarmerie were forced to proceed on the presumption that the two maniacs might attempt to somehow establish contact with His Majesty Himself.

The worst news of all was that the C.I.A. agent assigned to cover the man from the Deuxième Bureau who covered the French President had learned of a brilliant move on the part of the Deuxième Bureau. They had motion pictures of Boris Alexandrovich Korsky-Rimsakov, the close friend of Jean-Pierre de la Chevaux, mocking everything that Sheikh Abdullah ben Abzug held sacred. As shameless evidence of his scorn for all things Arabic, the singer had arranged for two men, in full and apparently authentic Arabian costumes, to accompany him on a six-hour-long drunken debauchery in New York City, during which one of the men costumed as an Arab had staggered into the Radio City Music Hall and, by gestures, offered to buy the entire corps de ballet. What he intended to do with the corps de ballet was evident from the gestures.

Once the Sheikh of Abzug saw those films, America could simply forget about getting so much as a drop of Abzugian oil. There was a particularly good (from the French point of view, of course) sequence showing the singer nearly in hysterics as the "Arab" stumbled and fell down the Music Hall main staircase, over and over, but somehow never lost hold of his bottle.

"And we can't get the films back?" the Ambassador asked.

"Not a chance," Potter replied. "All we can do is go to the party and hope for the best.

At six-thirteen, Chou-Chou, with quick little steps, went to the door of *Cher* Boris Alexandrovich's suite and pushed it open. She was proud of her strength of character. It hadn't been easy, forcing herself to be thir-

teen minutes late, but what would he have thought of
her if she had shown up on time?"

There was a figure in the dark room by the window.

"*Cher* Boris Alexandrovich?" Chou-Chou called,
thinking that the figure was somewhat shorter and fatter
than she remembered *Cher* Boris to be.

"Come in, madame," the figure said.

"You're not *Cher* Boris Alexandrovich!" Chou-Chou
said. "What is this?"

"Madame, I am Sheikh Hassan ad Kayam. I regret
that *Cher* Boris has been called away."

"Where did he go?"

"As a matter of fact, the French President had some
porno movies he wanted Sheikh Abdullah ben Abzug
to look at, and Boris went along to smooth things over."

"What do you mean, smooth things over?"

"Apparently, the President of France issued orders
that the Sheikh's airplane wasn't to be allowed to land
here. The Sheikh was going to cut his heart out for
that. Boris made him promise he wouldn't . . . what
with the party, and all, it would have been awkward
. . . but I don't think he believed him. He went along
to make sure that nothing . . . untoward . . . happened."

"But who are you? And what are you doing here?"

"Sometimes, madam, when ladies realize that *Cher*
Boris simply can't squeeze them into his busy schedule,
they are willing to accept, so to speak, a supernumerary."

"You're out of your mind!" Chou-Chou said.

"Well, you win some, and you lose some," Hassan
said, philosophically.

At that moment, the door crashed inward, and eight
of the largest members of the Marrakech Barracks of
the Gendarmerie Nationale burst into the room.

"Boris Alexandrovich Korsky-Rimsakov, we arrest
you in the name of the King!"

"I'm not Boris," Hassan said.

"You can say that again," Chou-Chou said. "Lock
this little twerp up and throw the key away!"

"Grab the broad, too," one of the gendarmes said.

"The Foreign Minister said to be sure she didn't get away. He wants pictures of them together."

"I assure you," Hassan said, as he was carried out of the room between two of the gendarmes, "that I am not whom you seek, and that there has been an error made somewhere."

Sheikh Abdullah ben Abzug howled as he watched the motion pictures of himself rolling down the flight of stairs.

"Wonderful!" he cried. "You will make me a copy, of course? And a copy for my good friend, Boris Alexandrovich?"

The lights snapped on.

"Your Highness is pleased?" the President of France asked.

"I am delighted," Sheikh Abdullah said. "I am so delighted that I will not cut your heart out, as I intended."

"Thanks a lot, President," Boris said. "You can send my copy over to the Opera House."

He put his arm around the Sheikh's shoulders, and they walked out of the room, still chuckling.

"That really was a nice thing for the French to do," the President heard the Sheikh say. "Maybe they're not all such black-hearted bastards, after all."

"What the hell is that?" Dr. Benjamin Franklin Pierce asked of Dr. John Francis Xavier McIntyre. They were on the sixteenth green of the Marrakech Country Club, on their second round of the day on those links.

"If I didn't know better, I would say that it is a full-grown man in formal clothes, crawling on all fours," Dr. McIntyre replied.

"Hawkeye, please!" the King said. "I'm putting."

"Zeekink, there's a strange creature crawling toward you on all fours," Hawkeye said. "Is it dangerous?"

"I don't see it," the King said, "because if I do see it, I will be forced to cut off its head. It knows that I'm not to be disturbed on the golf course."

He made his putt, which saw him go par for the hole, and that good feeling made him gracious.

"Off your belly, Foreign Minister," he said, "and speak your piece."

"Your Majesty, I would like to speak to you privately," the Foreign Minister said, "on a matter of the most urgent importance."

"I have no secrets from my golf cronies," the King said. "Out with it!"

"I have just learned of a grievous error on the part of the Gendarmerie Nationale," he said.

"What?"

"Mistaking him for a well-known American criminal, Boris Alexandrovich Korsky-Rimsakov, the Gendarmerie Nationale arrested Sheikh Hassan ad Kayam."

"What do you mean, well-known American criminal? Boris Alexandrovich is the world's greatest opera singer," Hawkeye protested.

"And my pal," Trapper joined in. "What kind of a country do you run here, anyway, Zeekink?"

"You know this man?"

"Very well," Trapper John said. "One hell of a drive; pretty good on the fairway, but rotten with his putter."

"You have locked up a golfing friend of my friends?" the King asked. "A man with whom your beloved King could play a few rounds of golf?"

"Not only him, Your Majesty," the Foreign Minister said, "but the wife of the President of France."

"You don't say?" the King said. "Before I have you executed, is there anything you wish to say?"

"It is still worse, Your Highness," the Foreign Minister said. "The whole incident was recorded on television film."

"Whose idea was that?"

"Mine, Your Majesty."

"Well, get the film back before you turn yourself in to the police," the King said. "I'll apologize for your stupidity tonight at the party."

"It's not quite that easy, Your Majesty," the Foreign

Minister said. "The film was taken by an American television journalist named Don Rhotten."

"That's Row-ten, I think," Hawkeye said.

"You know this man, Hawkeye?"

"From what I understand, he is not a nice man," Hawkeye said.

"I would be very embarrassed if television in your country showed such clear evidence of the stupidity of my Foreign Minister," the King said. "Is there anything you can do?"

"Not until we finish the game, Zeekink," Hawkeye said. "Then we'll have a whack at it."

"You heard my friends," the King said. "You will arrange whatever it is they wish arranged. If you do a good job, I will see that you are simply hung, rather than drawn and quartered."

"While we're finishing the round," Trapper John said, "round up a lady named the Reverend Mother Emeritus and a guy named Horsey. They'll help us to understand the situation."

"You heard him," the King said. "And don't bother crawling away, you idiot, run!"

"My shot, I believe?" Trapper John said, as he bent to address the ball.

It was going to be a Don Rhotten Special, a thirty-minute program beamed live via satellite from Marrakech (with time out for commercials, a total of 11.5 minutes of film, including openings and closings).

Don Rhotten watched it with great pleasure. It was all there: the crazy diplomatic broad, the dumb Frog broad going to the hotel-suite door, and then being carried out by the cops, the whole story. He was going to really zing them with this one. And since he had placed himself in the protection of the American Ambassador, he didn't have to worry about those nutty Abzugians wanting to slice him in six pieces, not that he believed that for a minute.

He watched himself, with a smile of deepest pleasure, as he closed the program: "This has been 'The Rhotten

Report,' and this is Don Rhotten, in mysterious Morocco."

"Great," he shouted. "Fantastic! Dan Rather, eat your heart out!"

The lights should have gone on at that point. They didn't.

"Put the lights on!" Rhotten ordered.

The lights didn't go on. Instead a slide of Don Rhotten, a still, flashed on the screen. There was always time for a few moments of that, Don Rhotten thought, and turned to look at himself again.

"Does he or doesn't he?" a voice which sounded very much like that of Benjamin Franklin Pierce, M.D., said. The slide changed. It showed Mr. Rhotten, bareheaded, so to speak, attempting to get his toupee back from the dog in the Casablanca Mental Sanitarium.

"Only his doggie knows for sure!" Trapper John's voice cried triumphantly.

"What the hell is this?" Rhotten demanded angrily.

"Has your rug slipped lately?" Hawkeye's voice inquired as a slide of Rhotten having his hair lifted by Boris at the airport in Casablanca filled the screen.

"Glue *your* wig with Ever-stick!" Trapper John cried as a slide of Rhotten, first chasing his wig under the airplane and then of him clamping it, somewhat cockeyed, on his head, flashed on.

"Lights," Hawkeye called.

"That ought to zing them, out there in TV land," Trapper said, "don't you think?"

"You wouldn't dare!" Rhotten said. "You wouldn't dare."

"Don-Baby," the Hon. Edwards L. Jackson (Farmer—Free Silver, Arkansas) said, "I know these guys. Believe me, they would."

"Where did you guys get those pictures, anyway?"

"That would be telling," Trapper John said. "Let's say a little sheep told us."

"What do you want from me, anyway? How much?"

"It's not money," Hawkeye said. "Perish the thought!"

"What then?"

"We have a few little suggestions for changing your story that we'd like you to listen to," Trapper John said, "a new slant, as I believe you call it."

"I refuse to do it," Rhotten said. "I have my television ethics; newscasting is my sacred duty!"

"As I was saying to Howard K. Smith just the other day," Hawkeye said, "the one thing a TV journalist must have is ethics, a sense of duty."

"That wasn't Howard K. Smith you said that to," Trapper said. "It was Walter Cronkite."

"So it was. I forgot all about him. Well, we'll give Howard the rug-and-dog shots, and Walter gets the scalping shot. We wouldn't want to play favorites."

"Let's hear your suggestions," Don Rhotten said. He knew he was licked.

"Bring in the new film, boys," Hawkeye said, "and the tape recorder. We have to do a new voice-over."

Two hours later, as the satellite passed overhead, the slightly revised story was telecast to Don Rhotten's 11,345,213 viewers. Monitors had been set up for the amusement of the guests of His Majesty in the hotel banquet room.

"Good evening," the familiar voice said, "this is Don Rhotten, and this is a special 'Rhotten Report' from Marrakech, Morocco. Americans have been much in the news here in the last day or two."

His face vanished from the screen, and there was film of the Sheikh of Abzug and Miss Penelope Quattlebaum signing documents.

"Through the brilliant personal diplomacy," Rhotten said, "of this beautiful and charming young American diplomatress, Miss Penelope Quattlebaum, the Sheikhdom of Abzug today signed an agreement with the United States for joint exploitation of Abzugian oil."

The Sheikh finished signing, stood up, leaned over, kissed Penelope on the cheek and raised his glass toward the camera. At this point, Mr. Rhotten diverted from the straight facts.

"The Sheikh here toasted Abzug-American Cooperation in the future," Rhotten said. Only those Americans who could read lips knew what the Sheikh really said with his benevolent smile: "Your mother wears army shoes."

"It will be," Rhotten went on, "sadly, Diplomatress's Quattlebaum's last diplomatic triumph. Her marriage to Sheikh Omar ben Ahmed, heir-apparent to the Sheikhdom of Abzug, took place earlier today, performed by the Rev. Mother Emeritus Margaret Houlihan Wachauf Wilson, of the God Is Love in All Forms Christian Church, Inc., in a joint Christian-Moslem ceremony.

"This correspondent has learned exclusively that to mark what he called 'a whole new era in Moroccan-Abzugian-American diplomatic relations,' the Secretary of State personally telephoned the King of Morocco to inform him that he is replacing all American diplomatic personnel in the area immediately. While the new Ambassador has not been named, it has been announced that it will not be the current Deputy Assistant Under Secretary of State for North African affairs, whose retirement has just been announced.

"And this TV journalist has learned, exclusively, that the King of Morocco, in honor of the Quattlebaum-Ahmed nuptials, has issued a general pardon for all Moroccan citizens under a death sentence. It is reported that he took this action at the request of his American medical consultants, Drs. B.F. Pierce and J.F.X. McIntyre, who came to Morocco on vacation, but have since devoted themselves entirely to Abzugian-Moroccan medical problems.

"The King was so impressed with what he called the 'nose-to-the-grindstone' attitude of the American physicians that he has forbidden them to do any further work while in the Kingdom. He says he hopes that they can now find time for a healthful recreational activity, such as golf, before returning to the loved ones they miss so much.

"And finally, there was a rumor that French interests were attempting to block the American-Abzugian oil deal, but they were laid firmly to rest tonight when the

President of France announced that, as a token of his all-around esteem for the Abzugians and the Americans, the Government of France is donating a maternity hospital. It will be named the Boris Alexandrovich Korsky-Rimsakov Memorial Lying-In Hospital, after the star of the Paris Opera, to be constructed in the Abzugian capital. As a token of his appreciation, the opera singer presented the President with a home movie of the President's wife, taken earlier today.

"And that's the news, the unvarnished news, from Marrakech. This has been 'The Rhotten Report,' and this is Don Rhotten."

His famous face vanished from the monitor in the banquet room. The lights were turned up. Horsey de la Chevaux got up, walked over to the Reverend Mother and asked her to dance. The band struck up "The Sheikh of Araby."